MRS BETJEMAN

Mrs Betjeman

Mary Alexander

Published by The Paris Press

Copyright © Mary Alexander 2019

Mary Alexander asserts the moral right to be identified as the author of this work

All rights reserved. If you have purchased the ebook edition of this novel please be aware that it is licensed for your personal enjoyment only and refrain from copying it.

Photographic portrait of Penelope, Lady Betjeman by Lafayette (1932) © The National Portrait Gallery

For translation rights and permission queries please contact the author's agent
Lisa.eveleigh@richfordbecklow.co.uk

About the Author

Mary Alexander lives in Oxford and London. She has an MA in Creative Writing, and her collection of short stories, *The Wind on His Back*, was published in 2016. She has also ghost-written several well-received memoirs. *Mrs Betjeman* is her first novel.

www.maryalexander.co.uk

"Two roads diverged in a yellow wood,
And sorry I could not follow both."
                                        Robert Frost

April 11, 1986. 5.30 am. Somewhere in the Himalayas.

"Do you believe in premonitions?"

It is a whisper in my head as I creak down the wooden stairs to the rest house kitchen. I need my morning cup of chai before my mind will start thinking anything that might pass for sense. Through the open front door I see the sky is a steady blue soaring high above the Himalayan peaks.

The kitchen is simple but spotlessly clean. I find matches, light the gas ring, put the heavy iron kettle on to boil, and turn at the sound of footfall.

"Jamie," I say. One of the tourists I am leading up through the mountains. We have been travelling for several days, on sure-footed local horses, riding higher and higher, reaching more and more remote parts. Today we will reach Mutisher, my favourite of all the Himalayan villages.

"Penelope. You're up very early."

"Yes. It's a wonderful time of day. Tea?"

"Peaceful," Jamie supplies. "Yes, please."

"Very peaceful." I agree.

I reach for the whistling kettle. Jamie interrupts me. "Let me make the tea, Penelope. You sit down."

I'm not in the mood to disagree. I feel slight, as if the wrong word might knock me down like a worn-out boxer in a ring. I reach for the wooden bench that leans against the kitchen wall and sit, the bench creaking under my weight. I am too fat these days. Perhaps not fat exactly, but stout. The result of being short, a good cook and seventy-six years old.

A crack winds its way through the plaster above the stone sink opposite me. Outside, the sun is looking in at me through the large rectangular window, as if it is waiting for me to come out to play. Come this way, it says. Follow me and I will show you Heaven.

Jamie presses a mug of tea into my hands.

"Thank you." I look up at him. About forty, I would guess. Craggy, friendly face wearing the early stages of a beard. This is understandable; it's hard to shave in cold water, and the rest houses we stay in get their water from their local well. Flecked grey eyes touched by sadness. No one gets to forty without sadness.

Last night I overheard him talking; he was sitting outside sharing his duty-free whisky with a couple of the others in our party, telling them about his divorce. His wife left him for another man two years ago, taking his two young boys with her. Now he only sees them a few days every school holiday, and they are awkward with him. He feels increasingly as if they are strangers. An everyday tale, far from unique, yet still uniquely painful.

I smile slightly at Jamie, and put my hand on his.

"I feel I may be going to Heaven today," I say.

Jamie looks uneasy. His eyes are bloodshot from too much whisky and too little sleep, and now he must deal with a mad old bag as well.

"Jamie, do you believe in premonitions?" I ask. He looks even unhappier.

"Penelope," he says gently "You need some breakfast."

I smile. I'm sure he's right. The kitchen staff will be in at 6, to make us chilli omelettes and banana lassies. I need to eat, because the way to Mutisher is a hard road. Many of the party will choose an easier route – there is more than one way to get there-but not me; not today. I will choose the hard road.

11.30am. Mutisher.
The air is soft and dark inside the temple, and smells of incense and wood. The Punjari is murmuring in Hindi in his low, throaty voice. My Hindi is rusty from lack of use, so I don't understand every word, but I am acutely aware that he is blessing me.

"Thank you" I murmur to the Punjari. I am a Catholic, but I feel the presence of God here, in this little wooden temple, as close as I have ever felt Him. I walk slowly back towards the open door. I stand for a moment in the doorway, blinking in the sunlight. It has been a long wait for spring.

I sit on the stones outside the temple, feeling their sun baked heat through the cotton of my thin trousers. I close my eyes, and my head feels heavy. It must be the mix of the sunshine and the incense and perhaps even the altitude. The air is thinner up here. The heart must work harder. My legs feel tired and my bare feet look wrinkled with age and pale from an English winter spent in roughly knitted Welsh socks.

The temple bells start to sound. The village has lapsed into a moment of stillness. The children are at school, and the adults sip chai at their stalls, waiting for the next batch of tourists to whom they can sell their wares. It has changed since I was first here, nearly 60 years ago now, but they are recognizable changes. Villages have sprouted where once there were just one or two simple dwellings; dusty roads that had once been open just to the Viceroy's car and a few others, have been tarmacked. Electricity cables make their erratic way up the mountain in slack loops slung between wooden poles, sited-infuriatingly-with no thought for the scars they make on the landscape. And all in the name of progress. I will write to the Indian district planners about this, even though I know it will do absolutely no good.

I sniff the air deeply, like an animal. I have always had a rapport with animals. John understood that. In our happy Uffington days, he told one of our sadly neglected visitors that had they been a horse, tea would have been offered hours ago. I laughed then, not simply because it was funny, but because-as with the best jokes-there was more than a grain of truth to it.

I sniff the air again and think a little more about my dead husband. Dead for two years now. I think of him every day and sometimes I still talk to him. Last night, I even found myself taking out my thin blue airmail paper to write to him at the small wooden desk in the corner of my room, before I remembered. It was not the first time I had forgotten he had died. As I put it away again, I thought about what I had been going to tell him. That nothing lasts forever, and that we shouldn't resist that, or blame ourselves. That change is the motor of life. An angular German man in our party told me that yesterday – they have had a lot to come to terms with, the Germans, perhaps it makes them a nation of philosophers-and I thought it good enough to share with John.

The air smells of bougainvillea and mountain orchids, of damp earth steaming in the sun mingled with sacred cow dung drying out on the road. I close my eyes, and the smells speak of my youth. They, at least, are as I remember.

I was not quite twenty years old and I had only recently and reluctantly arrived in India. I had been ruthlessly parted from my first love by my mother, Star; at the time I was furious, with the self-absorbed fury the young are so good at, but now, looking back from the distance of my old age, now I am so solid and take the long view on what matters in life, it simply makes me smile. My mother was right. That marriage would have been a disaster.

Now, I have a bosom that runs from my shoulders uninterruptedly to my waist and my grey hair is functionally short, and I don't let myself care a toot, really, for my appearance. I might occasionally powder my nose. But back then- I was young and excited and alive to everything the world could offer me; a world that seemed filled

Mrs Betjeman

with possibilities in a way that felt brand new; or new to girls, at least. The hard part was knowing which opportunities to choose. Did I choose well? How can one ever really know? By what yardstick does one measure the choices of a lifetime, a life that started over seven decades ago? I shake my head, trying to loosen the clouds that seem to have lodged between my ears. The past is in front of me, so close I can almost touch it.

Chapter One

London. The garden of Lansdowne House, Berkeley Square. 1928.

"Marry me, Penelope. You won't regret it, I promise". I looked at the expectant boy in front of me and shivered slightly in the cool night breeze as I wondered how to reply.

There was so much I loved about Johnnie. He was naughty, he broke the rules, and that immediately attracted me, because so did I. Last year, he had followed me to Italy, when I was dispatched there by my parents with a group of other girls, filling in that no-man's land of time between school and marriage. We were learning about the Renaissance, and I became bewitched by Giotto. Johnnie was a painter, and understood all about passion and art.

I blinked in the gloom as I watched Johnnie inhale from his cigarette, and reached out a hand to take it from him. I drew on it myself, and then passed it back to him. My chest started to wrack against my will. I opened my mouth and coughed violently.

"Penelope," Johnnie said. "I've told you before. Smoking simply isn't for you". I nodded in agreement, unable to speak. My eyes pricked and tears started to roll down my face from coughing, my throat stinging angrily.

Marriage to Johnnie would probably be rather good fun, so why didn't I just say, 'yes'? There were several reasons. Most of them to do with my mother. While it was huge fun to shock her – probably the only reason I persevered with the smoking, for example – marrying just for the shock factor might be taking youthful rebellion a little too far.

On paper, Johnnie Spencer Churchill was a good enough prospect. Extremely handsome, highly amusing and well connected-nephew to Winston, Father's friend-but nevertheless, Star wouldn't be happy. She most definitely didn't approve of him. She thought him a dilettante and had already told me so several times.

"He is not what we want for the daughter of the Commander in Chief of the Indian Army, darling, and that's that", my mother had said firmly just the other evening, as I was getting ready for yet another of these *debutante* parties, with Johnnie on my mind and a gleam in my eye.

"Oh Star, don't judge him so harshly," I'd said, brushing my dark fringe forward and ruffling it with my fingers. I'd recently had my hair cut into a fashionable bob in the barber's shop on the high street, and Star was furious with me about that, too. A barber's shop was gentleman's territory! Long hair would be back in fashion in a moment, and then where would I be, she'd fumed. Out of step with fashion, I'd replied, pulling a horrified face.

"Penelope, I'm certainly going to judge someone if there's a risk you might marry them. What's good fun now will seem rackety and penniless in five years' time when you've got three children to feed and clothe. I'm sorry, but he's just not quite, *quite*."

"Not quite, *quite*." I repeated my mother's words, the words she always used to sum up the inevitable, yet indescribable flaw of whichever man was courting me – the only thing I knew for sure was that they would definitely have one and quite possibly more than one. I was pretty sure that the fact that Johnnie was not quite, *quite*, was the reason Star was carting me off to India. To get me out of Johnnie's circle. I didn't want to go to India. Injer! More wretched parties. What I wanted to do was to go back to Italy and learn more about Giotto; but when did anyone ever ask me what I wanted?

I looked up at Johnnie. He was several inches taller than me, quite lean, no moustache, thank god. His eyes gleamed in the dark, like a stalking cat. The great beech trees in the gardens behind us cast menacing shadows on his face.

"Johnnie," I said. I smoothed the silky fabric of my *eau-de-nil* dress with one correctly-gloved hand. Of course, if I married Johnnie, it would give me the freedom and independence I craved. It would put me beyond the reach of my mother. With the status of 'wife', the experience of the world and all it had to offer, would be far more available to me than it was as an unmarried girl still living with her parents and requiring a chaperone. But marriage was for life, and I might be young and right now feeling reckless, but I did have some sense. Galling though it was to admit, Star had a point.

"Yes?" he smiled. "You're cold. Have my jacket, my darling." He shrugged out of his dinner jacket and draped it around my shoulders, the silk lining warm from his body, and waited for me to go on. It was undeniably nice having someone as handsome as Johnnie call me 'my darling'. Half the girls dancing away inside at that very minute were in love with Johnnie, but I was the one who had somehow got under his skin.

Why? I really wasn't sure. I wasn't the most beautiful of the debutantes – I was pretty enough when I made an effort, but I wasn't ever going to be lauded as 'a great beauty'; my legs were short and already a little thick, and my jawline was definitely not what you would describe as elfin. My mother said I was too hard on myself, but I simply considered myself to be realistic. I had my admirers, but I was not going to be Deb of the Year.

"Penelope?" Johnnie prompted. I still had to give him an answer. I sighed, and embarked on it reluctantly, gently.

"Johnnie, we're both very young. I'm only 18, you're not even 20."

I peered at him again through the dusk, which was deepening to impenetrable night now. Candles flickered all around us, and a white-jacketed waiter hovered close by with a tray of champagne. The sound of dance music drifted from the house. "Did you know, Robert Adam designed this house in the 1760's for the Marquis of Lansdowne?" I said to Johnnie casually. "It is in the Palladian design that had been considered so modern and fresh in Adam's day."

Johnnie drew on his cigarette sullenly. This was not the conversation he wanted to be having.

Never mind.

I was trying to hone my critical eye in between my endless round of debutante engagements. The white stucco of the house gleamed palely in the distance, and a couple of Romanesque pillars supported the porch. These were both classic Adam hallmarks, resulting from his own time spent in Rome – five years, if I was remembering my reading rightly. Yes, it was a fairly breathtaking example of the period.

Johnnie dropped his cigarette and stood on it.

"Are you turning me down *again*?"

An incredulous note rang through the words. We both knew Johnnie had recently been described by the social pages of one newspaper as being 'a talented artist with matinee idol good looks'.

One well-shod foot ground out the cigarette butt as he braced himself for another of my refusals. I wasn't being heartless. I just couldn't, for whatever reason – Star, youth, general unspecified confusion-say 'yes'.

"I'm sailing for India tomorrow. You know that."

Johnnie stamped a foot impatiently. "Yes, I'm very well aware of that fact, hence my proposal tonight. But you won't be gone forever. We could be quietly engaged during your absence. I could even come out to visit you. I will write to you, of course. Consider it, at least, Penelope. I'm not a bad catch."

I sighed, my eyes darting around the garden, taking in some shadowy shapes clustered on the other end of the terrace in the dusk. I squinted, and a young man bending over a girl's hand came into focus. He was lifting it slowly to his lips with a slow smile. She looked enchanted, as if it was precisely what she wanted to happen. I guessed I'd be reading about their engagement in *The Times* before the week was out. Why was it so easy for some people, and so hard for me? Perhaps they just made it look easy, and inside they were as confused as me.

"Penelope," Johnnie prompted.

I brought my gaze back to him.

Time to soothe.

"Oh darling, we both know you're a great, great catch. As I've told you before, I love you, I think the world of you, but there are things I want to do. I want to study. I want to become an expert in Italian art. I want to have a job. And quite frankly, I'm not sure I'll make anyone a very good wife."

Doubt crawled visibly across Johnnie's handsome face like a caterpillar traversing a leaf.

"Good God. You're not going to become one of those blue-stocking types are you? Or a woman who acts like a man? I know some women work these days, Penelope, but it's not because they want to, it's because they must, and it's not girls like you. Rather, sad old spinster types left bereaved after the war. The surplus two million."

"Don't call them that," I said, stung by Johnnie's cruelty.

I felt sure that if I'd been an adult twenty years ago I would have chained myself to the railings in the battle for Women's Rights, and I'd probably have been one of the women Johnnie was being so dismissive about, women whose fiancés had been killed in the trenches and were now destined never to marry. Women who had no choice but to carve out a meaningful life for themselves that would not include what they'd been brought up to expect, a life of home and hearth and husband and children.

"All these dances" – I waved my hand in the direction of the house looming behind us. "There is more to life than this, you know. This isn't really me; I'm always saying the wrong thing. Or going the wrong way."

Johnnie laughed in an unfunny kind of way, then straightened up and patted down his jacket, searching for his cigarette case. He took out a cigarette, tapped it on the monogrammed silver case that had been his 18th birthday present from his uncle, put it in his mouth and lit it. He exhaled noisily, slipping the case and lighter back in his inside pocket. This time I did not make the mistake of asking him for a puff.

"Penelope. You're still very young."

I remained silent. I felt he had decided to try and make the best of things.

"Could we say it's not a completely final no?" he said, taking one of my gloved hands.

I sighed.

"You will forget me before I've even arrived in India."

I felt a pang as I said this. I hoped it wasn't true, yet I also knew it to be more than likely: there were so many girls so much more suitable than me, girls who would undoubtedly make Johnnie a much better wife.

"Don't be ridiculous. I'll write to you all the time."

I looked up at him. He really was very handsome. Maybe I did love him. Maybe turning him down again was a mistake.

The man and the young girl at the end of the terrace were walking down the steps now, arm in arm, faces pressed close together, sharing secrets. They had none of my doubts.

"It's a no for now, edging towards a maybe," I said at last. It was the best I could do, and it proved enough for Johnnie. His beautiful face lifted, and a small smile played at the edges of his mouth.

"Have it your way, Penelope Valentine Hester Chetwode. I shall consider us to be unofficially semi-engaged. Shall we go back in and dance?"

The music playing now was the fast, hard, shimmery type of music that all us young shifted and turned to in a kind of mime of rising panic, laughter getting louder, shrieks more piercing, hands waving, as if to make sure no one could miss the fun we were clearly having. Growing up in the shadow of the Great War, the war to end all wars, we understood that our responsibility was to live each day as if it was our last. We had to have fun, to be fun, because that's what a life lived properly was-fun; if it wasn't, you weren't doing it right. We knew we owed that to the millions that had died. It was as if we had to have that extra bit of fun on their behalf.

It wasn't just like this in England. The world was at it. Hemingway was holding forth in salons in Paris, the Fitzgeralds ruled the Riviera, and across the Atlantic, New York was on fire with the Jazz age in full swing. Internationally, fun was compulsory.

I wondered if India would be fun.

The music seemed to grow louder.

"Oh Johnnie," I said. "You're quite right. Dancing's just the thing." Johnnie flashed me a smile, grabbed my hand and pulled me, quite urgently, into the house through the vast doors open to the garden. We pushed into the dancing throng and facing each other, began to move.

I quite liked dancing. When I was dancing I didn't have to talk or think. I could just feel the fast beat of the music, turn this way and that; I could just *be*. Even if I didn't know what I wanted to do with my life, or where I was going, or who to marry, for those few moments of turning and moving and spinning, I didn't really care. I had to concentrate so hard on getting the movements right that there was no space left in my head for serious thought. I turned and shimmied and bobbed and turned again, playing out the steps of the Charleston and then a quick Foxtrot that I'd perfected practicing at home with my protesting brother Roger as a partner. Dancing was, in that sense, all consuming, rather like horse riding; and riding, eclipsing even Giotto, was my most favourite passion of all.

Chapter Two

Delhi. September 1928.

I lay on my bed, grateful for the ceiling fan churning up the sticky air into lukewarm gusts that stroked my sweat beaded skin. I had been in Delhi for just a few days and already knew that everything everyone back home had told me about the heat was true.

Before I had left for India, people had queued up to tell me about their experiences of the country.

'Oh, the heat, my dear, the heat' warned a General's rather substantial wife, recently and gladly returned to the bosom of the mother country. At the time of listening, I'd been shivering in a too thin cocktail dress enduring another disappointing English summer, and had not considered heat to be a particular drawback. Others had talked of the terrible smells, the dust, the crush. At least a dozen people had recommended Forster's *A Passage to India*, and I'd been loaned not one but two copies of Murray's *A Guide to India*, the latest edition, which everyone said was indispensable. (They were right, it had already become my bible, the book I turned to when I wanted to know something about a monument I had passed or a custom I had observed). Strange though, I thought now, mildly hypnotised by the revolving action of the fan: not a single person had mentioned India's staggering beauty.

I got off the bed and started to run a bath. I saw in the mirror that my face was flushed and my hair needed a prolonged encounter with a hairbrush. I began to strip off my dirt-stained jodhpurs. I hadn't wanted to come to India, but from the moment I had stepped onto the Apollo Bunder pier at Bombay and walked through the Gateway to India I knew this country had something to offer me; something more than a superficial discussion about *The Just So Stories* and yet another round of drinks parties with the right set; I didn't know yet what it was, or how it would happen, but I had felt something undeniable, some internal jolt of promise and the feeling had stayed.

Several of my father's aides had met my mother and me off the boat; they shimmered in the heat; a sea of men dressed in beige beside the glitter of the water. The arch seemed both vast – the Gateway to India – and small when compared to the immense sense of life that lay behind it. I had stood still and let it all go on around me: the noise, the pomp, the people gathered to the sides of the red carpet eager to see us passengers alight, the men shouting "Chai, Chai" and holding up metal tea urns, the women mostly silent, wrapped in brilliant pinks and reds and oranges, colours from the earth and the plants that were flourishing energetically all around. The brass band playing, the liner we had arrived on sounding its deep throaty horn in celebration of a journey safely accomplished.

We had travelled from Bombay to Delhi by train. We slept on the train, my mother and I, sharing a wood paneled cabin, and swaying to the dining car in evening dresses every night for a formal supper of several courses. Outside, elephants and camels, temples, forts and monkeys rushed past, and every now and then, groups of silent people stopped a moment in the fields to watch us go by. It had been a gentle and visual introduction to India that had lasted three days.

I tested the bath water and added some bath salts before climbing in. My muscles hurt in a pleasing kind of way, from long hours spent in the saddle today. From the open window I could see the lush gardens, and hear the monkeys calling to each other.

My father had surprised me on my arrival with a horse, a spirited white Arabian named Moti, which meant 'pearl' in Hindi. An obvious bribe to cheer me up at being carted off to Delhi, it was love at first sight, and I had been riding him around Delhi every day. If only things were as clear with men as with horses.

Delhi seemed to be changing on a daily basis. Mostly I stayed within the new parts being laid out by Lutyens and his team, in wide boulevards surrounded by elegant planting, but occasionally I ventured into the crushing streets of Old Delhi with their compelling centuries of history of Moghul rule. I wanted to visit these parts more, but they were bewilderingly different and crowded, and I didn't quite know how to start. Today, Pa had come with me, and we had galloped out to the Qutb Minar and climbed up the five flights of the 12th century tower, puffing as we finally reached the top. It had been worth the effort. The view back towards Delhi across the dusty plains had been staggering.

I climbed out of the bath, wrapped myself in a towel and went back into the bedroom. Agrata, my maid, had laid out my dress on the chaise longue and was now hovering anxiously to do my hair. "No, don't worry Agrata, I'll do it," I said. She nodded and slipped from the room as silently as she had arrived. She didn't say much, and seemed almost frightened. I was used to the friendly chatter of my English maid at home, and her quietness made me uneasy.

Even from my few short days in India, I already saw how lucky I was – I'd seen the people huddled on the sides of the streets, and the children with missing limbs begging for food at every junction, while white men drove by in cars polished by their poorly-paid Indian servants. There was clearly a less comfortable edge to India than the luxurious life I had arrived into. But I wasn't going to shout at Agrata, or offend her. She didn't need to be afraid of me.

Flagstaff House had been assigned to my father on his arrival in India. Newly built, long and low, constructed of white stucco and marble, with tall and thin Arts and Crafts windows and a terrace overlooking the formally planted gardens at the back, it was elegant if ludicrously large. The ground floor held a series of drawing rooms made cool with marble floors that shone like dark glossy planes of water, and thick stone walls washed white and intermittently paneled with wood; the first floor held the magnificent ballroom with the terrace, my father's study, my mother's private sitting room and several suites of bedrooms, including my own. A ludicrous number of liveried servants ensured that we never lifted a finger unless we chose to.

I sat at my dressing table for a moment. I had chosen a long pale cream chiffon evening gown; I had powdered my nose and cheeks to hide the flush from the day in the sun. I had succeeded in untangling my hair. I would do. I stood up and left my room, making my way down the curving stone staircase to the sitting rooms, trying to feel elegant and not to trip on my long skirt. My parents had a party of people coming to dinner, and of course I was expected to join them. I hated these events as much as I had hated my season in London. Invariably I sat next to some Subaltern who had to be nice to me because I was the daughter of the god of their world. But somehow tonight, even the thought of the probable tedium ahead didn't dampen my mood. Something about India – the warmth, the colours, the smells, or the sense of the ancient still present in the modern everyday, made me feel like I wanted to sing.

I glanced into the dining room, and saw the table was set for at least twenty. Crystal glasses, crisp white linen, silver cutlery, towering candlesticks. White curtains gathered at the windows and fell to the floor, the cooling pale look broken only by the flowers in brilliant pinks and oranges. My mother might have had an army of servants to help her, but her hand was everywhere. Things always went smoothly under her guidance. Would I ever make someone that kind of wife? Capably running a house and home, entertaining and managing social situations effortlessly? Did I even want to? If I did, I wanted something else as well, something more than just a domestic life lived in the shadow of a man. I wasn't exactly against marriage, but my mother and her type of marriage hailed from a different age. Things were changing and I wanted something that didn't root me entirely in the home. The problem was, I wasn't quite sure what that something was yet. What, precisely, could I do?

I moved on down the wide corridor to the drawing rooms. Pa was standing by the drinks table in one of the drawing rooms, the windows overlooking the carriage driveway and the Catalpa trees. I hurried across to him, forgetting in my eagerness to reach him to pick up my long dress, and nearly tripping in the process. There was an ominous tearing sound. I looked round, but any tear was invisible in the yards of frothing chiffon.

"Daddy," I said, recovering my balance, and went over and kissed him. "What a fabulous outing that was".

He smiled benevolently at me. "You're happier on a horse than anywhere else in the world, aren't you darling?"

he said approvingly. "I must say Moti is turning out to fulfill his early promise. Drink?"

"Hmmm, yes please. Gin and tonic. Lots of tonic and not much gin." I was as bad at drinking as I was at smoking.

"He is, isn't he? So, who is coming tonight? Anyone I know?"

"No one you know yet, but there is someone who I think you will enjoy talking to, given your interest in old Delhi. Sir John Marshall. Archaeologist and a specialist in Indian art. Director General of the Indian Archaeological survey. He's been here for donkeys' years and is just coming up to retirement. Revived the whole Survey from the brink of collapse. Got the Indians involved in restoring their own monuments. Very good chap. Enlightened, forward thinking, not a Raj dinosaur, in fact quite the opposite."

I took a tentative sip of the drink my father had given me and coughed. The gin hit me like a blow. "Gosh. That's a very... fulsome... description for you, Pa."

"Hmmm. I rather admire the man. If you promise not to go all bluestocking on me, I'll ask your mother to seat you next to him at dinner. He's personable, intelligent, and was even considered a handsome fellow in his day, though he's a bit past it now. My age," he added, grinning at his own joke. His slight, burgeoning belly shook with laughter under his formal military evening coat.

"Oh Pa, thank you."

This man sounded like someone who could answer all my questions about India's arts heritage and be a welcome break from an eager to please subaltern.

Just then, Star swept into the room, immaculate in a dark blue evening gown, a pearl choker around her neck.

"Doesn't marble echo so? I'm still not used to this barn of a place, Philip. I can hear you two all the way down the corridor. What are you going to ask me?"

"Darling. You look delightful. Nothing of any substance, only to re-arrange the seating a little. Penelope would enjoy meeting John Marshall, I think. Can you organise it?"

Star eyed her daughter. "You've washed and brushed your hair," she said, pleasure warming her voice. "And I adore that gown. Hasn't it worked out well? Pale colours really suit you, Penelope. They bring out your eyes and flatter your complexion. You look beautiful, darling. Are you sure you want to sit next to Sir John? You'll be wasted on him, he's your father's age."

"Oh please, Star, I'd love to talk to him and learn more about Indian art."

My mother flicked her fan, irritation chasing pleasure across her face. "Alright, I suppose so, but really, Penelope, I don't know how you think you're going to catch a husband."

"You don't seem to like the sort I can catch," I retorted.

"If you're referring to Johnnie Spencer Churchill, you're absolutely right," said Star tartly. "I've heard he's set off on some travelling himself now you're out of his reach. Canada," she added triumphantly.

"Yes. He wrote to me about it. He's gone with his godfather," I said, determined to be better informed about my former boyfriend than my own mother. I felt the colour rising in my face. I wondered if he actually was a former boyfriend, or whether we were still, perhaps, just a little bit together. It was always so hard to know with unofficial engagements. A friend of mine had considered herself unofficially engaged to someone, right up until she had found out he'd gone and married someone else. That was the trouble with secrets.

"Alright, that's settled then," said Pa, frowning. "I don't want my two favourite gels in a spat." He put an arm around each of us and drew us towards him. For a moment I resisted, my body stiff with fury and my eyes watering, while Star glared at me across the distance of my father's body, but then I sighed, and relaxed against my father. What was the point of going up against my mother? She usually won, and despite her ability to make me furious, I also loved her for her outspokenness, her certainty, and the unwavering strength of her love. Once she loved, she never stopped. She was quite possibly the most loyal person I knew.

"You're the same, you two, that's the trouble," Pa said. He turned to his wife.

"Darling, I think you should try and recall that you were a little unconventional in your own youth, and that was quite what attracted me to you. It may just be a case that the apple does not fall far from the tree."

Star sagged against him. "I can see why you're a diplomat," she said, bashing him gently in the chest with her fan.

"I'm not. I'm military personnel," he replied, drawing himself up and showing off his medals.

"Same thing out here," my mother said, as a servant handed her a glass of her favourite gin cocktail. Star had none of my reticence about alcohol.

"Salut," she said. I knew the gin would cheer her up.

My father relaxed. The storm seemed to have passed, and just in time, as the butler announced the arrival of the first guest. We all straightened up and waited, smiles on faces. The evening's show had begun.

I stood behind my chair, talking politely with the young army officer on my right about the heat. He had been in

Delhi for four years now, and apparently this summer had been the worst he had known. "The heat has been relentless," he said, for the third time.

I kept one eye out for Sir John. I had caught sight of him over cocktails, when he had been pointed out to me by another guest, although the lady I had asked had thrown me a quizzical look at my request. My father might have described him as past it, but he looked anything but to me. Tall-over six feet, I guessed – still slim but well built, in a beautifully cut dinner suit that showcased broad shoulders, his grey hair still prolific on his head, his blue eyes alert, I had noticed him paying gentle attention to every woman he spoke to, stooping down in a flattering way to listen to them. In return they bloomed and blossomed like Indian Orchids given a drop or two of water. He may be old but he's a flirt, I realized with a start. A shocking flirt. My father had told me he had a wife called Florence, and two grown up children, all living back in England. Apparently, Florence couldn't stand India. Well, none of this was of consequence to me. He could flirt all he liked. It was his intellect I was interested in. To all else, I was immune.

He entered the dining room at last and I stood up a little straighter. Next to his great height, I felt even more diminutive than usual at just five foot two.

"Miss Chetwode," he said to me, looking down into my face with a twinkle. He had the benevolent, dignified manner of a friendly country vicar.

I smiled slightly. "Hello. You must be Sir John. I am afraid I may spend much of dinner picking your brains." Oh, why had I dashed right in like that? If only I had style and sophistication – like my mother. She would have held back about that until at least the second course, by which time she would have had him eating out of her hand.

"Pick away, pick away. Your father has warned me," he smiled at me. "And since I can never talk too much about archaeology, particularly with such a pretty conversationalist, I hurried over here the moment he tipped me off."

I laughed and smiled up at him.

Through the seven-course meal, I turned this way and that; one course spent in discussion with Sir John, the next with the Subaltern on my right. It turned out my initial impression had been unkind: He was a perfectly nice chap as Subalterns went. He was nearly 30 but still unmarried, and due to be posted to Calcutta at the end of the year. He was hugely in awe of my father, and clearly felt flattered to be invited to dinner and seated next to me. He could not have been nicer or more entertaining and put me at my ease. He loved to hunt, and when he discovered I adored riding, our conversation really took off. He promised to take me with him one morning, if my parents were happy for him to do so.

"We meet early," he warned, "5.30am. Otherwise the heat becomes too much for the horses and the hounds."

"Suits me," I said. I loved to rise with the sun. "That sounds the most wonderful fun." And it did. The idea of going hunting around Delhi, chasing down a fox with a pack of hounds, taking part in what was a quintessentially English sport in this exotic landscape, intrigued me.

The crab mousse gave way to the fish, and the Subaltern turned dutifully to the elderly lady, out in India for a lengthy stay with her son and daughter-in-law, on his right.

Which left me with Sir John again. I felt my stomach squeezing slightly with nerves, for no reason I could discern. I'd already discovered that he was a perfectly nice man, and that I had nothing to fear. So often at dinners of this kind, the diners talked down to me, because of my age and inexperience, in a way that made me feel quite furious, but with

Sir John it was the opposite. He addressed me as if I was the most interesting woman at the table.

I met his eyes and smiled.

"Your father tells me you like to ride," Sir John stated. I wondered if he'd been listening to my hunting conversation with the Subaltern.

"Oh yes," I replied fervently. I was more confident on a horse than anywhere else in life. On a horse, I might be a little more Sir John's equal.

"Then why don' t we ride out to some of Delhi's monuments, and I can tell you what I know about them? It might take a few expeditions, as there's a lot to see."

I reddened a little in my excitement. "Sir John, I would adore that. What shall we start with and when?"

"Well, we are spoilt for choice. But I suggest we begin close to home and work outwards from there; riding out from here across the Delhi Plains to the Red Fort is one of the great experiences of India, in my view. And it's something you must do while you still can. The way Lutyens and his lot are rolling out New Delhi, with its low white mansions that the powers that be hope will serve to underline the muscle of the British Empire, there won't be plains to gallop across for much longer."

"You don't approve of Lutyens?" I asked.

Sir John leaned towards me with a conspiratorial air. "Frankly, it's not a development I like, but what can I say? Beyond hoping that architectural gems that have survived 800 years will not be brought low by the modern city that is being built in these fading Raj years, there is nothing I can do."

"Fading?" I asked. "But the city isn't even finished yet!"

Sir John put down his fork with a quiet smile and spoke into his plate.

"The modern city. The latest incarnation of an ancient city. Are cities ever finished?"

Then he visibly collected himself.

"Just an old man rambling on, my dear. Disregard it. However, galloping across the plains – as I said, it's something I highly recommend. Do you have a horse?"

I wondered if Sir John was a Nationalist. "My father bought me one. A white Arab called Moti."

"A very good name. I imagine Moti to be luminescent. Just let me know when suits you."

"You speak Hindi? Is tomorrow too soon?" I asked. "I really would rather not waste a minute. I know so little about Indian Art."

"And there is so much to learn," Sir John said, one corner of his mouth lifting again in a slight smile. He gave me the feeling he had more than a little experience of impatient young women.

"Tomorrow. I don't see why not. We need your parents' permission," he added as an afterthought, but in a way that seemed to suggest it was simply a formality. He picked up his wine glass, breathed in its scent and took a sip. "Chablis. 1925, I suspect. Wine never travels well to India, you know."

"I don't drink wine often enough to tell, so I'm afraid I'll have to take your word for it," I said.

"Good for you. Nothing worse than a drunken female. I hope you don't smoke, either. At least, not in public."

I remembered Johnnie and the coughing.

"I smoke seldom and very badly," I laughed.

Then the fish course was taken away and the roast lamb arrived, and I turned back to the Subaltern.

"So, tell me more about this hunting," I said. "Are there really any foxes in Delhi? They must get awfully hot in all that fur."

Chapter Three

I woke at five. The Indian dawn had broken, the promise of heat was not yet in the air and a welcome soft breeze was toying with the linen curtains. I washed and dressed quickly and quietly. My favourite dark jodhpurs, a crisp white blouse, my light cotton riding jacket. I was going to ride astride, as was my preference, something my father disliked. In his opinion, a well-bred lady should only ride sidesaddle. I powdered my nose, brushed my hair, and picked up my hard white hat, which I wore largely to deflect the sun, although I'd recently read about an interesting safety development involving riding in hard hats. Pa had Horse and Hound magazine sent out from England every month and I read it avidly from cover to cover. I stood in front of the looking glass for a moment, turning one way and then the other, and smiled. These jodhpurs definitely flattered my legs, and my gleaming black riding boots were a close fit around my calves. The overall effect was to seemingly lengthen my legs. Pleased with my appearance for once, I skipped lightly down the marble staircase, past the dining room and towards the back of the house, my stomach flipping over in a way that still mystified me.

I left the house through a side door and walked through the gardens to the stables to find Moti. The air was damp and smelt of jasmine. Moti was standing in the yard, waiting for me, his pale coat gleaming in the early morning sun. Vikram, one of the grooms, was holding him loosely by the reins and combing through his mane, which already looked immaculate to me.

"Good morning, Vikram," I said, "and Moti, darling, how are you today, hmmm, my Moti?" I stroked his white velvet nose. "What an adventure we're going on this morning, my friend. Oh yes, we are." I took the reins, murmured a thank you to Vikram, and led Moti to the mounting block, while Vikram looked on in case I needed any help. I knew I didn't. As I gathered up the reins in one hand, and swung a leg over, settling myself firmly in the saddle, I heard the sound of a horse approaching. I guessed without looking up it would be Sir John, and sure enough, within seconds, he came into view, astride a distinguished looking chestnut stallion.

"Good morning, my dear. I see you're a punctual type. Jolly good. Can't bear hanging about. Well then. Let's get going."

Without pausing for an answer, Sir John turned his horse around and kicked it into a trot that took him quickly out of the stable yard. Hurriedly I turned Moti and followed him up the driveway and out onto the plains of Delhi.

The scrub grassland, with trees and wild flowers and chattering monkeys, contrasted with Lutyens' wide avenues and fast growing orderly new city.

"Soon this won't exist, this jungle," Sir John grumbled, as we walked along side by side on our horses. "It will have been beaten into submission by the Empire."

"I'm not sure you believe in the Empire, Sir John," I said, with a questioning grin.

Sir John laughed. "It's not for me to believe in it or otherwise. My job is simply to make sure that these archaeological gems – these priceless monuments, look, my dear, you can see the edge of the Red Fort against the horizon – which have survived five hundred or six hundred or even eight hundred years, survive just as long again. And that's not about Empire, that's about the Indians preserving their own heritage. Because it is their heritage, not ours, that will be lost, if these buildings and ancient cities and temples are allowed to fall into utter decay."

"Well, they won't be, will they? Allowed to fall down, I mean? You've been working on saving them for nearly 30 years, and as a result, they have been – saved".

Sir John threw me a look. "You've been boning up on me," he said.

"Just doing a little digging," I smiled broadly. "You revived the dying Archaeological survey of India in 1902, and since then have saved countless sites around India from destruction and loss. Notably, your policy has been to involve Indians in preservation techniques from the outset, rather than believing these to be the remit of the British Empire. Consequently, as you contemplate retirement, you are leaving Indian archaeology in the safe hands you have personally educated in the ways of preservation, to carry on the good work."

Sir John pulled his horse up short. "Right. I see. You are thorough, aren't you?"

I grinned again, rather pleased with myself. "I try."

"Well, I shall try and be the same. You are a well-bred young girl who has done one season in England. Sailing to India against your will, you left a string of broken hearts behind you, and were struck by India's magical seductive quality the moment your ship caught sight of Bombay. Some people feel it, others don't; you did. Searching for more meaning to life than a marriage and several children, you are now wondering if perhaps India may provide what you seek."

It was my turn to stare. "But how – " I began, feeling myself start to blush.

Sir John smiled. "It's not difficult my dear, to read the face of an attractive, intelligent young woman of good breeding raised to tell the truth."

Attractive? Intelligent? I blushed some more and smiled back at Sir John. Thank god I could ride so well I didn't need to concentrate. I felt a little light headed, and wondered if it was the lack of breakfast. I liked to think I was complicated, a little bit mysterious perhaps, and certainly different to other girls, but it seemed Sir John could read me like a book. I looked away from the tanned planes of his face, the neat ruggedness of his eyebrows, the Roman nose, the laughing, intelligent blue eyes with the lines around them that surely told a million stories, and focused on the surprisingly orderly chaos of the street around me despite the early hour. Beggars were shaking their tins, while stallholders were laying out their goods and calling to every passerby. Elegantly dressed Indian women wrapped in coloured saris were already going about their daily food shopping, selecting vegetables and fruits with practiced hands and haggling hard for the best price, while clusters of children too small to be put to work hung closely around them. The centre of the road was dominated by horse riders like ourselves, horse drawn carts and Indians on bicycles, and there seemed no rules as to who went first. Continuing our steady walk I felt grateful that Moti was not easily startled.

Sir John was speaking again: "Now we've established that, let's get down to business, hmmm? We are reaching the Red Fort. This particular city was begun in 1638 and finished ten years later, which was no mean feat given its size and the building materials of the day. For a century and a half, it was the capital of the Mughal Empire.

The walls of the city, red and crenellated, loomed large ahead of me. Above, the sky hung silent and blue; monkeys called noisily in the trees above us.

"It's stunning," I breathed, and it was. I fell silent and just looked as Delhi life clattered on around me. The endless red walls stretching away into the distance, the towers rising behind it, the expanse of land where most of the city's people would have camped, feeling safe behind the high walls.

Eventually Sir John broke the silence. "Yes. It is a great rarity. Perfectly formed and largely intact, this fort would have held the life of the entire city. Delhi has had at least seven cities cited on it in its time, but it is hard to imagine a finer one than this."

Moti twitched his ears to displace a fly and shifted from foot to foot.

The sun was rising higher in the sky now, and the city was lightening from a forbidding dark blood red to a warmer earthy colour.

"It is," Sir John said simply, unmoving, eyes trained on the fort. "I must have seen this fort a thousand times, but every time I see it, the impact is as great as if it was the first time. You will find that much of India is like that. "

It's been his life's work, I thought. Saving this, saving sites around India. I could feel the passion humming in his words, and when he finally turned towards me, I saw it in his eyes.

"Sir John. What you have," I said. "That's what I'm looking for. To know something so well that it becomes a part of you, perhaps the most important part." To discover and follow the thing that makes life … sing."

Sir John looked back at the fort, then back to me. For a moment I wondered if he was going to pretend he had no idea what I was talking about.

"My dear," he said. "If I have done anything remotely approaching remarkable in my life, I have done it for love. Not money, or success or title, or because it was expected of me; but because I loved it so much I could scarcely not do it. A love for bricks and dust and unearthing things almost lost to us. And while I don't regret it for a moment, it has cost me quite highly. That kind of choice can."

I knew that he didn't speak of money, but more likely of his wife, alone in England, and of the grown-up sons he never saw.

"Life is about making choices," I said, nodding. I wondered what I would choose. Husband or career? Could a woman feasibly have both, with the social odds so stacked against her, when Sir John, so much better placed as a man, still hadn't managed it?

"Quite," he said. "Quite so. Just make sure you make the right choices for you. You are so young, with your life ahead of you, and quite clearly a good head on your shoulders. The world is changing fast, which means that while old fogeys like me are about to be put out to grass, you – young women – have more choices than ever before. And about time too, if I may say so."

I felt dazzled and hot. "Thank you," I said, because I didn't know what else to say. I could feel I was blushing.

"A pleasure as always." He was laughing at me now. "Now come on. If there's any chance that archaeology is going to be your thing, let's get inside that fort and get cracking." Sir John kicked his mount into a canter and set off across the grass. Breathing in a mouthful of hot, dry and dusty air, I nudged Moti into life and hurried after him.

We were home by eight for breakfast. Sir John clattered up the drive just far enough to see me and my horse safely into the hands of the groom, before trotting straight out again into the awakening fray of the day.

"Can't stop. The Survey beckons" he said, waving. I watched his retreating back for a moment, before walking slowly back to the stables.

Giving Moti's reins to the waiting Vikram, I realized I was starving. I entered the cool of the house, took off my riding jacket and went straight to the breakfast room. My father was seated at one end of the long table, eating a boiled egg and perusing the Times of India.

"Ah. Penelope. There you are, dear."

"Yes, Pa. Here I am. I've been out with Sir John to the Red Fort. It was – astonishing."

"Jolly good. Beautiful place. Stunning. Sit down dear. Have something to eat."

I slid into the place to his left, and poured myself some fruit juice. A servant materialized at my side, holding out a letter.

I knew the hand writing immediately. My father winked at me. "Good thing your mother's taking breakfast in her room this morning, eh? My lips are sealed."

I flushed slightly. I realized I hadn't spared Johnnie a single thought since my quarrel with Star the previous night. I used my knife to open the envelope.

"Dearest Penelope". My heart lurched guiltily. I scanned the lines. Johnnie had arrived in Canada; it was cold and vast and beautiful; he was starting on some new landscapes.

"Oh. He's got a job," I said aloud. My father looked up enquiringly. "Vickers La Costa," I added, my eyes still on the letter.

It ended with him sending me his love.

"Jolly good set up, so I'm told," said my father, munching noisily on his toast. "That might improve the odds in your favour, Penelope."

I refolded the letter and put it down. I wondered whether I wanted the odds improving in my favour. I'd thought I'd hate India, and had protested loud and long about my parents dragging me here, but now here I was embracing it, embarking on the next adventure that was my life with every appearance of enjoyment. If I had married Johnnie, I would have had to settle down and play house somewhere, and I would have missed all this. As Sir John had said so clearly, life was about choices.

A servant was hovering with a pot of coffee. I smiled at him, and he filled my cup. Johnnie Spencer Churchill suddenly seemed much further than just a continent away. At this moment, the notion of any marriage seemed an impossibility. What would I write to him? Should I let him down gently, or just hope the problem would go away with time and my continued absence? I pushed the problem aside and reached for a piece of toast, slightly bemused at how fast love evaporated.

Chapter Four

That first outing set a pattern. Sir John and I quickly fell into the habit of riding out together two or three times a week. I never did get to go hunting with the Subaltern. After two of my polite but definite refusals, he gave up, leaving me free from any other morning engagements and able to throw myself into my explorations with Sir John. He took me to the tombs in the Lodi gardens and up and down the Chadni Chowk in old Delhi, to the Red Fort again, to the Humayun Mausoleum, and the Great Mosque. Much of each outing was spent listening to Sir John as he told me all about the kings who had created such masterpieces – Akbar, Jahangir, Shah Jahan, men dead for centuries but brought to life again in Sir John's retelling of their existence in his throaty, precise tones. But sometimes the conversation strayed into other areas and I learned how he thought India belonged to the Indians, and how much he missed his children, now adults he felt he barely knew; and sometimes we simply rode, side by side, in an easy silence, our breathing rising and falling, our horses moving companionably together in a quiet equestrian harmony.

I hadn't had many older friends in my life. My friends had, to date, all been my age or just a few years older. But very quickly, as Sir John dropped me off at home, or met me at the stables to set off on an early morning excursion, it felt as if despite the age difference, he wasn't merely a family friend, he was *my* friend. Our regular rides seemed a slightly strange arrangement that nobody seemed to comment on. Sir John didn't come in to see my parents, and because of his age, he seemed to have the freedom to ride out with me without the requirement of a chaperone.

It didn't make any sense to me, as the last thing he seemed to me was old, and therefore he was surely no less 'dangerous' than a younger man in terms of my reputation. Was there some cut off point when a man ceased to be considered a sexual being? If there was, Sir John didn't appear, to me at least, to have reached it. I wondered if this might have crossed his mind too. Once, I tripped up in the dark in the tomb in the Lodi gardens and he caught me just before I fell, by one arm, and with another around my waist, and pulled me close for a moment while I steadied myself.

"Steady how you go, Penelope," he'd murmured, and I'd felt his breath on my face, hot and dry.

One morning not long after that, riding beside him through the woods on the way back from old Delhi, I took the plunge and pondered aloud my thoughts on rules and age gaps. As we rose and fell together to the sound of the horses' hooves beating on the dry sandy tracks, age seemed an absolute irrelevance and Society even more incomprehensible to me than ever. What seemed important was how alike we were in so many ways, how we thought with one mind on all things archaeological. Sir John, of course, was the expert, but I was his more than willing pupil.

"Don't you think, Sir John? That some of society's rules are random and pointless and simply incomprehensible?" I said, panting slightly, as we paused at a stone drinking trough in the woods for our poor hot horses to have some water.

Sir John sat tall and still in the saddle and contemplated me for a moment with his usual steady, unreadable gaze before answering.

"As a matter of fact, Penelope, I do. But society likes rules, it makes the nervous and the dullards amongst us think that everything is fine."

"You aren't nervous or dull, Sir John."

In the trees behind us the monkeys called to us noisily.

"Neither of us are, my dear, which is probably why we enjoy each other's company so much."

"And because we know that rules are made to be broken?" I said lightly, before I could stop myself. Sir John looked at me before roaring with laughter.

"I shouldn't have said that," I said, blushing furiously. "That came out all wrong."

"Did it?" Sir John asked. His blue eyes were friendly, enquiring but persistent, and he was smiling, and I found I couldn't look away. The more we looked at each other, the more I started to think that perhaps what I had said hadn't been as wrong as I'd thought.

Very slowly and with great precision, Sir John moved his horse up close next to Moti.

"Did it?" he asked again, so quietly the monkeys stopped their chattering to hear us better.

I couldn't answer, and I couldn't look away. I just closed my eyes as he took off his hat, leaned towards me, and kissed me. He smelt of sweat and tobacco and a sharp kind of cologne, and leather and horse.

"This," I thought, even as his lips pressed against mine, as the slight stubble of his face rubbed against mine, "now surely this is love."

Mutisher. 1986.

"*Penelope. Penelope*"

I open my eyes and look into the face of the German whose pearl of wisdom, dispensed yesterday, I had wanted to pass onto my dead husband. I fumbled for a moment for his name. Leo. That was it. He was called Leo.

"*Ah. Leo. You made it. Well done.*"

"*Yes, what a climb, but what a view!*"

His grey eyes are alight with pleasure, which sparks an answering pleasure within me.

"*Isn't it? It never fails to stagger. I was remembering my first time in India.*"

"*This is my first time*".

"*Then it's particularly special. Although I find some places carry as much impact the hundredth time you see them, as the first. Parts of India are like that.*"

"*Are you alright? You look a little pale. Can I get you a drink?*"

"*Thank you, I'm fine, just a little hot, and a little tired. I didn't sleep very well last night. Some water would be very nice. Bottled, please. I have some rupees in my pocket.*"

As I struggle to reach into my jacket pocket, Leo flaps his hands at me. "*It's my pleasure. I have rupees,*" and clearly happy to have understood, dashes off at a pace to the small stall selling drinks across the road.

I watch him go, dust from the road billowing around his heels with every step. They can tarmac the roads all they like, but still there will be dust. Dry dust is in the air, on the leaves of trees, by the sides of the roads, churned up by school children walking to school, by cars, by bicycles, by cows crossing from side to side as slowly as they like, as if they fully understand their special status. Even the British Raj with all their pomp and ceremony were defeated by the dust. I remember my father's car, polished to a gleam by his driver in his own personal war against the dust. And yet, amidst this dust, *the dust that seems as essential to India as the spices and the noise and the swarms of people, the women walk, immaculate, in their brilliant pinks and oranges and creams, saris grazing the ground. I have never known how they keep so fine, so clean, amidst the mess. I look at my beige cotton trousers and see my own sandy handprints marking one leg.*

Leo will be a few minutes, checking the seals on the water bottles, and counting out exactly the right number of rupees. I have time. I close my eyes again. I want to be 20 again, and back in Flagstaff House, in the guest bedroom on the top floor, with Sir John.

Chapter Five

Sir John's lips against mine felt so right, as if I had been waiting my whole life for this particular kiss. When he drew back slowly, I remained still for a few seconds before opening my eyes to look at him. I hoped he wouldn't say something ridiculous like "I shouldn't have done that, forgive me," as they so often did in novels when affairs began. I felt sure this was the start of an affair.

He didn't let me down. With his usual combination of dignity and observance only for the etiquette that he considered useful, Sir John just drew back, and looked at me steadily.

"I have been wanting to kiss you for a long time," he said quietly.

"Well, please don't wait so long next time," I said. My voice sounded strange to my ears.

"If there is a next time," I added, not wanting to seem forward. I was so new to this and had no idea if I was behaving in the accepted way. All I knew was that I had this. It had never felt like this when I had flirted with Johnnie; then I had felt calm and deliberate, now I had clammy palms and butterflies in my stomach. I looked up at Sir John again and felt as if I might fall off my horse.

He was watching me, with a small smile on his beautiful flat mouth. He stretched out a hand and cupped my head.

The horses stood perfectly still, as if understanding this was an important moment in their riders' lives.

"I have no right, but I would like there to be a next time and a next time and a next time after that," he murmured, pulling me close against him and kissing the side of my neck. "I am falling for you, Penelope, God help me."

My heart soared. I gathered my reins in one hand, and tentatively reached out and put the other on the hand holding his reins. I looked up at him. He looked down at me, and I felt I could see what he was thinking. I shouldn't. I'm married. There's no future. She's so young.

"But I want to," I said. It was enough. He lowered his head, slowly, so slowly, and I slipped my hand around his back, and held on to the back of his riding jacket, feeling the warmth of his body for the first time, as he kissed me, and kissed me again.

Finally, we broke apart.

"Penelope –" His voice was a little hoarse.

"Don't say any of it," I pleaded. "I'm not stupid. I may be innocent, and young, but that isn't the same as stupid."

He said nothing for a moment. I wondered if I'd been too direct, and the dreaded blushing began again. "You're blushing, my love. Penelope, I would never think you stupid, but I did want to make sure you understood what you were doing. But if you are sure, then so am I."

I smiled, and he smiled back, and I felt everything melt away – our age gap, his wife, his children, my parents, the whole corset of social restrictions that ruled our daily lives. Nothing mattered in that shady spot, for that moment in time, but Sir John and me.

"Well then," I said. "I'm glad that's settled."

Sir John dismounted and I did the same, my legs feeling slightly shaky, as if I'd had a fright. We took the reins of our horses in one hand, and led them slowly through the shady paths, talking. It was the kind of talking that made me feel more alive than I had ever felt before. My body was pulsing with a new kind of energy, and I felt I could walk and talk forever. I wondered if Sir John felt it, and glanced covertly at him. He was in his fifties, yet walked like a young man, proving again that age was irrelevant.

"I knew, that first night at dinner," he said.

"I knew before dinner, when I watched you across the room, flirting with all the women," I teased.

"I was not flirting!"

"You most certainly were. What would you call it then, if not flirting?"

"Simply the attentiveness of good manners."

"Ah. And is this good manners, too?" I asked teasingly.

We had reached a deserted cave. Sir John looked about him, then let the reins fall. I did the same, and the two horses nosed to the edge of the cave and stood together, enjoying a sparse patch of grass. I watched Moti, as if to distract myself from the sheer nerve of what I was doing. But then there was no time to think. Sir John reached for me, and drew me in, putting his arms around me and holding me tight. He kissed my hair and then my lips, his hands sliding lower, to my hips, pulling me firmly to him, stroking my body as if it already belonged to him.

Finally, he answered.

"No, this is quite unconnected to good manners."

"Stuff good manners," I mumbled into his chest, inhaling the smell of him, wishing I could live there.

I returned to Flagstaff House that morning a little later than I usually did, to find both my parents were already at breakfast. I had hoped that today of all days my mother would have taken breakfast in bed. She was the more observant of my two parents and too often she read what I was feeling in a single glance at my face. I took a deep breath in the doorway, assumed what I hoped was a look of calm and composure and entered the room, sliding into my place, as I did every day.

"Hello parents," I said, with a calm I was far from feeling.

"You're late today, darling. Where've you been? And you've caught the sun," Star observed sharply. "You really must wear a hat and veil when you ride out. This heat is terrible for the skin. Oh, and jodhpurs, Penelope? I hope you haven't been riding astride again."

"I'm afraid I have, it's the only way to keep up with Sir John and learn the things I need to know," I said, filling a glass with cold water and drinking it fast. "You're absolutely right about the sun, though," I added, playing along. My face did feel hot, but I knew it wasn't the sun that was to blame.

I took some toast, and asked for a boiled egg. I was not remotely hungry, but an egg would keep up appearances and give me something to push around my plate.

"You must have seen every monument three times by now," my mother went on. I looked up at her carefully. "I don't see how you find it so endlessly fascinating. Piles of old rocks. Dusty temples. Once you've seen one, you've seen them all. There's so much more to do here. Balls, parties, tennis."

Find a suitable husband, I added silently to her list.

"I'm doing all those things too, Star."

It felt to me like I was forever slipping into some new pale silk dress to attend some social engagement. Life in Delhi could be just one long round of parties if that was what I'd wanted. "It's just I'm also learning something new every day," I said. "Sir John is so knowledgeable, as he's dedicated his whole life to these artefacts. It's like being with a very learned professor who wants to pass on a little of his wisdom just before retirement," I went on.

My mother nodded. I crossed my fingers under the tablecloth and hoped I had neutralized any possible threat that might have been forming in her mind.

"Yes. And such a nice man," she added. It occurred to me then that she, too, might not be immune to his legendary charm. Immediately I pushed the thought away. That was a complication too far.

"I have so much more to do. I've started writing an article on Indian art," I added. "On the things I have been seeing, and what I have been learning. Sir John says I might be able to get it published, in due course."

"Jolly good, my dear," said my father, who was clearly bored of this conversation, and more than ready to talk about something else. Horses or soldiering, perhaps. He held *The Times of India* in his hands.

"Have you seen this, m'dear? That fellow we met, last week at dinner at the Club? Something to do with tea in the East India Company? He's resigned his position to marry an Indian girl from Jaipur."

"What? Really?" My mother put down her piece of toast and held out a hand. She loved a juicy piece of gossip so long as it didn't directly impact on her family. "Oh, do pass it over Philip. Let me have a look." She took up the paper and scanned the article. "Oh. So I see. I blame the heat, myself," she said at last. "Stops a person thinking clearly."

I breathed more easily as danger, real or imagined, receded, feeling grateful to the unknown East Indian officer for drawing their fire. I stirred some sugar into my coffee and took a sip. It had been quite a morning.

And so, my morning adventures took on an entirely new complexion. They became the only part of my day that I truly cared about. We always made time to stop and sit somewhere discreet, to talk, and to kiss. My body folded against Sir John as if it had been designed to fit, and away from him I craved feeling the long hard length of him pressed against me. I was not a complete innocent, and I knew what happened between men and women. Of course, I knew I should be married, and that to sleep with Sir John without being married carried huge risks, but choices were few: I wanted to be with Sir John and marriage was clearly out of the question.

Ironically in the end it was my parents who made things easy for us, facilitating the very thing they would have been furious about if they'd only known. The idea came to me on a morning ride, when Sir John told me he had to give up his digs for a while, as they were due to be refurbished. That morning at breakfast, I relayed this to my parents.

"Of course, being a man without a family to accommodate, Sir John's lodgings are not a priority to him, but I do feel rather sorry for him all the same. I should not like to be ripped from my home at short notice with nowhere to go." I said.

"Absolutely not," said my father, frowning. "That's not on. Ask him here, shall we, Star?" he said, looking over the top of his spectacles at my mother. "He's been so good to Penelope. This house is so damn big we won't even know he's here. And he's fine company. I like the fellow. Would be rather nice to have another man in the house. Not" he added hastily, looking from Star to me and back again, "that I mind when it's just me and my girls."

I waited for my mother's reply. Persuading Daddy to do anything was easy. My mother was another matter. I held my breath.

"Hmm?" Star looked up from the letter, several pages long, that she was reading. "Yes, what a good idea. I'll send a note this morning."

I smiled. "Well, that's settled. I'm sure he'll be very pleased. And it's a nice thing to do, since he's been so decent to me." I felt I was gabbling, and told myself to shut up before I gave the game away. Mission accomplished, Penelope. Pipe down. I picked up my teacup a little shakily and took a sip.

And as easily as that it was done. Sir John was to spend at least two weeks in the guest room on the top floor.

He arrived three days later. Dinner that evening seemed interminable. Sir John was the guest of honour, of course, on his first night as a temporary resident with us, and had been monopolized by my mother. I could hear her regaling him with stories at the far end of the room where we were having drinks. I strained my ears and caught my name.

"Penelope has always been wild. Too wild, actually," my mother said. "I'll never forget the day when Queen Mary had called for tea. One minute we were taking tea, then before I knew how it had happened, Penelope was teaching her how to play Lacrosse. In the drawing room."

I grinned at the memory. Sir John glanced at me and almost imperceptibly winked. I smiled, sipped my G and T, and turned away to talk to our other guests.

One other couple, newly arrived in India, joined us that night, the husband serving in some important position in the army under the auspices of my father, the wife, Elizabeth, much younger than her new husband. At a guess I'd have said she was not much older than me; wide-eyed and startled and utterly unsure whether India was for her.

"I am terribly worried about starting a family here," she confided in me over coffee in the drawing room, blushing as she said this.

"Oh, why?" I asked.

"The dirt. The disease. The strangeness of the place."

"Are you here for some time?" I asked, wondering if they could wait to have a family until they went home to England.

"Five years at least. Charles loves it here," she said, gesturing in the direction of her husband. "It's in his blood. He couldn't wait to get back."

"Well, I'm sure it will all be fine," I said, not at all sure of anything but feeling this was the best tack to take. I glanced again at Charles, and recalled my father telling me that his previous wife had died of Malaria a couple of years ago. No wonder this new wife felt a little nervous. It must be difficult, walking in a dead woman's shoes.

"I've been here for a few months now and have never felt better," I added, hoping to give Elizabeth some confidence. The weak smile she gave me suggested I had failed.

Eventually, Elizabeth and Charles left. My father offered Sir John a nightcap, which he accepted, while I pleaded tiredness.

"Goodnight Pa, Star, Sir John," I said, exiting swiftly and making for the stairs.

In my room, Agrata had lain out my white lace and cotton nightdress as I had requested and was waiting to help me undress. Impatient to be on my own, I stood still while she unbuttoned my silver silk evening dress.

"Thirty tiny seed pearl buttons running from neck to the small of the back," the dressmaker had boasted when I had been fitted for the gown. Fiddly and difficult to undo, now I wished there were less. On about button thirteen, I heard Sir John's footsteps passing along the corridor, firm and confident. My breathing quickened. Finally, after what felt like an hour, I was free of the dress. While Agrata turned to put the dress on a hanger, I took off my undergarments and pulled on my nightdress.

"I'm very tired, Agrata," I lied. "I can brush my hair and put myself to bed".

"Yes ma'am," the maid said, but even then, she checked the bed was turned down correctly before she left the room a moment later.

The door shut behind her and I was alone at last. My parents would not venture up here. I went to the bathroom and cleaned my teeth, and used a cool flannel to wipe my face. I paused in front of the mirror. My face was a little flushed, and my eyes were sparkling. My dark hair was gleaming, and I felt I looked attractive, perhaps as attractive as I ever had. The white nightdress fell to my knees, but was cut for the Indian heat, a little lower than was usual around the neck and leaving my arms bare.

I opened the door to the corridor. All was quiet. I tiptoed along the corridor as quietly as possible, and reached Sir John's door. It stood open, and inside, I saw the lights were low. Sir John stood at the window, his back to the room, smoking.

"Penelope," he said, turning round.

I shut the door behind me.

Sir John looked at me for a moment, before throwing his cigarette out of the window and walking towards me. His dinner jacket had been discarded onto a nearby chair. His crisp white shirt was unbuttoned at the neck, his chest a little revealed. He touched my hair.

"Did you really teach Queen Mary how to play Lacrosse in the drawing room?" he asked.

"It was only a short lesson," I smiled, glad for the lightness of his touch. I felt dizzy, almost drunk.

Sir John's arms slid around me and after one more measured look, his mouth lowered to mine.

Hours later, as dawn was breaking, I crept back to my own bedroom and climbed into bed. My body felt a little stiff and sore, but the right kind of sore, as if I had ridden out for too long on Moti. The sheets felt welcomingly cool against my skin. I closed my eyes and relived the last few hours in my mind, and found I was unable to stop smiling. My life had taken an extraordinary turn. So much more extraordinary than the long round of debutante balls and parties followed by a 'good' marriage to some titled, landed man that I had feared it would be. Lucky me, I thought, rolling over onto my side, trying to get comfortable, to calm down enough to go to sleep. I sat up again, shook out my pillow, and lay back down on it, breathing deeply, my mind full of stars and my nerve endings recalling Sir John's touch like soft bruises.

Mutisher. 1986.

I may be old, but my body still tingles as if I was twenty when I remember that night. It marked the beginning of a wonderful chapter in my life.

John and I passed a magical few months, often left to our own devices, to explore caves and temples together by day, and, whenever we could contrive it, each other by night. Often, finding himself in between bachelor accommodations, Sir John would spend a few weeks at Flagstaff House, and those nights would provide us with undreamed of opportunities. We took each day as if it was the only one we had together, each one as if it was a gift, to be enjoyed without questions.

No questions, for the obvious reason that neither of us wanted the answers. So the time passed, and as the beginning had been magical, so the end, and our final night together, was painful and sad.

That is the flip side of love.

Chapter Six

Flagstaff House. Delhi. 1931.

Sir John lay on his back, propped up against several pillows, smoking and reading my essay. He sighed occasionally and I wondered what this meant. He turned the pages slowly, the familiar frown lines wrinkling his brow in concentration. By the time he reached the final page, I felt sick. After an absolute age, he put the pages down on the bed and stubbed out his cigarette, before turning to me.

"I like it. It's very good."

"Really?" I squeaked with relief.

"You are a very clever girl, Penelope. It needs finishing of course, but the bones are excellent, the structure is there, the points are good and well made, and I like your style. Polish it up while you're on the boat, and take it to the *Architectural Review* when you get back home."

"Do you really think so?" I asked, feeling like a greedy child wanting more. I pulled the sheet up over my breasts, although it was about a year too late for such modesty. A friend, Robert Brydon, wrote for the Archie Rev, as it was known, and had offered me an introduction.

I looked sideways at Sir John. Somehow there had never been a good time to drop the Sir, despite everything that had passed between us. So, he was still Sir John, even here, in bed with him, like this. The curtains billowed at the vast windows in the night breeze, mosquitoes buzzing and banging beyond the screens.

How many nights had we lain like this together, him smoking, me talking? As many as we could steal. Enough that I'd lost count over the last year.

"Yes. I do. It's a good piece and the subject is right up its street. You've got a fine brain, my dear. Don't let it go to waste."

I leaned in gently and kissed him.

"Thank you. You have given me so much. In every way."

He smiled and raised an eyebrow in that mischievous and questioning way of his that I adored.

"It's been a pleasure, my dear." We both laughed at this.

Then the eyebrow fell, and the laughter stopped. "Now off you go. It's late. You've got your packing to finish and an early start in the morning."

"What about you?"

"What about me? I'll be fine. You know my plans. I'm going to finish up my term here before heading back to England, where I shall pass my hopefully long and most probably extremely dull retirement writing books on the masterpieces of Indian Art and playing copious handfuls of Bridge."

With your wife Florence, I added silently. He didn't mention her out of kindness, and, I supposed, his legendary good manners. Sadness clutched my heart.

"Oh, am I wrong?" Was I wrong not to have run away with him to an obscure Greek Island, as he had jokily suggested early one morning not so long ago, and spent our lives together excavating newly discovered ruins? Only time would answer that question.

I threw my arms around him, felt his chest hairs tickle against my face, smelt that smell, of horses and cologne and sweat, the smell of the active outdoor, cultured man that I had fallen in love with, the smell that I would always associate with him. He gently unwound my arms.

"You are not wrong, Penelope. Now go, darling girl. Go."

"I was just waiting for the right moment."

"There will never be a right moment."

His voice sounded thick, as if he was suddenly very tired. He kissed the top of my head, and gave me a gentle push. Wordless, I slipped out of bed, stood with my back to him, pulled on my dressing gown, tied it firmly at the waist, and clutching my essay, left the room without looking back.

I knew that if I did look back, he would see that I was crying. That if I looked back, I might have *gone* back, back to his arms and for good. And then everything I knew would have been lost forever. It wasn't the age difference – that was nothing. The insurmountable problem was his wife and their two children, waiting for him back in England. No, no, no, I couldn't do it. I couldn't ruin the unknown Florence's life, and the lives of Sir John's children, and of course my own. Too many people would have been hurt.

I ran noiselessly down the corridor back to my own room, avoiding the floorboards that creaked with a second sense borne from experience. I had skipped this way so often I could do it with my eyes closed. Now I slipped back into my own bedroom and closed the door. My trunks stood open but nearly full, neatly folded clothes and shawls and saris stowed inside. I was mostly packed, and ready for the return journey to England. I lay down on my fully made bed and put my face in the cool cotton pillow. I wanted to howl, but I wasn't really a crier. I often envied people who could weep out their pain. Mine always seemed to stay within me, fading slowly over time like a bruise that was visible only to me.

I closed my eyes and breathed deeply. Already I missed him. Missed him more than I had ever missed anyone. Much, much worse than saying goodbye to Johnnie. But it couldn't be helped. There was nothing to be done. Why was it I always seemed to be running away from men I loved, or thought I loved, called John?

Mutisher.
Had I been wrong?

I squeeze my eyes tight against the tears of long ago. How I had mourned Sir John on the boat home. I had mourned him every time I had seen couples dancing or laughing, or walking along the deck, hands almost touching. It was as if I knew even then, at just twenty, that a love like ours was a rare thing in an average life, perhaps found only once in a lifetime or, judging by the number of couples who clearly had nothing to stay to each other, often not at all. For the three weeks of the voyage, I excused myself early to Star and the party of travelers she had assembled around her each night, slipping away to my cabin while she stayed up late playing cards or talking. I was preoccupied and I was wounded, and there was no one I could tell.

"Are you quite all right, Penelope?" my mother asked me more than once, frustrated as always at my refusal to dance with the eligible young men on the boat.

"I'm fine," I replied. "Just a little sea sick." It was a fiction. Physically I was perfectly alright, it was emotionally that I was in torment. I had left my lover, so like-minded, so talented, so upright, so remarkable; I had given up a great love for convention, and I was tortured by the thought that I might never find its like again. That I might have made the wrong decision.

Even now, so many decades later, the sun burning down on me, the temple wall digging into my back, I wonder how life would have unfolded if I had chosen differently. At the time, I had made the decision that had seemed the most sensible, but I was more conventional then. It is far too late, now, for it to matter anyway. Sir John is dead, and I am old, and those days are long gone, gone to dust with the Raj.

I shift on the hard ground, trying to get more comfortable, unfathomably tired, not ready yet to stand up again and get on with our tour. My body is old even if my mind is preoccupied with my youth. Sir John is in front of me, but I am shaking my head. I didn't make that decision, my life went a different way, along the road that led to John.

Chapter Seven

London 1931.

I looked out of my bedroom window onto the residential streets of St John's Wood. The gutters were running with water and the roads gleamed from the recent rain. Yellowing leaves were carpeting the pavement. The air had a chilly bite to it that felt almost spiteful after the heat of India, and London seemed almost antiseptically clean after a year spent in the crush and dust of Delhi's streets. On the pavement below I saw a man carrying a black umbrella hurrying past in a bowler hat. On the other side of the road, a nanny pushed a large pram with a dark hood purposefully towards Regents Park despite the ominous grey clouds building, and oblivious to the shrieked objections of her charge.

I had been home for ten days, but my mind had yet to catch up with my body. I was still half expecting sunshine and the sound of the gong calling me to supper, and I still woke each morning with a sense of anticipation that I was to ride out with Sir John. But before I had even opened my eyes I would remember, and I would lie there, in the safe, dark space behind my eyelids and think, 'England. I am back in England' and wonder how I felt about that.

I turned back to my room and crossed to my desk. My article lay in a neat pile, together with a letter from Johnnie

Spencer Churchill. I smoothed the letter open and re-read it. It was one more complication that we were still, in his opinion, unofficially engaged. I wasn't the same girl who had said goodbye to him at the dance at Lansdowne House 18 months earlier, and I felt sure that he wouldn't be the same person either. What would we make of each other when we finally met again?

I went back to the window and closed it against the brisk wind that was lifting papers off my desk and making my room decidedly too cold. If nothing else surely Johnnie and I could be friends. Seeing him would be a good distraction, to stop myself thinking about Sir John, wondering what he was doing, and who he was riding out with now I wasn't there to keep him company. Would he have found a new, young protégé to keep him company during his final months in India?

'Stop it, Penelope', I told myself. 'You're back in England now. Think of something else.' This, I was finding, was my best tactic when it came to Sir John, and the alternative thought of choice was something that felt really important – my appointment with the *Archie Rev*. Robert Byron had arranged for me to meet the editor, a slightly reclusive man, he had warned me, called Mr. Hastings. I was due at their offices in Queen Anne's Gate, Westminster, at twelve pm. I planned to wear a new patterned day dress with a blue knitted coat and my favourite felt cloche hat. In a manner quite unlike me, I had given considerable thought to my clothes for this occasion. I needed to look suitably business like, yet I had never dressed for a business encounter before. I wasn't nervous exactly, but nor was I sure what to expect. My parents would be furious if they knew what I was about, so I'd also had to lie to my mother. I'd told her I planned to go to Chelsea to visit an old school friend, Sylvia, for lunch.

Sylvia did at least live in Chelsea, but that was about the only particle of truth in the story. Luckily for me, Star had so much catching up of her own to do, after so long spent in India, that she was too busy and distracted to ask any of her lethally penetrating questions. If she had started cross examining me, she'd have been on to me in a moment. I'd delivered my tale with a convincing nonchalance-"I'm off to Sylvia's, her mother's giving a lunch" -but still, the less said the better.

Of course, there was the problem of our driver to deal with, but I'd thought about that too. I was going to pretend I was early and wanted something from The Army and Navy stores, which was round the corner from the offices of the *Archie Rev*, yet near enough to Chelsea for my fictitious lunch with Sylvia to be a reasonable short walk away. All this sneaking around was exhausting, and simply for a professional engagement with a magazine editor, rather excessive, but I knew it was what I had to do if I wanted to get on my way as an Indologist and writer. If I was to follow my heart, and try to achieve the thing that made my soul sing. My mother was from a different age, when, as she regularly reminded me, young ladies of quality did not 'swan about unaccompanied'. This felt rather ironic after a year of doing exactly that with Sir John right under her nose, but I wasn't about to point this out.

Just before noon, I stood outside the offices of the *Architectural Review*, which was housed in a large stucco building with several bells. I pushed through the open door, and a burly porter with a bushy grey moustache and a bad case of dandruff informed me that the magazine's offices could be found on the second floor. I didn't wait for the lift, preferring to walk, but took the stairs two at a time. On the second floor I found the door standing ajar, but it seemed rude to simply march in, so I rang the bell anyway and waited. After a moment's pause, I rang again, and faced with no response, I tentatively went in.

A long corridor with red carpet that had several balding patches and had clearly seen better days led into the distance. Several rooms ran off it to the left and right. There was an indistinct clattering of typewriters, like several people talking loudly to each other all at once, no natural light and a sense of energy that reached up to the high ceilings. I headed towards the sound of the typing. I followed it to a small room at the end of the corridor, where a girl of about my age with bobbed hair was bashing away at her typewriter so fast I could barely see her fingers. Through the open door behind her, I could see two more typists working away.

"Yes?" she demanded without looking up or stopping.

"Hello. I'm Miss Chetwode. I have an appointment to see Mr. Hastings," I said, with what I hoped was authority.

"Right-o" she said, never taking her eyes off her copy. Ker-ching went the typewriter as she pushed the roller back to the beginning of the line.

"Take a seat please."

I sat down on a pale wooden chair with a smooth curved back, my handbag containing my article clutched on my knee. I tried not to feel like a child clinging desperately to a security blanket.

So, this was the – well, a- world of work. I'd seen my father's, of course, but that was quite different. That involved smart uniforms, thoroughbred horses, lunches at Windsor with the King and his family, and commanding regiments of Indians in Delhi. This was the world of the office, of writing, of the intellect being expressed in a monthly format, bound and sold. Excitement interlaced with my nerves as my palms grew damp.

The girl got up and walked briskly out the room. I knew she hadn't gone far as I could hear murmurings.

A deep voice: "Well, Hastings won't see her, you know what he's like. He hates meeting new people. Besides, I know for a fact he's asleep on his chaise longue in his office at this very moment. Got a nasty head cold, apparently. I'd better see her myself. Ask her to come in, would you?"

Then the girl was back, and I was following her back down the corridor. She ushered me into a small room, not much more than a cupboard. A man who looked a little older than me, wearing two parts of a pale green woollen three-piece suit, the jacket cast casually off on his chair, white shirt sleeves rolled up, was sitting in front of a desk piled high with the most extraordinary mess of books and papers. He stood up as I waited in the doorway.

"Ah ha!" he said, as if he had just done something rather clever. "Miss -?" he enquired politely.

"Chetwode. Penelope Chetwode," I said. "I have an appointment to see Mr. Hastings. About an article I have written. On the Ellora caves in India," I added.

"Ah ha," he said again. "I am afraid Mr. Hastings is otherwise engaged, so you'll have to make do with me. John Betjeman. I'm an assistant editor here," he said, sticking out his hand. I took it. I tried to remember if Robert had mentioned him. He was taller than me, with dancing eyes and a mouth that looked as if it was about to burst into laughter. A battered looking teddy bear sat on the window sill watching us closely with his orange glass eyes. I wondered if it was his, or whether he had a small child who had visited him in the office and forgotten it.

"Grab a pew," he said, waving at a wooden chair at the next desk. He stuck out his hand again. "Can I have a look?"

"Oh, of course," I said, dragging my increasingly dog-eared manuscript from my black leather handbag and feeling even sicker than when Sir John had read it. Mr. Betjeman took the piece, and quickly flicked through it.

"Tell me something about it," he said, putting it down.

"Well, it's all about the Ellora caves. These caves – there are thirty-four of them – are just outside the medieval town of Aurangabad, and date back over a thousand years. The Indians call them the Verul Leni. You can walk through them all – and they absolutely take your breath away, because there's just the most fantastic amounts of intricate carvings. All done by Hindus, Jains and Buddhists between the 7th and 9th Centuries AD. That was the period of the Rashtrakuta Dynasty, you see, which was such a tolerant regime it allowed many religions to flourish simultaneously."

"They sound stunning. Personally, I hate Abroad, but I salute your adventurous nature. What are the carvings of?"

"The Buddhist caves can be quite plain in parts, and mostly feature stone carved images of Buddha, but the Hindu ones depict scenes with many Hindu gods, including Shiva, of course, a key Indian God, and Lakshmi for fertility, (here I started to blush slightly, recalling some of the explicit fertility images of naked large breasted women) as well as Kali, the goddess of death. The fact we can even see them, well, it's all thanks to this rather marvelous man, Sir John Marshall," I rushed on, "who has saved India's monuments across the country for future generations." It felt strange, uttering Sir John's name here, in this little carpeted box of a room, as if he were a relative stranger.

"He revived the Indian Archaeological Survey in 1902, and has been saving works of art ever since. He showed me around many of them himself, in fact, including the Ellora caves."

"Now you mention his name, I *have* heard of him," Mr. Betjeman said. "Does he happen to be a friend of Robert Byron?"

"Yes." I clutched at this familiar straw. "I know Rob too," I added. Which was true. Slightly.

John looked at me. His eyes crinkled attractively at the corners as he smiled. "We've a friend in common, then."

"It seems we have, Mr. Betjeman," I smiled back. His teeth had green bits at the sides. I wondered if he ever cleaned them.

"I've got some photographs," I said, diving back into my bag and pulling out a slight pile of them. "Why don't I show them to you, so you get a better idea of what I'm talking about?"

"Good idea," he said. "And please, call me John."

Did any mother ever call their child anything else, I wondered, as I handed the pile of pictures over to him.

He looked about the small room for a surface to put them on. The options were limited. His desk was piled high with paper, and the window sill crammed with dirty coffee cups and the rather disapproving looking teddy bear.

"Ah ha, the floor. That's the best place," John said, with the air of someone pulling a rabbit from a hat, and kneeling down, started to lay them out as if they were a deck of tarot cards and he was about to tell me my fortune.

I knelt beside him and began to comment.

"Now, that's Visvakarma cave, with carvings by the Buddhists dating from the 7th century. That's one of the finest examples of Buddhist art in India. These here, they are all from the Ramesvara Cave, also by the Buddhists. The most impressive Jaina Caves are caves 32 and 34 – see here, isn't that the most exquisite cave painting you've ever seen? And look at this carved lotus flower. Sensational." I kept pointing at the various photos and explaining things within them. Thankfully I'd got over my embarrassment, as the final image I laid down showed a man and a woman copulating while others watched. As I looked at it, I couldn't recall which cave it was from, and I knew instantly Sir John had slipped it in as a joke. I stifled a laugh, sliding it under another photograph.

"As I said earlier, they had an open approach to sex, quite different to that which prevails today," I explained, gathering up the pictures briskly.

John roared with laughter. "So I see. May I suggest you tell me more about this over lunch? There's a nice little fish place round the corner."

"Lovely," I said, grinning broadly back. He had that kind of smile, the type that made you smile back, as if you were united by the sharing of a good joke. It fleetingly crossed my mind that Star wouldn't approve of my dining with a strange man without a chaperone, but it seemed ridiculous to worry about that after we'd been poring over sexual images together for ten minutes, and at least I was smartly dressed and wearing a hat. Star didn't approve of most things I did, and besides, I liked this man in his dusty three-piece suit with trousers that looked like they had never seen a middle crease. So, I banished Star and her reservations from my mind, something I was in fact getting rather good at. John shrugged into his jacket and I picked up my bag. We walked side by side down the red carpeted corridor towards the ancient lift. He was several inches taller than me, I noticed, and his trousers were too short.

"You've got odd socks on," I blurted, before I could stop myself. What was I thinking of? I was trying to persuade this man to publish my article. Luckily John appeared unperturbed. Perhaps odd socks were a frequent feature in his life. John looked down at his feet with an air of wonder.

"So I have. Shall we take the stairs? This lift takes an age and I'm absolutely famished."

Mutisher.
Recalling the headiness of that first meeting with John, it is as if I am right there again, yet when I open my eyes the light is the brilliance of India, not the gloom of a drizzling winter day in London. But I can see the hairs on John's shins, protruding from his sock when he crossed his legs and his trousers hitched up an inch or so. I can hear him talking, often with his mouth full, as if he had so much to say it simply couldn't wait. He had ploughed through three courses – oysters, grilled dover sole, and an apple crumble – while I had been more interested in him than the food. So he had polished off my lunch too.

"Not going to eat that? Jolly good – mind if I do?"

And he'd forked it up and over onto his plate, and carried on munching and talking as if he hadn't been fed for a week.

Chapter Eight

"Right. Jolly good. Yes, that sounds rather marvellous. Thank you. That would be nice. At seven pm tomorrow? I look forward to it. Goodbye, then, John. Yes. Goodbye."

I put the phone back down on its cradle and thanked the Lord my mother was out and therefore not able to overhear my conversation.

Why, exactly, was the house telephone always sited in the most public part of the house, making privacy an absolute impossibility? I answered my own question – so no secret assignations could be made, of course. I clapped my hands together and jogged on the spot. I had just put down the phone to John Betjeman from the *Architectural Review*, who had told me that the magazine was going to publish my article.

Star wouldn't be impressed – she'd be worried that even such flimsy evidence of an intellect would be a major threat to my marriage prospects, which were, in her opinion, not looking good anyway. But Daddy might. I thought he would understand, as he understood so much about me. Whatever their reaction might be, I looked forward to telling them.

Sir John, I thought to myself, you might be impressed. (A pang here. I wished I could tell him. But we had agreed there was no point in letters.). At least my mind had some distracting things to focus on. I had to learn Sanskrit – it would help me in translating original documents into English. I had to improve my German too. Many of the Indian scholarship writings had been written in German, and I couldn't yet understand them well enough.

And then there was that rather nice man John Betjeman. Following the acceptance of my article. I had a feeling, a small, sneaking, growing feeling, that he liked me, and not just as an occasional contributor to his magazine. We had met several times since our lunch together, at my best friend Billa Cresswell's house for supper, at the theatre, at another friend's drinks, and the last time we had met he had given me a copy of his book of poems, *Mount Zion*. It was his first book, but there were "many more to come" he told me.

What did Star make of it? I told her a little about him, and predictably she wasn't impressed with the idea of him at all. She assumed an expression of martyrdom, as if I chose the most wrong-headed kind of fellow I could find, simply to annoy her.

"We ask people like that to dinner, Penelope, we don't marry them," she said to me, exasperation resounding through her words.

"Who said anything about marriage?" I snapped back.

No one would be good enough for me in my mother's eyes, unless they had a stately home and a pheasant shoot, together with some kind of title. John Betjeman's parents were – intake of breath!-in Trade and lived in North London somewhere, Highgate I thought, or possibly Hampstead, in a terraced house on a road with a small garden. Three generations of cabinet makers, apparently.

I'd reached the top of the stairs. I pushed into my bedroom in search of my coat and hat. Whatever Star thought of him, I liked him, even without the pheasant shoot (or maybe part of the attraction was precisely because he didn't have one.) John had inscribed my copy of *Mount Zion* in rather flattering, if humorous, tones. It was sitting on my desk, and I picked it up to look at it:

"Penelope Chetwode, I always think, is not only tastefully dressed despite the hours she wears out her clothes in the Reading Room of the British Museum, but is also the possessor of unique social charm that has made her the cynosure of all eyes – whether surrounded by the horn rims of Bloomsbury Spectacle frames or the paint and powder of a high class drawing-room. So compelling is her character that I am obliged to write for her this facetious dedication. I am that clever chap John Betjeman."

I put the book down again and shrugged into my coat. I wasn't going to flatter myself. My mother was a fool to even mention marriage. John Betjeman was a flirt and while he might like me, he certainly wasn't serious about me. In fact, he wasn't serious about very much. Conservation perhaps. He had a bee in his bonnet about that. Passionate about saving old buildings and loathing ugly new ones. Poetry. (He read me poems by some Welshman -, I forget his name- the whole taxi ride to visit friends the other day.) His old teddy bear, Archibald. (The bear in the office had turned out to belong to John). Supper out was just that – supper out. That was all. Still, as I turned to go back downstairs, my felt hat pulled low on my forehead, my coat buttoned, I couldn't suppress the flicker, just the smallest flicker, of something, a mix of hope, and laughter, and liking. What would a life be like, lived cheek by jowl with a curious intellect like John's?

I skipped downstairs, all the Johns swirling in my head.

Sir John, married, with children, and left behind in Delhi and very much out of bounds.

Johnnie Spencer Churchill, who had recently taken me to the theatre and to supper parties. Still as devastatingly handsome as ever. The trouble was, I felt pretty sure I didn't love him. Everything just felt different to how it had felt with Sir John, and how it was starting to feel with John B. The fact that Johnnie had started working for a bank in the City, and was trying to take it seriously although he clearly hated it, didn't help, as doing something he hated seemed to have made him awfully bad tempered.

Our evenings usually began well enough, but we had fallen into a habit of arguing about things, often small and unimportant. This was a new development. It was odd, because our backgrounds were quite similar and so I'd expected us to be like minded on most things, but it increasingly appeared not. Last week we had argued furiously over a play, which he had loved and I had absolutely loathed. But neither of us seemed able to simply agree to disagree, instead we had to flog whatever we were fighting about to death until we sat on opposite sides of the cab home in a charged silence. I'd thought it might mean that things were over and frankly felt rather relieved that a decision had been made for me. I preferred it when things were clear. But then just last week Johnnie had bought me a gorgeous pink sapphire engagement ring, to cement our unofficial engagement. It was so beautiful I took it, even though I knew I shouldn't have done.

I felt a stab of guilt as I recalled this. I hadn't worn the ring – it was on my dressing table, in my Indian silver jewelry box. Lots of people did this kind of thing, unofficial engagements were almost de rigeur at my age. At least half my friends had had at least one already – they seemed to be very much a part of the debutante scene and beyond. I knew that John B had been engaged at least twice, for about a month each time, and both broken off amicably enough. Still, as my thoughts turned back, yet again, to the John without a pheasant shoot, it felt wrong to be holding onto a ring from Johnnie, reluctant banker and would-be artist, but very probably not my future husband. I reluctantly suspected I had to find a way to give it back.

That brought me back to John Betjeman, or John B, or Tewpie, as I had already nicknamed him. Tewpie gave everyone a nickname. He had decided to call me Plymmie, I wasn't really sure why, except that he told me that Plymouth was the city which sat at the point where he crossed from sophisticated man of letters to the blustery carefree world of his childhood holidays in Cornwall. It felt like a compliment.

Imagine, imagine, that I did marry John B. Star really wasn't going to like it, but however much I tried to tell myself otherwise, I had a gut-churning feeling about this man that wouldn't quite go away – that if there was the tiniest chance he was serious about me, then he might be the man for me.

I decided to go for a walk. I left the house, turned towards Regents Park and wondered how one ever decided. There were simply no two ways about it, I was the kind of girl who got married, so that was not a question, but a given. The big question was, to whom? It was, as my mother had pointed out, a lifelong decision, so one really wanted to get it right. My parents had got it so absolutely right that it felt a tough act to follow. The sky was gunmetal grey and the air crisp, but I quickened my step. If I couldn't ride, and Moti was still in India, then walking was the next best thing to help me clear my head.

⚜ ⚜ ⚜

That night, Johnnie took me to the theatre again. He picked me up and it was clear from the outset that he was in an impossible mood. The taxi driver took the wrong route, his fish at supper was cold and had to be sent back, and when we finally slid into our seats in the stalls, the seats were too small.

"It's all those partners' lunches you're having," I teased, but he didn't so much as smirk. I knew it must be dreadful to have to do a job you loathed, but still I was glad when the house lights dimmed and the curtain rose a few seconds later, rendering further conversation unnecessary.

It was a production of *The Merchant of Venice*, a play I had always loathed. I'd been made to act in it at school, and it brought unwelcome memories flooding back of having to press my lips against those of Hilda Greville. I'd been Portia to her Bassanio, and there was simply no getting out of that kiss without a major rewriting of Shakespeare's script. Back then, I'd shut my eyes and imagined she was Laurence Olivier. Now, I was sitting next to someone as least as handsome, yet I didn't particularly feel like kissing him. I knew I couldn't let this drift forever – so many of my friends were already married, a few had even started on babies – and by some people's standards – my mother's, for a start – I was getting quite old. Did I care? Not really. Not as much as perhaps I should.

But something was urging me to decide. It was as if I was in danger of letting something – I didn't know what– slip irrevocably through my fingers. A sense of urgency was building within me, a sense that I couldn't put off this looming life changing decision for much longer.

So, as the scenes came and went, with each one I thought something different. With one scene I thought 'Johnnie Spencer Churchill' and the next I thought 'John Betjeman', as if I was pulling the petals off daisies – he loves me, he loves me not, he loves me, he loves me not.

Afterwards, Johnnie suggested we went to the Connaught Hotel for a quiet drink. Silent would have been a more accurate description.

"Oh Johnnie," I said, as he downed his brandy in two gulps, "I'm sorry you hate the job so much."

He fixed me with his handsome eyes, framed by those well-groomed dark eyebrows, but infuriatingly said nothing. Perhaps there was nothing left to say, but that seemed too sad to admit at the age of just twenty-two. To have no words left to share. But as we said goodnight, I slid the pink solitaire off my finger and slipped it into his dinner jacket pocket without him noticing. As I went up to bed, I felt tired but somehow lighter.

Chapter Nine

One cloudless morning a few days later, I woke up and just knew. Relief flooded me – the uncertainty had been dreadfully unsettling, and hard to live with. I dressed carefully, and even allowed my maid to help me arrange my hair. Usually I did it myself – I hated people fussing around me all the time, as if I was a helpless person who couldn't do a thing for myself. I powdered my nose and put on some lipstick. I wore a silk cream summer dress with a navy-blue velvet coat on the top, and my favourite pearls. I pinned my diamond brooch to the collar of the coat and stood in front of the mirror. The result was good. The dress fell to calf length and hid my legs, which I always felt were the worst part of me.

Charles brought the car round and we set off to the *Archie Rev*. He left me at the front door-I told him I'd make my own way home. I had no idea how long I would be, and the last thing I thought a good idea was for him to be loitering outside waiting for me. Besides, my mother was bound to need the car, and if things went well, I might be a while.

The porter let me in, and I climbed to the second floor up the by now familiar stairs. I breezed in through the open door, waved at the secretary whose name I now knew to be Maud, and continued straight into John's office.

John was sitting at his desk marking up an article.

"Penelope," he said, as he stood up to kiss me, not seeming remotely surprised to see me, "tell me this: don't they teach grammar at schools any more? This article is quite interesting, but appallingly written. I feel like I'm back at Heddon Court working as an English teacher trying to impress on a class of grubby kneed boys the small but important difference between 'who's' and 'whose'. I spent a summer term there after Oxford, and it nearly finished me off. This article might just succeed where numerous schoolboys failed".

He smelt slightly musty and his cheek was warm and scratchy.

"John," I said.

This was no time for nerves, yet I felt absolutely sick with them.

"I've come to say. Well, something a little out of the ordinary, I suppose. But I don't see the point in beating about the bush."

John was looking at me with raised eyebrows. "No, a dreadful waste of time, that," he agreed mildly.

I pushed on, encouraged. "So, the thing is. The thing is……., I think we should get married."

I'd done more than push on, I'd plunged right in.

John sat back down on his chair, and pulled one up for me. I sank into it, grateful for the support.

"Really? Alright then, Plymmie, if that's what you think," he said amiably.

"Oh." I don't know what I had expected, but this easy agreement surprised me. Then I remembered he had been engaged twice already, and broken it off both times. His agreement quite possibly meant nothing.

"Well, it is, John, really. I love you, and I think you love me, and most importantly, we're well suited. We both like to write, and to use our heads. And we like a laugh, you and Oi." I slipped into my familiar mock cockney at the end of the sentence and we both laughed. I could feel I was blushing slightly.

"Then I'm flattered, and delighted to accept and all that; so that's settled. Your parents won't like it though."

"No. I'm afraid you're right. We won't tell them yet. Then I will still receive my allowance and can carry on with my studies."

"You've thought it all out, you are a clever girl. Can I tell my parents? My father rather liked you when we went to lunch the other week, so he'll be delighted."

John took me in his arms. "Oh, Plymmie! We're secretly engaged. I think we'd better go out for lunch and get very drunk."

I laughed, excitement welling up in me. "We are! But I will still have to go back to India for a while, you know. Before we marry. It's all arranged, and I couldn't let my mother down. We've got a proper expedition into the Himalayas planned."

I wanted to go back to India, in the interests of my work. I knew it would be different this time – Sir John had retired and would be back in England, but now I was engaged to John, that didn't feel so bad. I was already a different girl – I had a published article now, and a vocation, but still a part of me longed for India, and if I didn't go on this trip, I had no idea when, if ever, I would return.

"Yes, yes."

"But you're not to fall in love with other girls while I'm away."

John assumed a hurt look. "Archibald would disown me. As if I would. Ninni noooni nooonii nooni, it's you I love."

I smiled. I couldn't help smiling when he played the fool, and made up rhymes, and generally made light of life. Who could? He seemed full of laughter, yet I knew that it covered up a darker, more complex, place, the place where his soul resided and his poetry began.

"Oi think this calls for a celebration, don't you?" I replied.

"Oi most certainly do, Nooni. Oi do." John pulled his jacket off his chair and held the door open. "Come on, my darling. Off we go into the sunset."

We walked along the red carpet together, laughing helplessly, and it really felt as if that was where we were headed.

Mutisher. 1986

"Penelope! Penelope. I've some water for you.

Leo is back. It feels like a long time since he went to fetch water.

"Thank you." I take the plastic bottle and sip from its open top. It trickles down my throat, deliciously cold, more delicious than any cold drink an American soft drink company could invent.

Things were quite different back then. Everything felt overlaid with this blanket of urgency, as if things had to be settled as soon as possible. Now, I have whatever time God gives me, but then, all I knew was that I couldn't wait too long for Tewpie to ask me to marry him. There were too many other girls who wanted him, and I was afraid he would be snapped up by one of the clever (blue-eyed)) Mitford sisters, or my equally clever friend Billa. Friendship seemed to come second when men were involved.

Once we were engaged, and I was on the way back to India, I wrote him a letter. I have always been a prolific letter writer – perhaps we all were, in those days.

'I have a love which can never exist for anyone else' I told him.

I take another gulp of the icy water and wonder now if that was true.

Leo sits down beside me.

In those days, you married for life. Back then, even the King couldn't marry a divorcée and keep his job.

"Leo," I say. "Have you ever been in love?"

Leo coughs into his water. Clearly not the question he had been expecting from his ancient, wrinkled tour guide with breasts down to her waist and legs that Tewpie always called 'the broadwoods' for their sturdiness and dependability. I want to reassure him. I'm not propositioning you, dear man, don't be so absurd. Those days are over for me. But I say nothing.

"Yes. Most recently-and enduringly -with my wife."

"That's good," I say. "That's very good."

Silence falls for a moment. Then.

"And you, Penelope? Have you ever been in love?" he asks.

I open my eyes to the accusing glare of the sun.

"Oh yes" I say. "Twice, I thought I was. And then-"

I fall silent quite suddenly.

It wasn't plain sailing. Of course John fell in love while I was away. He was an incorrigible faller-in-love. This time he fell for Billa and then for Pamela Mitford. He even got engaged to Billa. I should have known right then that things would not go smoothly for me with John, and perhaps I did, but I loved him, and it's a well acknowledged fact that love makes a person do things that their head may warn them against.

Love is blind.

When John wrote to me about Billa, I was so upset I considered breaking it off, but I also knew that I loved John properly. I had given up one man I had loved already, could I really risk doing the same with another? So I tried to think coolly, rationally. What did I want? What was I trying to achieve? Did one small dalliance really matter? And then I wrote back to him.:

'Do nothing until I am back – I know I can make you happy."

I really believed I could.

John listened to me. He broke it off with Billa, and I started for England. But three weeks on a boat is a lot of thinking time, particularly when you're twenty-three and engaged to a man who has already proved himself to be fickle enough to get engaged to someone else while being secretly engaged to you. Somewhere between Bombay and Egypt proper doubts crept in, and I wondered if I was being foolish. My father thought so. My mother had made her feelings quite clear. No one was encouraging me to marry Tewpie. So I got off the boat in Marseille in the South of France, to visit my aunt on the way home, to collect my thoughts and find a quiet space to ponder whether I could really marry this man, this man who fell in love with anyone and everyone, even when newly engaged to me. It was a strange time, because I knew I loved him properly, deeply and enduringly; that he was someone I admired and respected and wanted to make my life with; without that knowledge, I couldn't have gone so strongly against my parents' wishes, even with the delight I took in shocking them. Yet there was just so much that was clearly going to be difficult between us. He had so many friends who worshipped him, and I couldn't bear to be subsumed into that, to become just one more of his devoted followers. As I'd said to Johnnie Spencer Churchill before him, I had things I wanted to do, and that hadn't changed.

So I thought, and I pondered, but I came endlessly back and back to the same single point: this was a proper and real love, and they were hard to find. To have one was a blessing. Two was an abundance of gifts. How dare I pass it up?

It was Nancy Mitford who sorted it out. She sent John to France to see me.

"If you want her, you'd better go after her" she said to him. So he came and found me, even though he hated 'Abroad' and I found that so touching that we finally agreed it. We were to be together. No

more putting it off. We would marry, and soon. When he left, I had a ring made out of string around my finger and strict instructions not to take it off, even when bathing.

"Yes" I say to Leo, picking up the thread of my half-finished sentence. "I have known love."

Chapter Ten

July 29th, 1933. London.

I woke around dawn, and lay very still for quite a while, watching the light slide through the gaps in the curtains and feel its way into the room. I could tell by the hazy softness to it that it was still early.

I had no need to rush. Everything was organized and I had plenty of time. The dress and coat I was going to wear later hung in the cupboard, the new cream satin shoes sat neatly below.

The day would start as usual. Sara would bring me breakfast at 7am, I would eat, get up, get dressed. She would help me do my hair, and for once I would let her. Even I wanted to look as lovely as I could, today. But apart from that small deviation from my usual routine there seemed nothing very remarkable about today. Nothing to mark it out as my wedding day.

I traced the delicate outline of the ceiling rose with my eyes. I could have been marrying in St Paul's Cathedral or St Margaret's, Westminster, in front of a great crowd. That could have been my destiny. I could have had engagement announcements in the social pages of the broadsheets, and a round of engagement parties, as well as a towering pile of presents. But that would have required a different groom.

By choosing John – Tewpie-I had made a bigger choice than that of just a husband. I had also chosen a certain kind of wedding, and a certain kind of future. It meant that today, I would say my vows in Edmonton register office, witnessed by several people I didn't know, and John's parents, in a tailored dress and coat rather than a couture creation with a ten-foot train and my mother's tiara on my head. It meant I would not go up a long and ancient aisle to Elgar on the arm of my father, and down it to the sound of Mendelson's trumpets with my new husband at my side. It meant my own parents wouldn't be there at all.

My heart lurched with guilt at this. I didn't really mind the lack of pomp – I didn't care much for pomp – but I did feel a sense of sadness that I was deceiving my parents, and that they wouldn't be at my wedding day. But the practicalities of life demanded it. They so heartily disapproved of John and all he stood for that it just seemed simpler this way. Besides, they were still in India and we couldn't wait any longer. Who knew what John would do next if we did?

I reached for my diary, and the letter contained within its pages, the letter my father had written me when I'd first tentatively told him I wanted to marry John a few months ago. I had read it many times when I had been wondering how to proceed. Now I smoothed it open and read it once more, as if it was a way of getting close to Daddy, of hearing his voice in my head, however disapproving, on this day.

"Dearest Penelope.

I have just got your letter of May 4th in which you say you have made up your mind to marry John Betjeman. I cannot pretend to be pleased, but you are a grown woman with more than the usual share of brains, and if after all this time you have had for reflection you are not certain of your feelings you never will be.

I have told you the risks you are running, and it is useless to repeat everything I have said or written. I love you more than I can say and hope and pray you may have chosen right, and that you will be happy.... Bless you darling.

Your own Daddy.

I sat back against my pillows. My own Daddy, who hoped I would be happy, despite his opinion that John was a bad choice. I felt another pang, worse this time. Yet, however much I loved my Pa, I knew he hailed from a different generation, a generation when upper class married upper class, and anything else was unthinkable. He couldn't be blamed for that, but times were changing, and I hoped that he would come round to his soon-to-be son-in-law. I heard his note of caution, but I had weighed up the risks and made my decision in the face of them. Yes, there were differences between Tewpie and me, but there was also a great deal that was the same: strong opinions, a questing intellect, the same sense of humour, and a shared Christian faith.

Still, despite my confidence in John, I knew I was ducking things by marrying him while my parents were still in India. I just couldn't face the prospect of months of wedding planning conducted under a cloud of disapproval, of my mother's loudly whispered conversations filling in friends and family on her disappointment with 'Penelope's choice'. It was easier this way.

By one pm today I would be Mrs Betjeman.

My stomach flipped. Mrs John Betjeman. The name felt nothing to do with me at all, but I would, I supposed, get used to it. It was what I wanted, and with luck and hard work I would be as happy with my choice as my parents had been in their marriage.

I heard the rattle of china and the tread of Sara's foot on the stairs. My last breakfast as a single woman was approaching. After we were married, we were going to spend a few nights in a favourite hotel of John's, in Essex. My stomach churned again with a sense of the next stage of my life really beginning. I had a plan, and I could see it unfolding. John and I would be happy. I would become an Indologist and he a poet, and together we would support each other and look after each other. I would take him in hand about his ghastly suits-yes, that was one of the first things I would do, I had already sought out a good but inexpensive tailor – and make sure he had matching socks, and after I had spent a few months in Germany improving my German – I was adamant that I still had to do that even though John didn't like the idea, otherwise I couldn't progress my work-we would set up home together and at some stage start a family. My parents would accept my marriage, and all would be well. I would ride out every day – if my father forgave me, perhaps I could persuade him to send Moti home from Delhi- and work and write, and in the evenings John and I would sit down together and eat and talk and laugh. We would have children, and grandchildren together. Yes, there was an awful lot to look forward to. A lifetime of adventures.

Sara knocked and entered.

"Mornin' Sara," I said, in my mock-cockney. "Thanks so much for this. Would you be an angel and come back and help me dress in an hour's time?"

I wanted to tell her why, but I couldn't. This was my secret and mine alone. Sara bobbed out of the room, and I poured my tea before lopping the top off my egg. I was going to have to give up all this – this breakfast tray set with silver and a linen napkin, brought to me in bed, this fine, deeply comfortable way of living I'd known my whole life. I wasn't going into this blind. With my allowance and John's salary, we'd manage, but my married life wouldn't be like this.

I savoured each mouthful of egg as I thought all this. Very probably, I thought with a smile, not minding at all, excited by the adventure I was about to embark on, this was the last egg I wouldn't have to boil myself. I wondered how long eggs took to boil. I only knew they were boiled at all because they were called 'boiled eggs'. Did one completely submerge the egg in water? Hot, I presumed? I put the tray aside and swung my legs to the floor. Never mind all that. How hard could it be? There was bound to be a book or two on cooking. I'd find one and teach myself. Today there were more important things to think about. Today was my wedding day. I stood up, feeling light with excitement, and looked out the window to see a clear and brilliant blue sky. It felt like the gods had turned out one of England's finest days, just for me.

Later, I waited in the drawing room, internally a mixture of nerves and excitement, outwardly calm and serene. I had a suitcase packed and ready, standing in the hall. The doorbell rang, and I sprang up, brushing my skirt down, and walking to the door. John stood in the hallway, already ushered in. My stomach flipped and I beamed at him.

"Good morning. I'm not stopping," he said to Peters, the butler, who was attempting to take his coat. "I've simply come to collect Penelope."

"Very good sir."

John picked up my case.

"Goodbye, Peters," I said, walking out onto the stone front steps, knowing I was saying goodbye in a more permanent way than he could understand. I would never really live here again, not as I had before, as the unmarried debutante daughter of Sir Philip Chetwode. Next time I stood in this hallway, whether anyone liked it or not, I would be a married woman.

"Goodbye Miss Penelope".

"Goodbye, Mr. Peters," John said, grinning from ear to ear as he always did when he mocked me for being grand. Which was a bit of a joke, because we both knew that he not-very-secretly loved it – the deference, the comfort, the being waited on hand and foot much more than I did, and I'd grown up with it.

The heavy door closed behind us and John led me to his car, a dark blue Austin borrowed from his father for the duration of our nuptials and honeymoon.

He held the passenger door open, and I climbed in. The car smelt of leather and wax polish.

He went round to the other side, and got in next to me.

"Plymmie," he said, looking at me. "You look beautiful."

I smiled at him. The sun beamed down on us as John accelerated up the road and indicated to turn out of my street. I turned round to cast a last glance behind me at my sometime childhood home, and noticed Archibald, John's teddy bear, sitting on the back seat, the guest of honour at his master's wedding day. Then John swung left, and a little later took a right, and soon we were away into the sooty grubbiness of industrial North London, until finally the urban landscape opened out into the green, lush fields of Edmonton.

Chapter Eleven

There was just one picture of our wedding, taken by the wife of John's headmaster friend, Isabel Hope, on the steps of Edmonton register office. I didn't blush. Perhaps I was too happy. I simply clutched the arm of my new husband and beamed.

The reception took place in a local restaurant. We were a small group-John and me, John's parents, and Hubert de Cronin Hastings – I'd finally met him- from the Archie Rev, as well as a handful of our friends. John's father made a toast, and John stood up and made a little speech to our small assembled party, the spirit of which was how fortunate he was to have me as his wife. Somehow that made my sense of what I was missing – my parents, my past life – diminish. John loved me. We loved each other. A warmth stole through me. Despite a few hiccups on the journey, he had forsaken all others. It would all be all right. I was absolutely certain of it.

We waved off the last guest and turned to each other.

"Well then. It's just you and me, Plymmie."

We got back in the car and John drove us in his usual erratic fashion – frequently pressing on the horn, too often taking his eyes off the road to twinkle at me as he guffawed at one of his own anecdotes-to The Green Man, in Braxted, Essex. We were to spend three days there.

I had never set foot in a pub before, let alone stayed in one, so I had no idea what to expect. After a half hour or so, and feeling rather flung about by John's driving, we drew into the car park. The pub was a cream building, with a huge sign bearing an image of the head of a man with green hair on it creaking backwards and forwards. The landlord bustled forward to greet us. He clearly knew John well, and after offering us a drink, led us to our room.

It turned out we were the only guests, which I felt glad about. John and I had been so little alone together, and that was what I wanted most of all now. The room was perfectly adequate. The wallpaper was cream and covered with oriental temples depicted in a fine blue ink that reminded me of India. The curtains were unlined, so daylight began to leak into the room by five every morning. The bed was a solid brass one, with several thick blankets and a feather quilt, and a horsehair mattress that sagged in the middle. The sheets were starched and the window looked out onto a river that ran behind the pub.

Our three days quickly fell into a routine. Every morning, at seven o'clock, the publican's wife brought us a tray of tea, leaving it outside the bedroom. Lying awake together, John and I, not yet quite used to the other being there, listened for the rattle of china approaching. Together, we absorbed the sound of retreating footsteps with mounting excitement, and then John darted out of bed and retrieved the tray, and we sat in bed together, sipping delicious hot tea, with John calling me Mrs Betjeman as many times as he could in every sentence, as if it was some kind of child's party game.

"Oh do stop it, Mr Betjeman," I said.

"I'm just pleased you're my wife, Mrs Betjeman."

This was touching. I felt for his naked leg under the sheets. But I hadn't earned the reputation of being the most difficult debutante of my year for nothing.

"I'm not just your wife," I said, in amiable tones.

"Of course you're not," John said, just a little cautiously. "I know that. You're Mrs Betjeman who's also going to become an expert in Indian Art. An In-dol-o-gist," he said quite loudly, sounding out each syllable as if I was very deaf or rather slow or possibly both.

"That's correct," I said, sipping my tea.

"But you are my wife as well," John repeated, a pleased note throbbing in his voice.

I slid my hand higher and clutched his erect cock. I rolled towards him. We were both naked, having abandoned our sleepwear sometime during the night.

"Yes, Oi am, Tewpie," I kissed him between words. "Oi most definitely am."

We kissed again, and John pressed closer, his hands moving over my body. He stroked my breasts and sucked first one nipple and then the other, before rolling on top of me and entering me with a thrust, the first of many, until he let out a shout I had already come to recognise, and collapsed on me, dramatically still.

We lay quietly together, John's wetness sliding slowly out of me.

"I am your wife," I said again. "And I love being your wife."

A little while later, I added "I will miss you when I'm in Berlin."

"Berlin?" John said, roused, as if the notion of my going there was utterly foreign to him.

"Yes, darling. Berlin. Don't pretend you've never heard of it. You know perfectly well I'm going. Just for three months. To improve my German and to get a look at some of these crucial documents I need to study," I told him with as much patience as I could muster, which frankly wasn't much. He knew all about this plan, I'd told him many, many times.

Silence fell for what felt like a long time.

Finally, John said: "You know how I hate Abroad."

"Well, you don't have to come," I said, hoping he would, at least for a while.

"Although I'd like it very much if you did," I added, remembering something Star had once told me about men: 'Never assume they know what you are thinking,' she had said, 'because most likely, they are thinking something quite else.'

"I thought you might shelve Berlin, now that we're married," John went on.

Awkwardly, I leant up on one elbow and looked at him.

"Darling. I have to go. You know I do. It's only for three months." As I said this, I knew this was a feeble argument. Three months sounded and felt like an eternity to me, and so probably it did to John as well.

"Nor am I sure it's a very safe or savoury place to visit at present," John added, as if I hadn't spoken.

I swung my legs out of bed and tugged on my dressing gown. "It's perfectly safe for a non-political English person," I said crossly. "It's only Germans and communists who need to watch out."

"We all need to watch out," John said flatly, watching me as I washed my face. "That man Hitler is a dangerous lunatic."

"We agree on that at least," I said, starting to roll on my stockings. "His politics are alarming and he's rather unattractive with that black beetle moustache and barking voice. Yet he obviously has some kind of mesmerising quality, the way people fall for him. And not just the Germans either – look at Unity, for heaven's sake! And Diana's not much better."

John got out of bed and reached for his clothes. "So long as he doesn't mesmerise you. I'm awfully hungry all of a sudden. Let's go and have some breakfast."

I buttoned up my skirt, relieved the conversation had moved on. I already knew that changing the subject was John's way of heading off a horrid conversation, but today I thought he was right to do so. It was much better than a row, which was clearly going to be had at some stage, but our honeymoon was not the place.

I went down the corridor to the bathroom. It was narrow and cold, with a small misted window high up in one wall and hard bubbles of white paint on the skirting boards. The bath had seen better days. I washed my face and hands and returned to the bedroom to find John fully dressed in his grey flannel trousers and a sweater and tweed jacket.

"Eggs. I feel like eggs," he said, as we creaked down the wooden stairs. "Fried, not too hard. With bacon. And perhaps a tomato."

My mouth salivated. Dinner the previous night seemed a long time ago, and I had discovered that staying in bed too long made me hungry.

"Oh good idea, darling. Me too." I smiled up at him, and his eyes crinkled, and I knew things were alright again between us. I pushed away the thought of how much I was going to miss him. Surely the time apart would fly. And when I got back, we would set up home together in a proper way, somewhere outside London. Near enough for Tewpie to get to London for work, but just far out enough that we could have a house and a garden and a horse. We would have to buy crockery and linen, and I would cook. I'd find a daily maid and we'd have log fires and friends to supper. We wouldn't be too formal; I'd handwrite invitations and only ask people whose company we truly enjoyed. Clever people, friends of John's from Oxford, and new friends we'd make in the country, wherever we settled. I felt a flutter of excitement mingled with a sense of contentment. We were married and starting out on our life together, building something really solid. 'In sickness and health, forsaking all others, until death do us part' and all that. A little time spent in Berlin couldn't change that. John was right. I was Mrs Betjeman. Which meant I would get to live with this man for the rest of my life. All of this came at me in a great rush.

"Oh, Mr Betjeman," I said. "I do love being married to you."

We grinned at each other over a silver-plated rack of toast and descended again into our own silly, intimate little world.

"Mrs Betjeman. Oh so do oi."

Chapter Twelve

September 1933. London.

I had gone back home to London, and the days were tense. I'd told my parents about my marriage a few days previously, when they had arrived from India. They were upset, as I had known they would be.

- Why had I kept it a secret?
- Why couldn't I have told them?
- They only had one daughter to marry off, and now they had been deprived of that joy.
- Did I understand how selfish I had been?
- And after all they had done for me.

My mother did the talking, but my father's eyes reproached me silently, and that silence, those looks, hurt far more than my mother's words. I felt sick that I'd caused so much upset, but still I couldn't help also feeling madly happy and madly in love. I wished my parents would just accept it, so John could come and stay. I missed my husband, and didn't quite understand the whole fuss of it. I hated being cast back into life as a single daughter, when I was now a married woman. It had happened, I'd done it, it couldn't be undone, and nor did I want it to be, so couldn't we all just make the best of it? And it could have been worse – it could have been Johnnie Spencer Churchill, who was now travelling in Spain with his already pregnant wife. But somehow now didn't seem the time to mention that. Now was the time to grovel.

"I'm so sorry," I said, again, for the hundredth time, at breakfast, lunch and dinner. "It just seemed the easiest way."

The telephone in the hall was in constant use as my mother rang up relatives she hadn't spoken to for years and bellowed the news into the handset.

"Penelope's eloped – yes, ELOPED, I said". Either at least half the relatives were deaf or the line very bad, but my mother determinedly persevered until her statement was met by what I assumed were gratifying gasps of horror at the other end.

After several days of this, I decided to try and bring things to an end by speaking directly to my father. I went to his study and knocked on the door.

"Come in."

I entered. My father was sitting behind his mahogany desk topped with green leather, motionless.

"Penelope," he smiled at me slightly. The bags under his eyes were particularly pronounced today.

"Oh Pa."

"Take a seat."

I sat in the leather chair opposite him, feeling as if I was in the headmaster's study.

"Please try and understand," I said.

"I am trying."

Silence. Then: "What I don't understand, and perhaps never will, is why you did it. I look to my own behaviour, and wonder how I must have let you down in order for you to have done this. If I recall correctly, I wrote to you, telling you how I wished only for your happiness if this was to be your choice. That I would support you, even though it wasn't my first choice for you."

I shifted in my chair. "I know. I can't really explain it. It just seemed – easiest."

"That's what you keep saying. But it doesn't feel very easy now."

"No." I looked about the familiar study, with its wall of books and worn Arabian carpet. Evidence of India was everywhere, in the silver elephant on my father's desk, to the yellowing wall hangings of Kali that hung either side of the door. The burgundy drapes were tied back with thick golden rope and early autumn sunshine was streaming in.

My father sighed heavily. "Well. It would seem we all have no choice but to try and adjust. We had better put an announcement in the papers. Let everyone know the marriage has taken place. Even your mother can't telephone the news to everybody."

I smiled, grateful for his joke, however half hearted. We were united for a brief moment against my mother, always the most comfortable emotional position for me. My father and I lined up against Star, and, sometimes, my brother Roger, too.

"Oh, it's much too late for an announcement," said Star, bustling in, that day's copy of the *Daily Telegraph* hanging limply from her fingers and missing my father's jest completely. "This has just been delivered". She raised the paper to eye level and read out a headline:

"Field Marshal Chetwode's daughter. Married after Broken Engagement.".

My father closed his eyes, nodding his head in indication of a kind of painful acceptance, as if he had expected this very thing.

"How?" he asked.

"I can tell you that, too," Star said, holding the paper at arm's length again and preparing to read further.

I flushed. My mother was clearly enjoying herself now, embarking on her story with evident relish.

"Let me see, ah yes, here we are: "Lady Birch told the paper: "My niece and Mr John Betjeman became engaged quite a long time ago, but the engagement was broken off. This wedding was a complete surprise to all her relatives. Not even her parents knew anything about this marriage until after it was over. It took place very quietly indeed on July 29th."

Star lowered the paper again and glared at me, then lifted it again, carrying on reading very slowly in a high, sarcastic kind of voice. "The happy couple took their honeymoon in a Public House in Essex."

I said nothing. What was there to say? A Public House just didn't have the same *cachet* as a tour around Europe. I was clearly going to have to endure a period of disgrace with my parents, and on a wider level put up with being the latest sensational story doing the rounds. I took a deep breath. As Sir John had always said, 'all things passed'. This too would pass. I simply had to remember that. My parents were returning to India in a matter of days, and everyone knew that today's headlines was tomorrow's fish and chip paper.

I looked between my parents. My mother, with pursed lips and frowning brow, my father, fingers steepled on his lap, eyes now closed. His thinking pose.

I took a deep breath and resolved to make one last effort.

"Look. Mummy, Daddy. Can't we focus on the most important thing, which is that I do love John, very much, and I believe we will be happy. I know he's not the sort of man you hoped I'd meet, but the world is changing and I think a marriage such as mine will become more and more usual. He's a very talented poet who is clearly going to make his way in the world. I wouldn't be surprised if he ended up as...well, as Poet Laureate or something. He's also, and may I remind you that to some people this is the most important thing when settling on a husband, a wonderful man. I love him. What I suggest is, could we all please try and get past how my marriage has begun, and concentrate on that, instead? I feel sure you will like John once you know him better."

My mother swung round to look at me. I wouldn't have been surprised if her jaw had dropped open like an actress in a silent movie, hands rising to expressing the sheer horror of it all. Like him? Her face seemed to scream. Like him? His parents are In Trade! He's a Nobody. (I could see the capital letters in my mind's eye). You, who could have made a glittering match, have chosen this, and now you ask us to *like* him?

Star opened her mouth to speak, but my father, my ally all my life, hadn't completely deserted me now. He opened his eyes very slowly, as if his eyelids were being wound up manually by an invisible pulley, and held up a hand to stop her. He looked at me thoughtfully for a moment, before sighing heavily and starting to speak.

"My darling Star. I think Penelope has a point. What we have here is, as the French say, a *fait accompli*. We must ask Penelope's husband, Mr John Betjeman, to dinner before we leave for India, and welcome him to the family."

Star said absolutely nothing which of course said more than words ever could.

I broke the silence.

"Thank you, Pa. I am sure you will get on famously."

I was not forgiven, but it was a step along the path towards forgiveness.

I went off to telephone John, to see if and when he could come to supper. My brow furrowed a little as I stood in the hall and waited to be connected to him. Although I had declared with such certainty that my parents would love Tewpie, this had just been bravado and in fact I was sure of nothing of the sort. In truth, I had huge misgivings on this front. My father, usually so warm and forgiving towards me, was clearly furious at my elopement with someone he considered so unsuitable, and I suspected he would show John his rigid military front. My brother Roger always went against whatever position I took on anything and everything, on the grounds that siblings were born to be rivals, so he would be no help to me. And as for Star, she had already declared her hand.

John might be charming, but it was a great deal of hostility even for him to overcome, and his usual stance when faced with dislike was to fall into a pattern of mockery. So when John came to supper two nights later, I was extremely nervous. We were in the drawing room when Peters announced his arrival. My mother was, deliberately I felt, at her most imperious. A dark velvet evening dress, hair up, long white gloves. I was amazed she had stopped short of a tiara. My father was in uniform. He stood up and shook John's hand firmly.

"Welcome. Come. Have a drink. Whisky? Now I've been wondering what you should call me. Sir is too formal, and Philip wouldn't do. You can't exactly call me Father since I'm not your father. So I think you'd better call me Field Marshal."

Roger, standing by the drinks tray, snorted with laughter. This wasn't the opening gambit I'd been anticipating, and a glance at John's face told me this wasn't the kind of start he'd been expecting either. I caught his eye and made a pleading 'don't make a fuss' face behind my father. I hoped he wouldn't respond badly, or make one of his jokes, which could be hilarious but more often than not were at least in part at the expense of the person he was making the joke to. At the same time I felt a bolt of irritation at my father. What on earth was the point in asking John to supper if he was then going to insult him? Even if John didn't make an obvious joke he was more than capable of rising to the gauntlet Daddy had just effectively thrown down, by calling my father 'General' or 'Colonel' at every opportunity here on in, which would lead to a very uncomfortable and probably extremely short evening. My mother raised an eyebrow and smiled at me for the first time in about a week.

I glared crossly back. I longed for these two men, so important in my life, to get on. For my father to invite John shooting, and for John to talk about my father with warmth and appreciation to our friends. They were both my family now, and I wanted them to like each other, even if they were only doing it for me. Instead, they were like a pair of male lions, squaring up to each other, ready for a fight.

I looked at John again, who was now clutching his cut glass tumbler of whisky and taking a large slug, with an expression on his face that I knew meant he was formulating his response. He looked thoughtful but his mouth was twitching, as if he might combust into unstoppable laughter any second. Perhaps something of my churning feelings reached him then, across that immaculate drawing room, because he took pity on me. There was no mocking reply. Instead he simply said,

"Of course, Field Marshal, that will do very well," with one of his best smiles, before adding after a lengthy pause: "And you must call me John."

Now it was my turn for sudden, unexpected laughter, quickly swallowed. My father frowned, but said nothing. I felt he had got off lightly. I knew that later, there would be many, many jokes made in private between John and me. But that was a problem for later. For now, I would settle with tonight being a success, an evening to mark the beginnings of a new stage in our family relations, so my parents could sail for India with good feeling towards my new husband, and I could embark on my marriage with their blessing.

Chapter Thirteen

Berlin.

February 1934.

I sat at the small battered wooden desk situated under the window and wondered what to write to Tewpie today. I had been in Berlin for ten weeks now, and with John left behind in London, at times my husband seemed remote to me. I was shocked to find how much I missed him. In our short marriage I'd got used to him being there each night when I fell asleep, and when I woke in the morning. I missed the intimacy and closeness that was ours alone, to be shared with no one else. I was making progress in learning German and in my research, but it was much slower than I had hoped, largely as a result of numerous unimagined distractions.

Before arriving in Berlin, I had pictured myself diligently passing weeks poring over documents in the appropriate libraries and immersed in an intensive German course. While I was managing something of that, there were just far too many invitations to parties and dinners that somehow I found it awfully hard to decline. As a result I was out too much and working too little, and since all these invitations came from English friends, my German was underused and improving at a snail's pace.

The trouble had begun with my mother-didn't it always? She'd written to everyone she'd ever met with even the slightest of German connections to let them know I'd gone to Germany to study. This had followed hard on the heels of the news that I had run away with John and married him. While we'd later put it about that I'd married John quietly as my father had been ill, I wasn't naïve enough to think that anyone really believed this. So not only was I a new face on the social radar of Englishmen and women living in self-imposed exile in Berlin, I was a curiosity and a focus for a fantastic amount of gossip. Why had I married in secret? Were my parents furious? And was the marriage already over? Was that why I was in Berlin? As a result, invitations poured in and my diary was packed.

Few people were rude enough to ask me these questions directly, but I could often see in the eyes of whoever I was talking to a ferocious curiosity as to the state of my life. As a debutante I had acquired the reputation of being unconventional, and now, to everyone who relished any whiff of scandal (and that appeared to be most people), it seemed I was living up marvellously to that early promise.

Berlin itself was also very distracting. I had only been there once before, during my travels across Europe during my Art History course, and that felt like a lifetime ago. I had been younger, innocent, unmarried, and not so attuned to the atmosphere of the place. I had also been chaperoned and sheltered. But most of all, Herr Hitler had not been so evidently in charge. I had recalled it as a hectic whirl of culture and cakes, and in many ways, it still seemed to be that. I had been to the opera just a few nights ago, and I met one friend or another for patisseries almost every day – but at the same time, not very far underneath the surface, things felt very different. The distinctive red, black and white Nazi flag draped from every flagpole, and troops of soldiers marched through the streets on a regular basis in a rather alarming manner. The Reichstag, a beautiful building I had sketched from several angles on my previous visit, now lay in ruins, apparently as a result of the random act of one mad communist. Adolf Hitler had used this as an excuse to declare the country under a severe threat from communism and invoke Emergency Powers. Now the man was being tried, and would very probably be executed if found guilty, which everyone knew he would be. Every day the newspapers reported the trial, and just yesterday Hitler – had any star ever risen more quickly? – had taken the stand and given evidence in support of the theory of a communist conspiracy against Germany.

Hitler. Fast becoming a byword for power, and of the ruthless and absolute variety. Opinions on him remained divided. Tewpie had been quite clear – 'The man's a lunatic' – but my friend Unity Mitford worshipped him, having first seen him at the Nuremburg rally the previous autumn. She'd gone to the rally with her sister Diana, who had rather scandalously (wonderful-someone more scandalous than me!) left her husband Bryan Guinness for Oswald Mosley, the leader of the British Fascist Party. The rally had happened before I arrived in Berlin, but Unity was still eulogising about it weeks later when I got there. Almost as soon as I arrived, she took me to tea at the coffee house that Hitler frequented, and told me she went there almost every day in the hope he would eventually notice her. We ordered tea and waited for Hitler to put in his usual appearance, which he duly did, but for reasons I couldn't quite explain I didn't feel his reputed magnetism, only a sense of invisible menace. The way everyone jumped about him made me nervous. He had walked into the teashop with several companions and taken a table in the far corner, before greeting the waitress by name and ordering a number of cakes and a pot of tea. He had spoken quite softly to the waitress and smiled at her. I wanted to look away, but I couldn't, my eyes were impolitely glued to his every movement. A few moments after arriving, he got up – his companions all immediately leapt to their feet-and went outside for a moment, and then stalked back in. I thought he walked as if the world was his and his alone, and while Unity practically swooned, I sat there chewing my lower lip and wondering where all this was heading.

Then there had been the unpleasant incident concerning a university lecturer who had been going to show me some Sanskrit documents. Some days previously, I had walked over to the University of Berlin to keep our appointment, which had been made by letter from England some weeks before. The Professor was an expert in the field of Sanskrit documents and sublime at the translation of them. There were few people as knowledgeable as him on the language and issues surrounding it in the whole world. However, when I had called on the Porter's lodge to announce my appointment, the Porter had quickly looked at something over my shoulder and told me in rapid German that the Professor did not work there any longer.

"He doesn't work here anymore?" I repeated slowly, in my rather basic German, certain I must have misunderstood.

"No longer here," the porter repeated more slowly, still looking over my shoulder. "Departed."

And with that he turned away, presenting me with his back, returning to shuffle a pile of papers in what appeared to be a completely purposeless way.

The back told me the conversation was over. But I knew there was something uncomfortable, even furtive, about the way the Porter had refused to meet my eye or elaborate, and in the way he returned with such relief to his nonsensical task. I retraced my steps home again, turning the incident over in my mind like a coin in my pocket, and wondering how odd it was that the Professor had not seen fit to let me know that he would not be able to keep our appointment after all.

A few days later, I met a journalist friend of Tewpie's, Will Chalmers, for drinks. Will was a foreign correspondent for *The Times*, and his work sent him all around the world to wherever something was occurring that needed reporting. He was now in Berlin covering the Reichstag fire trial and John had asked him to check on me. Clutching a gin and tonic, I told him what had happened.

"This professor was Jewish, I presume?" he asked shortly.

"I suppose it's possible," I said slowly.

"Then that's your mystery solved. Rules have recently been brought in disqualifying Jews from holding a variety of professional positions," Will said, frowning at me. "Your professor probably had no choice but to stand down."

My mouth gaped. "What rules are these?"

"Hitler's Rules, Penelope. He makes them up as it suits him."

"But how ghastly. Just for being Jewish? How very unfair."

"Yes. But this is happening all over Berlin – and Germany – I'm afraid. The man's got a vision for a new world order, and Jews – and gypsies, and homosexuals, for that matter-don't play any part in it."

I squinted at Will, frowning, a sickening awareness flooding through me. The flags, the marching, the rumours, the emergency powers. The menace, the fear that underpinned everyone's deference. It had seemed so obviously appalling that I had made the mistake of not taking it seriously enough. But could Hitler really be such a monster? Diana and Unity were very English girls and they both adored Hitler. I looked up at Will who was watching me intently. I've always had one of these annoying faces that reveals everything I'm thinking.

"It seems unbelievable," I said rather helplessly.

"Believe it," Will replied shortly, knocking back his whisky and gesturing to the barman for another.

I thought back to what John had said. Was this man Hitler really that dangerous? Was he determined to take us all back to dark times, to what, growing up, all the adults in my life had always described as the worst of times and the worst of times (to misquote Charles Dickens). Was Hitler mad enough, God help us, to start another war, even though the Great War had been the war to end all wars? I shook my head slightly. I wanted to dismiss the idea outright and to concentrate on my weak gin and tonic and eating the bowl of olives in front of me. It just didn't seem possible that anyone could ever consider war as a viable option again. I was too young to remember the start of the Great War but by 1918 I was eight, and old enough to remember the end. Nor could I avoid knowing about it-the consequences of it had been with me my whole life. I thought of all my female cousins, with their lost fiancés and the spinsterish lives that had resulted; of my elderly relatives with their dead sons, of the generation of boys lost before they'd really begun their lives. Of Vera Brittain's recent and brilliant memoir, *Testament of Youth,* which I'd read just weeks before coming to Berlin. Of Johnny Spencer Churchill's dismissive talk of the surplus two million. The images piled up like dead bodies on the Somme, and I looked at Will with a sense of dawning horror.

"Oh Will. We can't do it all again," I said. "It's not possible. Is it?"

Will said nothing. He just looked at me, frowning, his head nodding slightly, swirling his whisky in its heavy cut glass tumbler. It said it all.

I didn't eat the olives. I left Will soon after that, and hurried back along the darkening streets to my room, a heavy knot of nerves in my stomach, my mind churning over what I had learnt, feeling an acute longing for home. I turned a corner and ran into a platoon of marching soldiers, and I had to force myself to walk calmly past them. I had done nothing wrong, so what had I to fear? (But then neither had the Jewish professor, his only 'crime' was to be Jewish.) As fear walked across my shoulders, leaving a trail of goosebumps on my arms, I suddenly felt utterly certain that terrible things were starting to unfold. Berlin as the world knew it might very soon cease to exist.

"Darling Tewpie," I wrote, sitting up straight at my little writing desk. There was so much to say. So much to tell him. I wished he was here, that we could spend some time together, talk over what was happening to our world once again. I'd tried and tried to persuade him to come and visit, but he wouldn't. He hated Abroad, he told me in his letters, time and again; I'd known that when I'd chosen to go to Berlin, he said, and that was that.

Instead he'd been working hard, and had found us a home for my return. We were to move to Berkshire, to a house in a village called Uffington. John had written enthusiastically about it, and how he was busy getting it ready with the help of a local girl called Molly Higgins. Now I longed to be back in England with him, enjoying the domestic fun of putting together our home, to give in to the appeal of being married; but if I did, I knew I would lose a foothold in my own plans. Too much was happening here to leave. I felt a new sense of urgency, that I had to stay on and finish my research as quickly as I could, in case Berlin was about to become a place where an English girl could no longer go. Tewpie, so committed to his own work, would surely understand that.

A knock sounded on my door.

"Come in," I said.

"A letter, Mrs Betjeman," said a maid, walking towards me, making the floorboards creak, holding out a silver salver with a letter on it.

John's writing.

"Thank you." I slit it open, greedy for news, and started to read it quickly. The house was ready. He missed me. He was longing for me to return to him and see it. He was very sorry, but he'd been a little too taken with Molly. But it was over now. Could I please forgive him and would I come back soon?

I put the letter down on top of the papers on my desk and rested my head in my hands. I couldn't quite take it in. How could this have happened? Tewpie and I were together, unwaveringly, forever, the same, however much the world changed around us, whatever Hitler did. Weren't we? That was our commitment – wasn't it? That was the commitment I had made. But if this kind of thing was possible, what had John meant by marriage?

I closed my eyes and breathed in deeply as my whole world seemed to rock. I had so many feelings swirling in my chest I didn't know which one to start with. I tried not to think of John, entering the body of some other girl, thrusting into her as he did with me, but the image felt violently, lividly, obscenely alive in my mind. Had he kissed this Molly, held her, stroked her, as he had me, before finally possessing her in the way a man should surely only possess his wife? My breathing felt shallow and heat climbed my cheeks. My chest tightened and I closed my eyes, trying to shut out the truth. I felt just as I had when we were first engaged, and John had proposed to my friend Billa. Billa had later told me they had never progressed beyond a kiss. But still. I had felt a sick sense of betrayal then, just as I did now. Was my husband an incorrigible ladies' man? Was my marriage going to flounder before it had really begun? I wasn't naïve, I knew men did these things – the irony of my friendship with Sir John was not lost on me. I knew they had little flirtations on the side of their main life, so to speak, but my husband – my new husband of a matter of mere months – seemed to have them in such proliferation and with no regard for who knew or what I felt. Had my father, with his doubts about John, been right all along? He certainly would not understand, he who had been married, and, I presumed, faithfully so, for over thirty years. Moral outrage rose in me as, at the same time, I felt guilt seep through me like damp through a wall. Perhaps it was my fault. I shouldn't have left him alone all this time. If I had been there, the physical thing between us was good enough to keep him out of the arms of some village girl. I knew men had needs. Star had told me that. I hadn't been there, and John was simply not the sort of husband you left unattended. This – I glanced at the letter again–was what happened if you did. Husbands like John needed constant looking after. I pictured my mother's face, showing not a scrap of surprise. "What did you expect?" she seemed to say. And I knew she was right. What had I expected, leaving my new husband? What had I thought would happen?

"Husbands," my mother's voice boomed in my head, "are a kind of work, Penelope. And if you don't do the job properly, someone else will."

I looked at the letter I had just started, telling John about the political situation in Germany, and wanting to stay longer, and my own growing interest in Catholicism.

"There is no chance of my going over for two years at the very least", I had written, in a bid to reassure him, since my new husband was not at all happy about my growing attraction to Rome. My new, neglected, unfaithful husband! I picked up my pen, and wrote on, pushing down my anger, ignoring my hurt, setting my face against my desire to learn, to drink in knowledge like a thirsty elephant at a waterhole, turning my back on Berlin in favour of practicality – and, I supposed, love. My marriage could not, would not, fail. Of that one thing I was certain.

I crossed out the sentence about staying longer. "Read your letter," I wrote shortly. "Never mind all that, I miss you. I miss our jokes and our talks and I miss being close to you at night. I have decided to come home early."

That day I understood that John, and my marriage, came first.

Mutisher.
I realise I am frowning as I remember this, even though it is over a distance of more than fifty years. It wasn't a fashionable view then, and it isn't a fashionable view now, but it has always seemed to me that the sting of a husband's infidelity, once discovered, never quite fades. When I was growing up, in my privileged upper-class world, a discreet affair within the framework of a marriage was considered perfectly acceptable, once the heir and the spare had been provided. Yet this made no sense to me – if I had wanted someone other than John, I would have married them-and when John chose other girls over me, each time hurt as much as if it was the first time. So I cannot help but frown, even now, when I think about Molly Higgins.

I remember sealing the letter and calling for the maid. She took it downstairs for posting, and I went to telephone the agent to organise my ticket home. I remember meeting Unity to say goodbye, dodging the soldiers on the way there. I remember urging her to come home with me, to open her eyes and to see what was going on, but she simply laughed as if I was mad.

"You are silly, Penelope. Of course there won't be a war," she said. "If there is, I will kill myself. Germany – Herr Hitler – " she gesticulated round the café I now referred to as 'Hitler's café' – "all this, here, is my life."

I laugh, a short barking noise that sounds odd to my ears, as I recall this, even though there is nothing to laugh at, nothing that is funny. But I was not the mad one. I was a young woman, alarmed by what was happening in Germany, and in love with my husband. I needed to get home to him, to feel his arms around me, and to feel safe. I wanted to be an Indologist, but that day in Berlin, my desire to make my marriage work, to be with John, revealed itself to be greater than my professional ambition. If that meant going home early, then that is what I would do. It turned out I wasn't so different from other girls, after all.

Unity, meanwhile, stayed in Germany, and she had meant what she had said. When war was declared, she took a pistol and shot herself in the head, just as she had told me she would. She didn't die immediately from that bullet. That might have been a blessing. Instead she was wounded, but not yet terminally. She came home, severely brain damaged, and lived for several more years, cared for by her devastated, exhausted mother, before finally dying. A short life, ruined by an obsession with a lunatic. Just one more casualty of Hitler's war.

I breathe deeply to try and still my rapidly beating heart. The noises in the village are floating up to me: children calling to each other as they start on the short journey home for lunch from school. Mothers talking while they heat the water for the rice. Life is very *simple here. You live, you eat, you pray, you learn, you work, you sleep. You wake up and it starts again. Being alive is a privilege in itself. Perhaps we make things too complicated in the West, far more than it has to be. We live on our whims and our passions. We do not abide by the rules.*

I know now that life is easier if rules are observed. As I learned to my cost in those distant days with Sir John, so I endured it with Tewpie, too: Breaking the rules usually means someone gets hurt.

Chapter Fourteen

Uffington. March 1934

"What on earth – Penelope, what is that horse doing here?" John bellowed. It was just after six o'clock on a blustery spring day, days that were finally, thankfully, getting lighter. John had just returned home from work, and stood at the open doorway to our house, looking into our drawing room, a look of incredulity on his handsome English face.

"Pa sent him over from India," I said. "I told you he was coming."

John put down his bag with a snort. "Well, yes, I knew that. But I had thought – I mean, I had thought – clearly foolishly – that he would live outside – …" he trailed off, uncharacteristically lost for words.

"Oh he's only in here while he's settling in," I said, unable to hold back laughter any longer. "I'm just showing him around."

"Showing him around? I see. Can I suggest you show him out before he decides to relieve himself on the floor?" John urged, not enjoying the situation anything like as much as me, but too scared of horses to be able to do what he wanted to do: to take charge and march Moti out himself.

"And where's Molly? Molly!" he roared. "Molly!"

"She's in the kitchen," I said. "What do you want her for, anyway?" I said in a *faux* suspicious tone. I had, on the surface, befriended Molly, and in doing so I hoped I had neutralised any remaining threat she presented. I had yet to let John forget his transgression completely but outwardly made light of it for the most part. I didn't want to be the kind of wife who was always angry and untrusting and now I was back, I was determined such a thing wouldn't happen again. Certainly John had no lack of interest in me in that department. Still, it was a mildly uncomfortable setup.

John glared at me harder.

"Penelope" – now I knew he was cross – "do please get that horse out of here."

"Oh, do shut up, John. You make the most dreadful fuss sometimes," I said, suddenly furious with him. I took up Moti's leading rein and started to coax the horse to the door and out into the evening light.

"Come along, Moti," I said, loudly and pointedly, walking him round to the back of the house and through the garden to the paddock. "We know when we are not wanted."

Outside I inhaled lungfuls of the cool, damp air, and my anger with John subsided as quickly as it had flared. I knew it was best not to think too much about him and Molly, but sometimes I still found that difficult. The grass was soft under my feet, and Moti left a trail of small hoof-shaped prints behind him. We reached the paddock. I took off Moti's rein and set him free. I shut the gate behind him and watched him graze for a moment. It was wonderful to have him with me, but this was the first time in my life I was going to have to look after a horse myself, and I wasn't quite sure where to begin. I would just have to work it out, I told myself. After all, I'd got to grips with the kitchen, and had even been learning to cook, thanks to a combination of

Paula, whom I'd met during my trip to Berlin and had now come to England to be my housekeeper, and a brilliant bible called *Elizabeth Craig's Cookery and Household Management book*, which I had purchased in Blackwell's in Oxford. This was stuffed full with recipes and household cleaning advice. Cleaning was something I could delegate to Molly (with some pleasure, it has to be said, and the harder work the better), but I'd learned a lot about the management of a household. Apart from the odd minor disaster – like the time the Aga had run out of oil, or the day Paula forgot to collect the meat from the butcher's when the delivery boy was off sick – things had gone fairly well. John always had a meal to come home to, something I considered to be the bare minimum, and sometimes the sum total, of my wifely duties.

Even so, life didn't run as smoothly as they had in my mother's households, but then the resources at her disposal were far vaster than those available to me. I didn't mind particularly-I wasn't the only person making do with less. Life was changing all around us. Many of our old family friends were selling off their large London houses. Developers were carving up ballrooms and card rooms and turning these once beautiful private dwellings into blocks of flats, sometimes even with shops on the ground floor. Lansdowne House, where I had danced with Johnnie in such splendour just a few years ago, admiring its ancient and seemingly unassailable beauty, had recently been sold. I'd walked passed it just the other day and had stopped and stared when I reached it – it had been literally chopped in half. The front rooms had been entirely removed to allow for the construction of a new street. Apparently, the remainder of that grand atmospheric mansion was now in the process of becoming a Gentlemen's club.

I had turned away slowly and walked towards the open space of Green Park, full of sudden, stabbing sadness at what was lost, never to be recovered. It was irrational, because I knew that life never stood still, that change was all around. It also had to become fairer. Why should a few of us have so much, and so many work hard to make our lives comfortable? The need to correct the gross inequality so apparent in life had been screamingly obvious in Delhi, and that was simply an outpost of the British society I'd grown up in, so why be surprised if it was happening here, too? It was only from a nostalgic point of view that I mourned the backdrop to my girlhood, slowly being dismantled and never to be the same again.

Everyone said it was a result of the Great War. Certainly, many families I had grown up with lived differently these days, and it was proving more difficult to find any domestic help of any note, as those formerly in service took advantage of the freer life and better wages offered by a job in a factory or a shop. I had been lucky in persuading Paula to come back with me from Germany, even if she was bad tempered at times, spoke about three words of English and continually reminded me she could only stay for a year.

John and I were living on my small allowance, which my father still made over to me despite my marriage and the circumstances of it, and John's salary from the *Architectural Review*. This was enough to employ a cook and a maid, so I could hardly claim to be managing things single-handedly. I wondered what Star would make of my domestic set up when she came to stay in April, as she was due to do. It was certainly modest by her standards. I wasn't sure how I felt about that impending visit. I longed to see my parents, particularly my father, but I also relished the freedom marriage had brought me, and being a wife and an adult, rather than a daughter and a dependent.

I returned to the house to find John sitting in his favourite leather covered armchair reading a copy of the *Evening Standard* that he had brought from London. A tray of tea sat, un-poured (and no doubt cooling), in front of him.

"Paula made it," he said in a voice that seemed to be striving for cheerfulness but failing miserably.

"Oh for heaven's sake. Let me pour," I said, setting cups on saucers and picking up the large China teapot. Sometimes the irritations of husbands seemed endless, despite the advantages of being a wife. Couldn't they even pour out their own tea?

"How was London?" I asked brightly, to cover my impatience, although I knew John would pick up on it.

"The train was very full."

"Are you finding the journey a bore?"

John had always lived in London, and I had wondered how he would adapt to living in the country.

"It's worth it," he said after a moment. He'd gulped down his tea and I'd poured him a second cup, and now he was crunching his way through a plate of shortbread biscuits I had made. Pale round buttery discs, I had been pleased with how they had turned out. I had eaten several just out of the Aga, and had to resist taking another one now, as I was afraid that country life was making me fat. The waistband of my jodhpurs was definitely tighter than it had been. Unless, of course, there was another reason for that tightness. I felt a little jolt of hope at the thought, and smiled suddenly at John, who smiled tentatively back at me in surprise.

"Jolly good biscuits," he mumbled through a mouthful of crumbs.

"Worth it? Oh Tewpie, I do think so. I know we're slightly at sixes and sevens, but we will straighten out. This is the perfect place for us, near enough to London for you, yet rural enough to be real country, wonderful for Moti and the chickens, and what a special place for our children to grow up in."

Tewpie's face clouded again, so I hastened on, even though I could see it all in my mind. "And we've a few of your friends coming to stay this weekend. Evelyn, I think-"

"- So long as you don't spend the whole time talking about bloody Catholicism with him-"

"-and Bryan, and I can't remember who else. How is Bryan? Have you seen him?" As a rule I had very little idea who Tewpie saw on his days in London.

"Briefly. He put a brave face on it, but anyone could see he was pretty down."

I settled back into my chair and sipped at my tea.

"It was a dreadful shock. I still can't quite believe that Diana has left him like that for Mosley."

I wasn't sure I approved of Diana's behaviour. I admired her commitment to love above all else, but I also disliked the pain she'd caused Bryan and, no doubt, her small children.

"She's no longer allowed to see her children, you know. She's been deemed a bad moral influence."

John nodded, making a sad face.

"Yes. I did know," he said. "I've always liked Diana. She's not wicked. She just married the wrong man."

"It does happen. Look at Evelyn and his experience with She-Evelyn. She simply changed her mind about him after a year or so and went off and fell in love with someone else."

John nodded.

"Yes. Divorce may be becoming easier, but it's a high price to pay for freedom, particularly for women, Plymmie, as Diana's finding out. It seems a bit much to deny her access to her children." He put his cup down and drew his hand across his mouth, dashing away the few crumbs of biscuit that were clinging there.

He went on: "I hope Bryan relents soon. Anyhow, it certainly puts our elopement into the shade. If this has reached *The Times of India*, your mother and the Brigadier will be feeling very glad you are no longer the most scandalous debutante in their social circle. Not by a long shot, tally ho, eh?"

"Oh, shut up, John," I said. "And however much you may like Diana, I feel sorry for Bryan too, and those poor little boys. It must have hurt them all very much," I said pointedly. John only liked Diana because she was beautiful, I thought, trying to ignore the all-too-familiar jealousy climbing up my insides.

"Anyway, we'll do our best to cheer him up," I added.

"You can start by keeping that bloody horse where it belongs," John said.

"Oh, SHUT UP!" I said again. Sometimes it seemed as if this was all I said to John. No wonder Paula, with her extremely slight grasp of English, had thought Shut Up was John's name for most of the first month she was with us. When I'd found that out, I couldn't wait for John to come home so I could share it with him. We had both laughed for ten minutes flat, till tears ran down our faces. Since then I couldn't resist using it even more.

"You need a groom," said John.

"Yes. Apparently, there's a local lad looking for work. He's coming to see me in an hour or so. I'll try him if he's interested. I'll have to train him up."

"How on earth will you do that?" John asked. "The blind leading the blind." He knew I'd never cared for a horse myself before. I shrugged and waved my hands in the air.

"I'll manage. I must, so therefore I will. I'll get a book on it. Teach myself. Can't be that hard."

"Good idea. What's the lad's name? Do I know him?"

"Jackie Goodenough. He's just left school."

"A promising name. Let's hope he's good enough."

I swatted at John with my hand.

"Ouch. I hope you're not the type to turn violent. I've heard about wives like that. Husbands going to work with unexplained black eyes. Sounds like this Jackie fellow might work out, then."

"Let's hope so."

"Perhaps his first job could be to find a home for some of the tack that seems to have arrived with the horse. Get rid of that stink."

"What stink? Oh that. It's from the Cochaline, the leather polish I use, that's all."

"Be that as it may," said John. "Does all of the horse's stuff have to be draped around the house?" He gestured in the direction of the hall, where a bridle hung over the banisters, and down the corridor to the kitchen, where a saddle sat in the middle of the tiled floor.

"You act as if horses aren't your thing," I said. Sir John flashed through my mind again. Two men I had loved, who couldn't have been more different.

John glared at me, cross again. "You know they're not," he said shortly. "Things I don't like, Plymmie – let me make you a short list: horses, Abroad, offensive modern architecture, the pulling down of beautiful old buildings, and horses, or did I mention horses already?"

I sidled up to John, winding my arms around him.

"Darling, let's not allow Moti to come between us," I said.

Sometimes it seemed as if everything we said needled each other and made a situation more prickly, until it appeared that we didn't like each other at all.

John looked at me for a moment, then sighed.

"No."

"A quick lie down before supper?"

An answering smile spread across his face, and we fled upstairs before anyone – Moti, Paula, or Jackie Goodenough, who was due any moment – could stop us. There was a kind of magic about bed that brought us back together again and restored our marital equilibrium. Fortunately, Jackie Goodenough was late, and by the time he arrived, John and I were both downstairs again, John in his comfortable favourite green sweater, just about to settle by a well stoked fire, with the by now cold tea exchanged for a glass of wine, and positively wreathed in smiles.

"You must be Jackie," I smiled, smoothing down my hair and hoping I didn't look too flushed. It had been worth it just to see the transformation in John, but it was times like this, when the different parts of my world threatened to crash into each other as I rushed hectically from one thing to another, that I thought, had I missed something? Was my dress tucked into my knickers? Had I done up my zip at the side? I tried not to let my ruffled state show. I pulled on a coat, which fell to below my knees and provided wonderful cover for any oversights in my outfit.

"Excellent. Let me show you the horse."

Our life in Uffington settled down into a routine. On weekday mornings, John took the car to the nearby railway station, which invariably involved a great deal of cursing over the starting handle. When the engine finally kicked into life, he set off to Challow, which was just a few miles away, and from there he caught the train to London to spend the day at the *Architectural Review*. After a few months, he was asked by the *Evening Standard* to write film reviews and then he branched out even further by going to work for Shell. Supposed to be writing advertising jingles for the oil company, instead he came up with the idea of writing motoring guides for the various counties of England. He decided to start with a county he had known and loved since childhood-Cornwall.

And all the time, in the background, there was his poetry. Scraps scribbled as they came to him, found later on loose pieces of paper in jacket pockets and at the bottom of his briefcase, and worked into something more. Slowly the scraps grew into poems and the poems grew into several poems that multiplied like butterflies, and seemed to me to reveal the very beating of John's heart. If the poems were coming, the rest of his writing also flowed and John was as happy as he was capable of being.

He wrote about all sorts of different things – the arrest of Oscar Wilde, the hideousness of Slough, the death of George V. Something stimulated a thought, and then the poem grew, like a mushroom, in the dark recesses of his mind. Some I liked more than others. Some I thought too light, almost as if John was being flippant with his ability. Sometimes I thought John took the easy route to the public acclaim that I could already see he enjoyed, through well-paid journalism, just a little too often.

"We need the money, Penelope, that's all," he said frostily, when I mentioned it. His tone told me all I needed to know. This was, in his view, nothing to do with me.

As our married life began to carve its own groove, John and I learned to bend a little. I didn't bring Moti into the house when John was home, and John bit back sharp remarks about the mess everywhere – piles of books and newspapers that seemed to grow with a life of their own, and of course the tack that was still draped around the ground floor, even though I did my best to confine it to the boot room.

John stopped complaining about my devotion to Moti, or at least stopped making complaints directly to me. Occasionally I overheard him making them to other people. One day the vicar called to discuss church business with John (we were regular worshippers). As I staggered in the back door under the weight of Moti's saddle, which was overdue a clean, I heard John say to him: "I'm so sorry to keep you waiting, Vicar. If you were a horse Penelope would have given you a cup of tea by now."

I bit back laughter as I dumped the saddle in the utility room and went into the kitchen to fill the kettle and set a tea tray.

"Good afternoon, Vicar," I said, entering the room a minute later, the laden tea tray rattling in my hands. John, taking in the pile of homemade scones, the egg sandwiches and the uncut Victoria Sponge cake, smirked with satisfaction, and I smiled back, briefly transformed into the model wife for all the world to see.

Chapter Fifteen

My parents were due back from India in April. Their stay with us would be their first visit to Garrards Farm, and their first time under the roof of my marital home. While their visit implied they had forgiven John and me for our clandestine wedding, I knew my father had not yet warmed to my husband. My mother, more pragmatic, pretended she had, but my father, whom I loved so dearly, was a tougher challenge and winning him round was proving difficult. My husband didn't help. John's response to the hostility between him and my father was to mock Daddy to anyone who would listen. Now one of his jests had, most unfortunately, reached Daddy's ears all the way in Delhi. He had written to me about it in a temper not long ago:

"Your John is a fool," he wrote furiously.

John denied ever having said anything, of course, but this cut no ice with Daddy. Consequently I was both dreading and looking forward to their visit.

Both the blessing and the problem with family was that ties were lifelong and could not be broken. However angry my father was, however much my husband labelled my parents as antiquated snobs and mocked them behind their backs, everyone had to at least appear to get on. All families faced the same challenge-of coping with other family members they didn't particularly like. I reminded Tewpie of this whenever he complained of the forthcoming visit, and begged him to be at his most charming.

"It's terribly important to me," I told him, and he had said he understood. I hoped he really did, and prayed to God nightly that things would go well.

The weekend of my parents' stay arrived.

"Ah, Field Marshal," John said. In private he favoured the mocking 'Brigadier'. "How very good to see you." I scanned his face for sarcasm, but saw nothing other than an open friendly expression of welcome as he pumped my father's hand. My father smiled, and after a while had passed and he had said nothing about the rumours, I exhaled, hoping we were all moving on.

I showed my parents to the smartest spare bedroom. I had been tidying and polishing, with Paula's help, for several days, and the house, usually so messy with piles of books and papers stacked precariously in every corner, was practically unrecognisable, like a scruffy child cleaned and pressed into a new suit with hair flattened down in readiness for some great occasion. Books sat on shelves, dust had been swept away and I had even confined Moti's tack to the pegs in the kitchen corridor, prompting John to make pointed remarks about how my parents should come more often.

"We don't have electric here," I told them, as we came back downstairs from the Grand Tour. "We still have oil lamps."

My parents exchanged a silent, horrified glance that seemed to say: "But in India, we had electric. In London we had electric. But in *Berkshire*, we cannot have electric?"

On the first evening of their stay, we dined at home. We had a complicated meal involving *consommé*, poached fish, roast lamb, meringues with bottled berries (my first attempt at preserves and a moderate success) and finally, cheese.

John, like most men, liked wine, so a succession of bottles accompanied each course. Paula managed admirably. I didn't want my father and John to have a chance to row over the port, so I suggested, since it was just the four of us, that we all took a glass into the sitting room, where a fire was roaring, and played cards. Since it was a cold April night, and perhaps because John and Daddy were as reluctant to be left together as I was to leave them, everyone readily agreed, and we had a few spirited rounds of Racing Demon.

By the time the church bells had chimed midnight and I had lit my parents' oil lamps, I felt it safe to consider the evening a success. At the foot of the stairs, just as I was about to bid them goodnight, I was struck by a thought.

"Hold on a second, let me just fetch you a box of matches. In case your lamp goes out in the night," I said.

I dashed off to the kitchen, smiling to myself. As I rushed back to the stairs, matches in hands, my father's voice floated down the corridor to me in a low, urgent hush.

"I quite agree, Star. But we've done our best with that horrid little Dutchman. There's nothing else to be done. He's Penelope's choice and we've just got to hope he doesn't let her down."

I slowed my pace, my footfall seeming to grow louder and echo down the corridor, reverberating in my ears.

I drew to a standstill in front of my father. I handed the matches to him with a stern look.

"He's not Dutch. He's English," I said quietly.

My father had the grace to look slightly uncomfortable for a second in the ensuing silence. Star said nothing, for once perhaps deciding it was best to leave my father to do the talking.

"Goodnight, Penelope my dear," he said clumsily, after a moment, a shade of emotion reflected in his eye that I couldn't quite identify – embarrassment?-before he turned and hustled my mother upstairs to bed, complaining loudly and unrepentantly about the stench of the oil lamps. I turned slowly back to the sitting room, where John was still waiting, and hoped like hell he hadn't heard. That I had, was bad enough.

The following evening, we were invited to drinks by a new local friend. Lord Berners – Gerald-lived at Faringdon House, by far the grandest place in the neighbourhood. John and I had quickly discovered that he was an accomplished painter, composer and writer, and ran the smartest `*salon* in the county.

Lots of people we knew enjoyed his legendarily colourful and generous hospitality, and it wasn't hard to join in the high jinks. Nancy Mitford, Osbert Sitwell, Cecil Beaton, Evelyn Waugh, the Spanish painter Dali, were just a few amongst those who might be found there, together with Gerald's pet giraffe. I had never liked a smart social life, which was partly why I was so thrilled by our move to Uffington, away from London and the endless round of parties that had dominated my life since my coming out, but Gerald was so enchanting that I instantly made an exception for him, and loved going to see him. He was fantastic fun, and his parties the best I'd ever been to.

That we had been invited to Gerald's, with my parents, was sufficient to raise John somewhat in my mother's estimation (I had to concede at this point that Tewpie was right, she was a terrible snob). We arrived amidst the loud blowing of the car heater and some idle conversation, coupled with a few sharp intakes of breath from Star at John's driving. John loved a party and proceeded to dazzle and generally get on brilliantly with everyone. He took my father around the room with him and introduced him to Diana Guinness, always the most beautiful girl in any room, and my father quietly dissolved. My mother stood by me and watched as John joked with Evelyn and Gerald.

"He's really... quite charming with his friends," she said in reluctant admiration.

John was holding forth to the little group gathered around him. I caught Evelyn's eye, and he winked at me before yawning ostentatiously as though utterly bored by whatever John was saying, and I found myself smiling disloyally. Sometimes I wondered if Evelyn actually wanted to be friends with John.

"I don't know why you're so surprised, Star," I replied sharply, sipping my cocktail too fast and feeling the gin hit the back of my throat. "What did you think he'd do, start assessing the quality of the cabinets?"

Even as I said it, I knew I was being unkind. The landslide that was my mother's changing life was too much for her to take in. When she was a girl, she'd have been disinherited if she'd eloped with the cabinet maker's son. But there was no point in continually harking back to her day, it was long gone, and nothing would bring it back.

'God save me', I thought, tucking my mother's arm in mine and heading towards my old friend Billa, whom I had spied in a far corner by the grand piano, 'from getting old and stuck in my ways'.

John knew many of the guests that night, but a new friend to come out of the evening was Gerry Wellesley, heir to the Duke of Wellington. Obviously, my parents knew his parents. Gerry had been invited to design a folly for Gerald, and was full of excitement about the commission. It was as if this son of an old family friend of ours, warming to John, was the last barricade that needed to be brought down for my mother. By the time we left, well after midnight, more than a few gins down, my mother had understood at last that I wasn't the only one who had fallen for John. He was a man capable of charming whomsoever he chose, and the moment she allowed him to, he started turning his sparkling eyes and gentle wit onto her. Together they tottered down the steps together, my mother's aristocratic tones trailing back to me and my father, who followed more slowly behind.

"Simply the most divine party, and so nice to meet some of your friends, John dear," we heard her say.

I looked at my father, and couldn't help grinning triumphantly.

"John dear!" I echoed. "My mother seems quite taken with the horrid little Dutchman."

"Oh, do pipe down," my father replied, reddening. I burst out laughing and hugged closer to my father's arm, cuddling the soft Indian cashmere of his coat.

Despite this thaw on my mother's part at least, John's shoulders visibly collapsed with relief when Monday morning came round and it was time to wind up the car and head for the railway station. I watched him leave from the doorway, leaning against the painted portal, in my printed silk dressing gown. My parents were still asleep. Above the roar of the motor car, he shouted:

"Quite busy this week, Plymmie. I might stay in town."

Then he sped off before I could say anything. I watched him disappear from view, before turning and going slowly back inside, shutting the door on the rising sun just visible behind the downs. A week without Tewpie would be a long week. What I didn't know, on that April day, was that this was just the beginning of a permanent alteration in the daily pattern of our marriage. It marked the start of John not coming home every night. Instead he started staying regularly, one, two or even three nights a week, up in town, with friends. It was as if, despite the seeming success of the weekend, feeling shut out of his marital home by the in-laws opened his eyes to everything in London he had temporarily forgotten. I wondered if he had heard my father's remark after all. Whether he had or hadn't, that Monday his joy in all things urban was reignited, and from then on, John maintained a dual existence: in London, enjoying the parties I loathed with a variety of our friends, and then spending time at home in Uffington, with me.

Mutisher

A few of our group have arrived in the village, and Leo has wandered off to greet them. They stand, a small assortment of Westerners in this very foreign field, wondering what to make of it all. Will they love it and long to understand it, or will it just be one more sticker on their suitcase? What are they searching for? A holiday, or an enlightenment of a deeper kind?

How many loves can a person manage in their lives? Love for people, for places, for things. How big is a heart? Does it have limitless capacity, or is it like a suitcase, and if you fill it too full, the buckles break? If you are lucky, loves pile up as you get older – places, friends, children, horses – but I suspect our human hearts are finite. And if we have our limits, we must choose wisely how we portion out our affections.

If I had to choose just one place to love, it would be India. It has held my heart since my first visit. Perhaps it is even my most enduring love. I have known it longer than I knew Tewpie, and truthfully – whisper it- it has loved me better.

Gerald Berners, long dead now-so many of my friends are dead these days that the world feels half empty – Evelyn, John, Sir John, Nancy: the list goes on-had a passionate love affair with Italy. Gerald was a man of many, many passions, admittedly most of them superficial – for his pet giraffe, for dyeing the doves in his dovecote brilliant jewel-like colours, for entertaining, for practical jokes. But Italy, that was a different thing altogether: along with Robert Heber Percy, his 'mad boy', I think it was his real and true love. He spent the entirety of the Second World War clinically depressed because he couldn't get to his house in Rome. Superficial, perhaps, in a time of war, but Gerald responded stubbornly first and last to his own reality.

What about Tewpie? Tewpie crammed a lot into his heart. He always loved London. He never really left it, despite our married years being played out almost entirely elsewhere. Cornwall was perhaps the place that possessed him, while Oxford had touched him since his days as a Dragon school boy, with the Cherwell river running across the bottom of the playing fields; that ancient city with its beautiful old buildings, its echoing quadrangles, its timeless mystical quality and well preserved ways that inspired John's hated tutor C S Lewis, to write the brilliant and elegiac Narnia series.

Then of course there were the people John loved. The women (I don't want to think about the women), the long-standing friends, some of whom dated from his University days, and others who were collected as he journeyed through life.

I often played host to friends from John's time at Oxford. Evelyn, of course, (although John liked Evelyn less and less as the years passed) and Maurice Bowra in particular – as well as newer ones found scattered about the county, like the Pipers and a clutch of Mitfords.

My mind feels dull and clouded, with things I haven't thought about for years, suddenly as pressing as if they had just happened. Why did John turn against Evelyn? Was it because Evelyn professed to love me, or because Evelyn objected to how John treated me? Or because Evelyn liked to put it about that he and I had had an affair? I try and snort with laughter as I remember this, but no sound emerges. Or, most likely, did John's gradual disentangling begin when Evelyn made his journey to Catholicism in 1930?

John – religious, but stoutly Church of England – distrusted Rome and those who worshipped at her shrine. Of course, over time, that included me.

I stretch my legs out in the sun, enjoying the intensifying of the heat as the sun rises higher and higher in the sky, my mind soaring like a bird flying into the blue.

Back in the 1930s and '40s, converting to Catholicism was something of a minor trend. England in those days – much of Europe, in fact – was a rapidly altering place, and there was a feeling that almost everything was up for grabs, for reconsideration and re-evaluation. It gave the business of being alive a new energy, a sense of vibrancy, of freshness. It was the energy of change, and we were still young enough not to mind too much change. Some people were drawn to communism, others to religion or its polar opposite, anti-religion, to a life of atheism. For me, it was Catholicism. It probably seems odd now, in these increasingly secular days. What does religion matter, you may ask? The answer is, it matters a great deal. It mattered then, and it matters now, it is just that, at present, the Power and the sense and the Glory of it has been temporarily forgotten, eclipsed by the power of self. But God has faced down much worse. It is a temporary setback.

When we were young, there was still time for God in our day-to-day existence; for many of us, for John and me, for Evelyn, for the Pipers, Church was central to our lives. In our Uffington days, when John and I were both Church of England, John liked that very much. It sat well with him and his own sense of spirituality. Church was something we did together. John became a bell-ringer and I was responsible for the flowers. Together we befriended the vicar or perhaps he befriended us. We worshipped together, kneeling side by side in our pew, every Sunday morning. John often went to Evensong too. Sometimes I would play the organ for Evensong. It was jolly, it was comforting, it was regular, it was unchanging. It *could be relied on. And for John, who took his religion seriously, it was just right.*

The trouble was, I already knew the pure and ancient embrace of Catholicism was waiting in the wings of my life for me. I had read GK Chesterton, I had discussed God at length with Evelyn, and I knew Catholicism to be the rightest, truest thing in the world. So true, in fact, that once, later, in a period when I wondered whether everything I had done in my life had been a mistake, I had thought, if only I had given into God earlier, I could have become a nun. But in the early days of my marriage, I accepted my life as it was. I knew I would convert to Catholicism, the 'when' of the thing was the only part that troubled me. I asked myself sometimes why I was waiting, what was I waiting for? Now of course I know, as perhaps I had known then. I held off as long as I could, because I understood that the road to Rome was the same road that led away from John.

Chapter Sixteen

Uffington. Spring 1936.

"Darling."
We had recently had a telephone installed. I already regretted it, as my mother was making good use of it. She called me most mornings, with some vital piece of news she felt compelled to share with me.

"Good morning, Star."

"Darling." This morning she sounded excited and I wondered why. "Have you seen *The Sketch* this week?" She didn't wait for an answer -I hadn't, since it didn't arrive in the local newsagent until at least day after publication and sometimes longer-but steamed on regardless.

"Oh darling, it's a hoot! There's a huge piece on what they call the Uffington Set, and there's a picture of John, and another of you driving around in your little cart. And Gerald, with his coloured doves. Too funny."

I smiled into the receiver.

"It's not a little cart, it's a phaeton. It does sound fun; will you save me a copy? I'm coming to London tomorrow. I rode Moti over to see Gerald last week, and he asked me to bring him into the drawing room for tea."

"Your horse?"

"I'm afraid so. No need to panic, Star, of course I said no. It's one thing for him to come into Gerrard's Farm (my mother had heard this story from the newly-befriended John), but going into Faringdon House, Moti's hooves all over Gerald's fine silk carpets – well, that's quite a different matter."

"He really is very eccentric, isn't he?" my mother sighed happily. She had always warmed to eccentrics.

"The genuine article," I replied. "Evelyn was there again, too."

"He always seems to be there at the moment. Either visiting Gerald, or you." My mother's tone had turned disapproving.

"I think he's a little lonely. I suppose he's still getting over She-Evelyn."

"That was years ago now. I have my suspicions he is getting rather keen on you, Penelope. Which won't do at all."

"Don't be ridiculous. He's simply a friend, Star. That's all there is to it."

"Hmm. Well, I did hear a rumour he had fallen in love with a Herbert girl. A cousin of his first wife – a little awkward, but perhaps a happy ending looms, nonetheless."

My eyes widened slightly in surprise. Evelyn hadn't mentioned a word of this.

"How can it? It's very sad but now he's a Catholic, he can never marry again while She-Evelyn is alive. He really is very committed to his beliefs to have made such a sacrifice."

"Perhaps he can get an annulment?" my mother suggested, but I could tell she was losing interest. Evelyn wasn't her favourite of our friends (that lofty position was currently occupied by 'Dear Gerald' although my father thought him rather silly and wasn't anything like so keen) and now she had extracted the reassurance she required that there was nothing between Evelyn and me, she was keen to move on to the next thing on her daily to-do list.

"I'll keep *The Sketch* for you darling. Pop by for tea," my mother said.

"Marvellous."

"Any other news?" she asked. I hated it when she said this, as she always, unfailingly did. She meant, "Are you pregnant?" or, more recently, "Are you pregnant yet and if not, why not?"

I felt her implicit criticism and resented it. "Nothing to report," I said shortly.

Then, just as we were about to say goodbye, she added, "Oh, and how's John?"

"John's fine," I said, my irritation evaporating and unable to prevent myself from grinning into the receiver. My mother had finally started asking after my husband.

"Goodbye then, darling. 'Til tomorrow."

"Goodbye".

I replaced the receiver, and went back to polishing Moti's tack which was spread across the dining room table. My mother was right, I mused, as I rubbed in the pungent red Cochaline cream that stopped the leather from cracking. Evelyn was often visiting us or staying with Gerald. But it made perfectly good sense – he was recently divorced and was therefore in need of constant company. Besides, I enjoyed spending time with him, he made me laugh. He drank too much and could be appallingly rude, but he could also be side-splittingly funny, and he was attractive in the traditional English way I liked. We also discussed religion in general, and more specifically, Catholicism, our common passion.

Of course John loathed these conversations and wouldn't join in. When we started up, he usually left the room. He had been both annoyed and bemused by Evelyn's conversion, and that hadn't diminished with time.

"He arrived at Oxford an Atheist!" he'd exclaimed furiously when the news first reached him, and then proceeded to sulk in his study all evening with just Archibald the teddy bear for company.

In fact, anything to do with Evelyn seemed to annoy him these days. Nevertheless, an annulment. Would that really be possible? I knew divorce was easier and that the newly introduced divorce bill was responsible for that, but I couldn't believe many people would want really want to take advantage of it. In any religion, wasn't marriage for life? And there was no denying the stigma of the divorcée – one only had to think of the new King and his mistress, to understand that. If he couldn't get round it, no one could.

I couldn't bear to imagine unpicking my marriage. Things might be changing but in the world I came from, people didn't divorce. (And yet, Diana had.) Besides, it felt as if our union was an entity cast in steel, linking John and me forever, and I loved the definiteness of it. Oh, we rowed a lot – but we were bound to, we were both strong personalities. Sometimes, it felt as if we were in competition with each other, rather than on the same side. We had things to work out. But there was time: we hadn't even been married for three years yet. We were still at the start of our adventure.

I closed the lid of Cochaline and hung the bridle back up on one of the hooks in the back corridor. Our marriage was still in its infancy, but we were laying things down: we were a couple, a man and a woman joined together, two people who had taken vows that, in my opinion, could not be annulled, even though they had been said in a Civil setting. We were united for life, and the assembling of a shared history was part of that process, of building a life together that would last until we died. Our house here in Uffington, that had so quickly become home. Our shared friends, and the new friends we were making together. (I pushed John's nights spent in London from my mind.) And, surely, one day, we would start a family.

Jackie Goodenough appeared at the door, startling me out of my thoughts. "Hello Jackie. It's done," I said, "I've just finished it. Will you tack him up? I need to ride."

I quickly changed into jodhpurs and went out to the paddock where Moti was waiting. Sometimes, I simply had to ride, and today was such a time. I needed to gallop across the downs and feel the rhythm of Moti and hear the sound of his hooves. I needed to feel the wind on my neck and smell the spring grasses, until unsettling thoughts about marriage and its difficulties and any potential impermanence and why children didn't come, had been blown from my head. John loved me and I loved him, and that was all that mattered. We were well suited; Molly Higgins had been an aberration; Evelyn was just a good friend who sopped up some of my loneliness when John was away in London during the week. Between John and I, all was, and would remain, well.

Chapter Seventeen

I was lying in the bath, submerged to my neck in hot water. Occasional drops fell intermittently from the tap onto my toes. The room was cold but the water scalding hot, so hot I could see my skin turning a bright pink. The bath was just about the only place to get properly warm at this time of year. It also had the added advantage of putting a locked door between me and the rest of the world. Away from the help, asking me questions about the running of the house. Away from Jackie Goodenough, asking me if I wanted to ride Moti or whether he should rub him down for the night. Away from the vicar who dropped in at inopportune moments for a sherry or to discuss bell ringing schedules with John. Away from John, wanting things. Only mundane things, that husbands always wanted – a cup of tea, a clean shirt, an audience for his latest poem, a cuddle in the bedroom – and most of the time that was fine, but just occasionally, as now, I needed to be completely alone, in a world that was absolutely quiet apart from the drip-drip-drip of the tap and the clamour of my thoughts.

Pride and Prejudice, an old favourite, lay on the floor beside the bathtub, bearing my damp fingerprints. It is a truth universally acknowledged, I thought, washing my arms, the smell of carbolic soap rising to my nostrils, that every woman in possession of a husband is in need of a child. While I wasn't desperately broody – I wasn't one of those girls who went seamlessly from dolls to real live babies-I wanted children, and days like this, when my period had just arrived, were becoming difficult days. I couldn't help wondering why a baby hadn't yet put in an appearance. It wasn't for lack of trying. Whenever John was home, we tried. I'd visited the doctor recently, to enquire if I could do anything to help things along, but apparently *keeping* trying was the only thing to do.

When I had been with Sir John, unmarried and vulnerable, we had been so careful, terrified of an accident that would finish me in the eyes of my parents and the rest of the world. Sir John, equally unwilling to have the scandal of a baby out of wedlock, had faithfully used what he called, rather hilariously I thought, 'Johnnies'. Nevertheless, despite these precautions, I had still celebrated every time my period had arrived. Even the most careful use of preventative methods could fail. I had heard too many stories at boarding school, (that early source of information on all things to do with reproduction), about older sisters and household maids and their ruinous brushes with trouble.

Now, however, I was married, I was 26 years old and I was ready for a child. Most of my friends had had at least one baby by now, if not two or even three. Usually, with no way to prevent it, they had started reproducing within a year of their marriage, and I suppose I had expected the same to happen to me. It was starting to dawn on me that perhaps, for John and me, the process wasn't going to be as straightforward as I had assumed.

It wasn't something we had ever discussed, but increasingly I felt he gave me a certain look, when he knew that, once again, I had the curse. Did I imagine it, or was John thinking about children, too? He had said, once, when I had asked him, that of course he wanted children, adding how unnatural it would be not to, although he had then quickly changed the subject. But if that was truly the case, was he as disappointed every month, as I was? If he was, with my period here yet again, I wondered if this would be the moment when he would actually articulate this thought. Would he say the unsayable, the thought that was starting to haunt me: that perhaps, between us, we weren't going to manage to have children?

I frowned and stood up abruptly, water cascading off me. I got out of the bath and wrapped myself in a stiff white towel, hard and scratchy from being dried on the line.

I knew there were people for whom children didn't happen. My parents were close friends with a childless couple, and had taught me early on that while it was not something to comment on publicly, it was also something of a tragedy. Childlessness was, I understood, to be pitied. Retrieving the damp curling copy of Jane Austen's novel reminded me that even only producing female children could provoke regret and even represent financial disaster. A century and more after Austen's day, a son remained the gold star of reproduction for most people. I didn't give a fig for that-for me, a child of any gender would do.

Whenever I thought this way, I turned to logic. There was no history of childlessness in my family. As far as I knew, my parents had had no problem conceiving. There was no reason to suppose I would have prolonged difficulties.

I pulled on my dressing gown and prepared for the cold dash along the corridor to the bedroom. It was unfashionable to think that the problem, if there was a problem, lay with the man, but Star, always so bold, had already intimated this to me, and it had to be faced: It was at least worth observing that John was an only child. Had his parents struggled to have children? I tried to imagine asking John's mother this question, and failed. Mrs Mabel Betjeman and I weren't exactly the close confidantes that this kind of conversation would require us to be.

Back in my bedroom, I dropped the towel and, shivering, rolled on my stockings, trying not to snag them as they kept sticking on my damp, hot skin. Gerald Berners and his lover Robert were coming for supper, as well as some friends from the village. I pulled on thermal knickers and a vest- a strange mix with the stockings but the cold demanded it-followed by my favourite pale grey velvet dress that fell gracefully to my ankles. I reached for my pearls and fastened them around my neck. I dragged a brush through my hair, and put cream on my face, leaving it to sink in a moment before dabbing powder on top. I added lipstick, and looked at my reflection. The powder toned down my flushed cheeks and the lipstick made my mouth more prominent. My hair was rather untameable when long, and was much better cut short as it now was. It was dark and glossy and didn't yet need dying.

It had once been an anxiety that I didn't fit the mould of the fine boned, pale faced English rose, and sometimes I wondered whether it was feeling less than classically beautiful that had partly inspired my choice of John, a member of the intelligentsia who appreciated my brain as well as my body, rather than a man from my own class, where girls were expected and required to be highly decorative, wonderful hostesses and not much else. I smoothed down a stray lock of hair, then dropped my hands to my lap. I had John's plain wedding band on my finger, but otherwise my fingers were unadorned. My nails were cut short and stained faintly pink from Cochaline. A residue of dirt from riding Moti was visible under several nails despite the hot bath, and however much cream I put on them, my hands remained rough.

I sighed. Although I didn't rate looks alone – they couldn't ever be sufficient on their own to make a person interesting, and I didn't pursue them as much as I might, having other things on which to spend my time-I sometimes wished a little glamour came more easily to me. Tonight, Robert would look far more resplendent than me. Although Gerald resembled a small, rather squat frog (unkindly, this brought some comfort), Robert was utterly beautiful in a purely aesthetic sense and paid great attention to his clothes. His Savile Row tailor's bills were paid by Gerald, and therefore his budget was limitless, something Robert made full use of. It was awfully easy to write Robert off as a young boy (he was 25 years younger than Gerald) who had made a good marriage (and too many people did), but the truth was he was so amusing, and so handsome, and gave Gerald such pleasure, that even if that was the case, what did it matter?

I took a final look in the mirror. My eyes were shining, and if I didn't look glamorous, then at least I looked well, and the soft lighting from the oil lamp helped. Country life suited me, even if John still answered to the siren call of the metropolis. As I brushed my hair one last time, I heard a crunching of gravel and glanced at the clock on the wall. It was just after seven thirty. The new girl, Betty, would have prepared the drinks tray, but I needed to go downstairs and greet the guests myself. It was something John hated doing alone, even though he was far more sociable than me. I stood up and left my bedroom, heading for the stairs. I could already hear John grumbling loudly.

"Plymmie? Plymmie? They're here. Do get down here. You're running late as usual."

I left the room and hurried downstairs to where John waited, immaculate in his black tie. He had very good legs, I thought, which, coupled with his humour and the naughty twinkle in his eyes, combined to make him very attractive. I felt a stab of something in my groin. Bed wasn't always just about making babies.

Chapter Eighteen

John was a strange mix of the gregarious and the reclusive; he seemed happiest if he could find some solitude even while amongst friends. Our weekends were busy, with John sneaking off to his study or for a walk when it all got too much. We gave a lot of dinner parties, we often had housefuls of weekend guests, and we regularly went out locally to dinners and drinks. We were also involved in village life, with the church and the youth club that John and I started, for all the young who seemed to be hanging about with nowhere to go.

The weeks, by contrast, were so quiet that I didn't bother with supper and was usually in bed reading by 9pm. I didn't mind the peace. I rode Moti every day, and with John away much if not all of each week in London, I frequently rode over to Faringdon House to see Gerald, who was becoming a close friend, and of course Evelyn who was often there too.

One day, I arrived there for tea, to find Evelyn and Gerald waiting on the terrace for me. It was a cool day that had tipped its hat to spring, starting off warmer than usual and clear but subsequently clouding over. Within moments of my arrival, rain began to spit. Gerald looked at the sky.

"Grey, grey, grey. We'd better go inside," he said, turning on his well-shod heel. "Follow me."

"I'll just take Moti to the stables," I said. It was too late to worry about the effect of the rain on my hair, I was dishevelled and a bit of a state already. Frankly there wasn't much more damage that could be done and one of Gerald's lovely qualities was that he seemed to like me for me, and didn't care that I wasn't really a chic kind of girl, like Nancy or Diana, who were also his good friends.

This cast Evelyn, who was looking elegantly rumpled in his green wool suit, into a bit of a quandary. I could see him wrestling with himself, wanting to be gallant and escort me to the stables and embark on sharing some scurrilous piece of gossip with me as he usually did, but at the same time, not wanting to subject himself to a drenching. Gerald inadvertently came to his rescue:

"No, no, we don't want Moti to miss the party. Bring him in."

"Oh Gerald. Don't be ridiculous. He'll ruin your floors, and the potential damage to your furnishings is unlimited."

"Now don't be a spoil sport, Penelope. I know you have Moti indoors at home. John told me as much. He wasn't thrilled about it, I might add."

"My house is quite different to yours".

At Gerrard's Farm there were no silk rugs and no priceless Chinese vases. Only piles of books with dirty teacups balanced on the top.

Gerald waved my words away. "Nonsense. There's absolutely nothing you can say to change my mind. I'm quite set on it now. Moti is my guest for tea and that's that." He stepped backwards, holding the door open with a flourish and addressed the horse: "This way, Moti, please."

I shrugged tiredly. I hadn't slept well, and didn't feel like an argument with anyone, let alone Gerald. He could be very stubborn when he wanted something. I decided to give in.

"Oh, alright then. It's your house," I said, and started to lead Moti up onto the terrace. Evelyn went through the glass French doors ahead of us, laughing like a drain. He seemed in surprisingly good cheer and I suspected he'd already had a whisky or two, despite the fact it was only four in the afternoon. Moti and I followed, his hooves sounding gently against the delicate wood floor. Once inside, Moti moved his heavy white head from side to side, looking around him curiously. I sat down on the sofa next to Evelyn and watched as a maid put down the tea tray and set it out for us without showing even a glimmer of surprise at finding a horse traipsing round the salon as if he was admiring the paintings.

The maid poured us all a cup of tea. Gerald picked up his cup, took a sip, and surveyed the scene. Moti was now browsing the books.

"A photo. We simply must have a photo. Otherwise no one will believe us," said Gerald, clapping his hands like a small, delighted child unwrapping a much longed-for present. He dashed to his desk and took out a Box Brownie. Then he gestured to the maid who was just at the door making her escape.

"Lydia, come back, come back, just for a moment. Can you take a picture of us all? Just hold it up like this – that's it – and look down into it- perfect – and make sure we're in the glass square. Then, press, and hold very still. See? Got that? Marvellous. Now just wait while I get in position. Penelope, bring Moti a bit closer," he bossed, absolutely in his element now.

I put down my cup of tea and fetched Moti, who looked at me with haughty bemusement.

"It's alright darling," I whispered, stroking his nose. "Trust me." Moti picked his way slowly across the unfamiliar surfaces – the slippery parquet floor and the contrasting white rug, until he stood next to where I sat on the sofa. "That's perfect," Gerald cried excitedly. "Now, Lydia, have you got us all in?"

Evelyn had come to stand by me on one side, while Gerald stood regally on the other.

"I take a terrible photograph," I muttered to myself.

"You look beautiful, Penelope," Evelyn whispered quietly.

"Don't make me laugh," I said. I looked even worse laughing – eyes closed, mouth open.

"Stop talking, you two," commanded Gerald, "you have to hold still for the camera. Ready Lydia? Three, two one-."

The bemused maid bobbed. "Yes, sir, I think so, sir," and pressed the shutter. We all sat, frozen, waiting for Gerald to give us the all clear.

"One more, just to be sure," Gerald ordered. We all stood up a little straighter. At last, the photo call over, Lydia departed and I noticed the sun had come out and that the rain had stopped. Tewpie would think this was a fantastic joke, Moti being in Gerald's house and practically sitting on the Chippendale chaise longue. But I hadn't forgotten that Moti was a horse, or what he was capable of – and frequently did – at home. I was terrified that at any moment he would lift his tail and relieve himself on Gerald's immaculate white silk carpet. Whatever Gerald said about it now, clearly still feeling the effects of the three glasses of wine he had no doubt had at lunch, he would surely feel quite differently tomorrow, when he was sober and the housekeeper was in a filthy mood. Gerald's housekeeper was particularly terrifying.

"Come along Moti," I said purposefully. "Time to take you back where you belong." I took his reins in one hand, and began to make our way through the Chinoiserie, past the cut glass candlesticks on the sideboard, out of the drawing room and back onto the stone terrace. Past the stone lions and down the steps to the gardens.

"Oh you are a spoil sport, Penelope," moaned Gerald, following me out. "I've never had a horse to tea before."

With Moti safely outside, albeit on the immaculate square of lawn in front of the terrace, my shoulders relaxed. Moti, as if reading my body language, immediately left his mark steaming on the lawn. Gerald roared with laughter.

"It's funnier out here than it would have been inside," I said drily.

Evelyn appeared in the doorway behind Gerry. "What's the joke?" he enquired. Gerald gestured at the lawn.

Evelyn looked thoughtful for a moment, then said: "Penelope, you are quite extraordinary. You remind me of Helen of Troy."

"Did you know Helen of Troy?" I asked with a smile.

"Of course not. But I have an idea for a story based on her life, and when I have written it, I am going to dedicate the book to you."

"That's very flattering of you," I said. I had never been any good at accepting compliments. One simply didn't, yet Evelyn was dishing them out like guineas today.

"You are. Quite extraordinary. With your horse and your cart-"

"- it's a phaeton" I interjected.

"-driving around the countryside as you do. This is the age of the motor car. Have you noticed that your own dear husband writes for Shell-Mex, which as I'm sure you are aware is an oil company that sells petrol to fuel today's ever-growing number of keen motorists as they crisscross the countryside? John is writing motoring guides to England, for heaven's sake. Squandering his talent, of course, but that's not the point I'm making."

"Of course I've noticed, Evelyn," I snorted with laughter. "I'm not a complete fool. I just happen to like horses more than cars."

Evelyn nodded. "Yes, I can see that."

"They don't leak oil onto the driveway," I added.

"No. They just leave other kinds of deposits," Gerald smirked. He continued: "I want to paint you, my dear. You and Moti, in my drawing room. You can't refuse. I won't accept it. I simply won't take no for an answer."

This was a new idea. Gerald painted in quite a serious way and had had a very successful exhibition in London the previous year. I had seen some of his finished pieces. They were delicate, finely executed portrayals of his subjects, most often in watercolours.

"Oh Gerald, really, what an idea," I said, rolling my eyes. But a small part of me was captivated by the notion. I adored Moti – John said I loved my horse much more than I loved him – and while that wasn't entirely true, the idea of having Moti immortalised on canvas was engaging. Of course I might not be able to afford the picture-Gerald's pieces sold for considerable prices. But that didn't mean it wasn't a worthwhile exercise. There was also the uncomfortable fact that I didn't have quite enough to do with my weeks, and to sit for Gerald in easy silence would be a welcome distraction from everything that was currently preoccupying me.

"Why not outside?" I said, preparing to negotiate. "Why does he need to be painted inside?"

"It's the most perfect setting for him. A remarkable setting for a remarkable horse and his even more remarkable owner. Besides, I like the unexpected nature of the image. You don't *expect* a horse to be indoors."

I smiled, getting drawn into the idea, despite its absurdity or maybe because of it. Evelyn looked cross. He obviously felt his book dedication was being upstaged.

Once again I gave in. "Gerald, if you're really set on it, let's fix a time. But please remember this – when the inevitable happens, don't say I didn't warn you."

"Oh darling, you are very ill-bred to keep bringing that up. I expected more from the daughter of the commander in chief of the Indian Army. And anyway, what's a little shit between friends?"

I burst out laughing. Even Evelyn couldn't maintain his cross expression and broke into a grin, while Gerald was rocking backwards and forwards, convulsed by his own joke. It felt like the three of us were co-conspirators, united by some naughty plan.

"Alright. You've quite persuaded me. Just let me know when to come and sit for you."

"As soon as you can, m'dear."

I thought for a moment. "Towards the middle of next week," I suggested. "Wednesday?"

On Mondays I sorted out the house after the weekend, and on Tuesdays I often went hunting. By Wednesdays, I had generally exhausted my list of things to do, and apart from trying to further my research into Indian arts, which wasn't easy to do from a small village in Berkshire, I had time on my hands. I touched my flat stomach instinctively. John's weekly absences didn't help in the matter of starting a family. It was one of the things we had argued over the previous weekend. But John had insisted he needed to be in London during the week, at least for two or three days and sometimes for the entire working week, which meant we could only 'try' at the weekends. I had become accustomed to his ways of arguing by now, and I knew that whatever I did or said, once he had made up his mind, he would not budge. Sometimes, his refusal to even countenance a different arrangement made me wonder if he really wanted to be a father, or whether he was simply paying lip service to the notion; that reproduction was the done thing for a respectable married couple. I'd shouted as much at him on Sunday after church, and the remainder of the weekend had passed in a state of chilly politeness.

Anything that took my mind off the lack of a baby had to be a good thing.

"Wednesday it is."

I led Moti to the mounting block, and sitting astride, I set off home to the sound of my horse's hooves clip-clopping comfortably along the pathways. The sky was darkening once again in a quietly threatening manner. As we began the climb up into the Chilterns, my thoughts wandered back to babies and I wondered what kind of father John would make. From what Tewpie had told me, and from the little I had known Mr Betjeman Senior, it was obvious that they had had a complex relationship. John had felt close to him when he was a child, but as he grew up, he also grew away from him. As an adult, he had found his father argumentative and difficult, or perhaps it was just that his father couldn't manage his disappointment when Tewpie had said he couldn't go into the family firm.

"Come along, Moti," I encouraged. We were nearly at the top now, where the land plateaued and all of Oxfordshire and Berkshire fell away beneath us.

"Trot on".

Moti pricked up his ears and picked up his legs a little more quickly. Rising and falling in the saddle, I hoped that whatever the trouble had been between John and his father, Tewpie wouldn't replicate the domineering kind of behaviour he complained of on any child of ours. His father was dead now – he had died two years ago, quite suddenly, from a heart attack. But behaviour didn't always die out with its originator. More than just biological patterns were handed down in families. My own relationship with my parents had generally been warm and supportive; in fact, it still was, despite the friction caused by my elopement. It was a pattern I hoped to mirror with my own children, pray God we were able to have them. My parents remained central to my life and were by far the better parental role models, I decided, cresting the last hill separating Faringdon from Uffington.

My hands were cold inside my leather gloves and by the time we turned into the lane that led us home, I could hardly feel the reins. But we had taken this road numerous times, Moti and I, and thankfully Moti continued to trot towards Uffington with minimal guidance from me.

A thought had been bubbling in my mind, and I had been trying to ignore it. I was a practicing Christian, and believed in the principle of one God. But my need for a child was growing and swelling to fill my mind and seemed to be overcoming all sense. Rationally I knew I shouldn't, but still I found myself pulling on the right rein and heading up slightly into the hills behind Uffington. I was so near, it would only add ten minutes to the trip. Moti pricked his ears in surprise – he had probably been anticipating a rub down and some hay – but altered his direction agreeably enough. I wanted to spend a few moments at the White Horse of Uffington, the pre-historic carving that sat above the village, which the local people swore was a fertility symbol. Of course I thought the whole thing absurd- how could a pagan image have any real meaning to a Christian like myself? —but still I pressed on. A person of any faith understood that logic and prayer did not always mix well. What had I to lose?

We reached the carving, and I drew Moti to a halt and dismounted. I threw his reins over his head and after a curious glance at me, he lowered his white velvety head to graze some grass.

I walked closer to the carving. No one knew why it was here or how it had got here, but the lines of the prehistoric horse, up close, were even more beautiful than when viewed from afar. I fell to my knees by the horse's head and tentatively put my hand out to touch the chalk. It felt dry despite the drizzle. I opened my eyes and looked about me. Only sheep and Moti were watching me. Feeling slightly self-conscious, one hand pressed flat on the chalk, I closed my eyes and began to pray.

"Dear God," I prayed silently. "Please, grant me the joy of a baby."

I opened my eyes and looked at the sky, at the hard earth, at the rough, white surface of the chalk horse, as ancient as anything I'd ever touched, at the short grasses on the hillside, and took a deep breath, amending my prayer, injecting greater humility. "Please, Lord. If it is your wish, grant me a child."

The cold was permeating through my jodhpurs and Moti was advancing on me, nudging against me with his soft nose, as if to say, enough, Penelope, I'm tired and cold and hungry, can't we go home? I was all those things too, but on top of it all, I also felt a deep sense of calm. I gathered up Moti's reins, put a foot in the stirrup, and leapt back into the saddle.

"Thank you for waiting, darling," I said to my horse, stroking his white, white neck. "We're going home now."

It was Friday afternoon, and school children were spilling out onto the street, their voices shrill with excitement at the prospect of two days freedom.

"Hello, Mrs Betjeman," several of them called to me, and I smiled and waved at their familiar faces as I passed. John would be home soon; .he always tried to leave London by 4pm at the end of the week. By six I should hear the chug of his car pulling up in front of the house. I hadn't seen him since Monday so my desire for him had sharpened. I had asked Paula to prepare a casserole and leave it in the bottom of the Aga, to change the sheets on our bed, and to lay the fires.

It was now getting colder and trying to snow. Small isolated flakes drifted down and settled, almost invisible, on Moti's white neck and back. How could a day that had started like spring end as winter? Despite his coat and the exercise, I knew Moti would be feeling the cold. He had been bred in the lowlands of India, where snow was unheard of. He was much less used to England's cold, damp climate than I was. I flicked the reins and Moti quickened his trot. We passed the last of the school children straggling on their way home and the road lay empty ahead as we sped the last short part of our journey. We reached Garrard's Farm and I guided Moti round the back of the house to the stables. Thankfully Jackie was waiting.

"Could you deal with him for me, Jackie?" I asked, passing him the reins. "I think he should be in the stables tonight – he'll freeze in the fields. Will you make sure he's got plenty of hay?"

I usually rubbed Moti down myself, believing quite firmly these days that if an animal gave its efforts to you, the least you could do was reward it with efforts of your own by looking after it, but today, with John soon home, and having run a bit later than I'd intended, I had other things to do. I needed to bathe, not only to dispel the deep chill I was feeling in my bones, but also to wash my hair. It was so easy in the country to spend days at a time feeling cold and damp and looking totally unkempt. For Tewpie, coming from London, and the world of central heating and ladies maids who artfully arranged a lady's hair, and proper social evenings out that didn't involve having to wear several layers of clothes just to keep warm, the change to rural life was marked enough. I dreaded the thought of him comparing me with all the women he would have been fraternising with all week. I was all too aware of Tewpie's susceptibility to female good looks. I wanted to look attractive by the time he arrived rather than sweat-stained and smelling of horse.

I dashed into the house by the back door. I hung my coat on a hook and put my gloves in the kitchen on the rail in front of the Aga to dry. Betty was nowhere to be seen, but the room was warm and permeated with a comforting savoury smell. A fish casserole, I guessed. I took out some matches from a kitchen drawer. I lit a taper and started to light the oil lamps that sat on the kitchen table. Things always felt better if I managed to light at least some of the lamps before complete darkness fell. I went into the sitting room and dining room and lit the lamps and the fires. The rooms were freezing. I drew the thick velvet curtains closed, put the guards in front of both the fires, and carried a lamp carefully into the hall. It was smoking a little-I really had to remember to remind Betty to trim the wicks at least once a week – and the smell of burning oil hung in the air. As I turned for the stairs, I heard the sound of wheels on gravel: John's car was swinging into the drive. I looked down at myself – stained damp jodhpurs, unkempt hair – but there was no time to do anything about it. I ran through the house to open the front door, thinking it was a good thing that I had never wanted the life of a decorative lady aristocrat. And that John hadn't wanted a decorative, aristocratic wife, rather than the rather scruffy, domestically challenged, argumentative one still wearing filthy Jodhpurs that he had got.

I flung open the front door. "Tewpie," I called. "Tewpie, my darlin'. Oi 'ave missed you. Welcome home."

My husband was clambering inelegantly out of the car. I could tell immediately by the stiff hunch of his shoulders that he was in a bad mood.

"It's bloody cold here," he muttered, "much colder than in London." Bloody London, I thought. I could tell immediately that his heart was currently in some salon in Kensington, at some party he was missing; he'd rather be charming a number of ladies with his poems and witticisms, than on the threshold of a draughty country house in the middle of nowhere. But I would change that. Love would conquer all, as Virgil had written two millennia ago.

His arms were full of books and a messy pile of papers.

"Here, let me help." I took half the armful from him, but in doing so several loose papers fell to the ground.

"Oh hell," I said, bending to scoop them up.

"Here, let me, Plymmie. It's my manuscript for the *Shell Guide to Cornwall,* for god's sake, please get that sheet out of the puddle, before all the ink runs and I have to write the lot again."

I scrabbled the papers up, dripping and, I saw with alarm, ink clearly running in some places.

I carried my damp burden inside and straight to the kitchen, setting it down by the Aga. "They'll be dry in no time," I said with a breezy false confidence.

Tewpie was scowling. "It's bloody freezing in here. Like a tomb," he said. "Haven't we got any heating?"

"No" I said shortly. He knew perfectly well that we didn't. Did he think I'd magically had it installed during the five days he'd been away? I didn't want to kick the weekend off with the row, but I was starting to feel annoyed.

"This isn't London, with its modern central heating systems, I'm afraid. You know we manage with fires and the Aga. Look at you. You're simply underdressed. You need to go and put on a few extra layers. I'm perfectly warm with my thermals on under my riding kit."

I was lying, as my jodhpurs were damp, but for the sake of winning the argument I wasn't going to admit it. Instead, I raised my shirt a little and flashed John a glimpse of thermal vest. It didn't have the desired effect. He reddened and looked even crosser.

"What?" I said, smiling, "can't you write a poem about Mrs Penelope Betj, snug in her thermal vest? You're always writing poems for other girls. I'd rather like it if you wrote one for me for a change."

"Where's the drink?" John asked. I noticed with relief that the pile of papers was looking a little less limp already, drying out next to the Aga hob. I raised the lid to release extra heat.

"There's a drinks tray in the sitting room, and a blazing fire just lit, so why don't we go and sit there? Or would you like a bath to warm up?" (We could share it, I thought. Despite his grumpiness, I hadn't seen John all week, and I longed to touch his skin, to get close, to get naked.)

"I haven't yet managed to have one, I'm afraid", I continued. "I got held up at Gerald's, he made me take Moti into his sitting room for tea, and that rather delayed us. You must have told him how Moti came into the sitting room here, because he knew all about it, and you know how competitive he can get. He's been begging me for weeks, and I couldn't resist any longer, he just had to have his own way sooner or later, so it was easiest just to give in. How was your week, darling? Busy?"

I was trying on wifely hats. Regaling him with an anecdote. Playing the solicitous wife. I really wanted to be a good wife, but sometimes, I worried it didn't seem to come as naturally to me as to other girls. I had to keep trying. Marriage was a kind of work, and I had to keep at it.

John shuffled off in his three-piece suit to the sitting room.

"Take off your jacket, Tewpie. Put on a sweater!" I called after him. Honestly, didn't the man have any survival skills? "Your navy-blue jersey is upstairs in your drawer."

Something muffled and indecipherable floated back to me down the corridor. I shrugged – I couldn't put the sweater on for him-and opened the Aga door to stir the casserole. At least that smelt rather good. John loved food, and loved to eat well. The baked potatoes had crisped up nicely. I only had to cook the kale for a few minutes before we decided to eat. It was only John and me tonight, although my parents were coming to stay in the village pub tomorrow, which had a couple of decent rooms. Just for one night. Extraordinary decision, I thought, since they'd never stayed in a pub in their lives (and I recalled the fuss about my honeymoon). But they'd decided they couldn't stay in the house as the smell of the oil lamps upset Daddy's asthma. I'd never heard of my father having asthma before. My mother said it dated from too many years inhaling the smog of Delhi, but it seemed a ruse to me, a cover for the fact that they were used to greater comfort than our farmhouse offered and the pub, however lowly, was preferable to our spare bedroom. As, I admitted to myself, sniffing the air – was that burning? – John was, too. He was a sybarite. The more comfortable he was, the better, in his view. There was no merit in suffering unnecessarily, he often reminded me. It mattered less to me. I wondered if, because I had come from a life of extreme comfort, I found it possible to let luxuries go easily enough, while John was from a more Spartan background, and therefore snatched up all comforts on offer and hugged them to him as if his life depended on it. In fact he positively sought them out in the friends he made. His enemies called this social climbing.

Footsteps sounded in the corridor and John reappeared "There's no soda in the canister," he grumbled. Another strike against me, I thought. Then, John stopped in his tracks and started to shout: "My papers! Penelope, my papers!"

John rarely called me Penelope. Plymmie, or Pethrillappy or Yellow, but hardly ever, in fact, almost never, Penelope. I couldn't remember the last time he'd called me by my given name. I spun round to look for the source of the crisis and was confronted by orange flames rising to the ceiling.

"Oh hell," I cursed, rushing to the sink and dashing back with a damp cloth. I threw it onto the burning pile, and sprang backwards as black acrid smoke started to fill the room. John was standing helplessly by.

One look at his face told me a row was now inevitable. I wondered if, by the time we'd finished shouting at each other, we'd even remember to eat the casserole, let alone make up sufficiently to try and make a baby.

The smoke diminished, I ventured back to the Aga and carefully removed the tea towel, which was now black in parts, and had a large charred section in the middle.

I wasn't going to say anything soothing to John. There was simply no point. We had to face the situation as it really was. Platitudes weren't something either of us could abide. I looked at the papers. Blue ink streamed across the top page, words running together unrecognisably, and at least the top third of the page – the edge nearest the Aga hob, which had clearly caused the fire – was missing.

"Not too bad," I gulped. Perhaps platitudes had their place in the lexicon of language, after all.

"I'm sure we can salvage something," I continued, lifting the top page and looking at the pale blue wash on the page below. I made out 'where' and 'architec-' and a few other half-words, but the book was clearly, mostly, gone. John had slumped onto a kitchen chair.

"Where's the soda?" he asked in a small voice. "I really, really, need a drink."

I found the soda and we went to the sitting room and sat in silence, John clutching a whisky and soda. I rarely drank – I didn't like the taste of it, and it went to my head very quickly – but to keep him company, or perhaps to try to avoid annoying him further, I held a small whisky and soda in my hand as well. Conversation was sparse, but it wasn't, at least yet, a row.

"You could apologise" John said, in a whine.

"I have," I said shortly.

"Hemingway's first wife, Hadley, lost a suitcase full of his novel," John grumbled on.

"Oh, am I to be the first wife, then?" We had both heard the story about Hemingway leaving Hadley not long after the papers were lost, for a woman called Pauline, who Hemingway had married the moment his divorce came through.

"You could hardly blame me, could you?" John moaned. "Fortunately for you, I am a Godly man, and divorce is against my religion. Even though you have set fire to my latest Oeuvre."

"You call that good fortune? Don't be ridiculous. It's not as bad as that. Whoever typed up the Shell guide will have taken a carbon copy, I always see the typists doing it when I come and visit you, so it's really only a few pages of hand written notes that are gone. I know it's not ideal, but then, Tewpie, life ain't."

John sat back in his armchair more comfortably. The whisky was obviously hitting the spot.

"Oh, alright. I promise not to sulk all weekend."

"That's a good decision," I said, stretching out a hand and smiling at him. He took it. His hands felt rough and sandpapery, with calluses on the end of his fingers. I held it for a moment, and breathed out. I could feel him warming towards me now Peace had been brokered. My leg muscles ached in my rain dampened jodhpurs, but this wasn't the moment to say I had to go and change. We had so little time together, John and I, we had to make the most of it. Even if I caught a chill in the process. I put down my drink and went over to my husband. I knelt before him, between his splayed knees, and put my hands on his legs.

"In which case, if we're friends again, is there something I can do to make it up to you?"

John took a large sip of his drink, his eyes meeting mine. His bird's nest hair stood up on his head, and he smiled to reveal his uneven teeth. I smiled back and one of my hands stole up under his jumper to his belt buckle.

Afterwards, we lay side by side in the gloom, half undressed, smelling of each other, my hand in his, and I knew that for a little while at least, I was forgiven, and all was right in the world again.

Chapter Nineteen

Over the following weeks I spent quite a lot of time being painted in Gerald's drawing room. I had wondered whether Moti would be able to keep still, but it quickly became evident that he enjoyed being admired and recorded for posterity by a hand as fine as Gerald's, and he was not only happy to pose steadily for some time, several days a week, he also seemed to understand that indoors was not the place to 'go'.

So I relaxed into the experience, and began to look forward to the sittings. They broke up the long week without John, giving them a focus. Gerald was always a source of scurrilous gossip and cheering anecdotes, and often had house guests who added to the general merriment. And little by little, the image of Moti-tall, pale and proud-and myself, unnaturally pressed and clean and smiling in my jodhpurs, emerged onto Gerald's canvas.

"It's a very good likeness," I commented, at the end of one sitting, as Gerald was standing back, paint brush still in hand, admiring his handiwork.

"Don't overwhelm me with praise, Penelope dear," Gerald replied.

"Oh ha!" I snorted. We both knew over-effusiveness was a pet hate of mine while Gerald could gush for England.

"I must admit I'm pleased with it," Gerald said, putting his brush down.

"You should be. It's very good."

"What will John make of it, I wonder? I know he's very thick with John Piper, and he's a Proper Artist of course. My little daub isn't going to stand up to any kind of comparison."

Gerald was evidently fishing, inviting me to contradict him. I took a verbal step sideways. "He's longing to see it."

I started to lead Moti outside. "How many more sittings do you think we will need?" I called over my shoulder.

"Why, are you finding it a little arduous, my dear? There's quite a lot I can do without you, if you have other fish to fry. I need to flesh out the background, and the carving on the mantelpiece is going to take some time."

"Not arduous, nor other things to do," I replied lightly. "I was merely asking out of curiosity, that was all."

Moti's heels clattered onto the flagstones of the terrace and the cold March air bit into my crisp cotton shirt. Brave yellow daffodils waved from the flowerbeds.

"We're a long way from spring," Gerald grumbled.

"You're an impatient man, aren't you?" I teased. "I am afraid the seasons are one of the few things that remain immune to your charms and powers of persuasion. They're in the hands of someone more powerful than you."

"Don't start, Penelope. I'll only put my hands over my ears," Gerald said. "I don't want any of that God stuff here. Do you know what God has to say about homosexuals?"

I flinched slightly. It was rare for Gerald to speak so baldly of his sexual orientation. Since Oscar Wilde's trial and conviction, there had been a general unspoken widespread social agreement that, whenever and wherever possible, any mention of homosexuality was best unsaid. That's not to say two men couldn't live together – Robert and Gerald did – only that there was a greater fear and awareness of the consequences of being too visible, of flaunting one's love too publicly.

"Leviticus: I paraphrase, but the spirit of it goes something like this: "You shall not lie with a male as with a woman; it is an abomination. ... If a man lies with a male as with a woman, both of them have committed an abomination; they shall be put to death, their blood is upon them."

"That's not God, that's the Old Testament" I said firmly. "I am sure God would love you if you would allowed him to. Oscar became a Roman Catholic before he died, and so has Bosie, as well you know. If they didn't object to Him, why should you?"

"Ah, but did it make them happy?" Gerald demanded. "Did it? Bosie seems rather a miserable old man these days."

"Happiness is not life's only goal," I replied.

Moti was now cantering round the park in front of the terrace, clearly having found happiness himself.

"He," I said, "Is a manifestation of God's beauty. Look at him. Long legs, effortless muscular movements, his incredible mane of hair. A work of art," I breathed. "Only God could create him."

"Darling, that's exactly how I feel about Robert," Gerald replied, laughing. "The legs, the muscles, the hair."

"Oh I don't know why I bother," I said crossly. Gerald was not going to be an easy convert.

"Help me, Evelyn," I called, as Evelyn, replete from too many sandwiches and cakes, his stomach pressing against his waistcoat, struggled up from the chaise longue where he had been lounging and eating, and joined us on the terrace, tea cup still in hand. He clearly couldn't quite bear to declare himself completely finished.

"Jolly good tea," he said. "Help you with what?"

"Helping Gerald to see the beauty of God."

Evelyn looked at me, and then at Gerald. "I think there is a slight chance he will get there in his own time, Penelope, just as I think you will one day turn to Rome. However, you are far the closer on your journey of the two of you," he pronounced, his eyes half closing, whether with assumed mystic insight or indigestion from overeating I wasn't sure, but the result was to give him the appearance of a plump sage.

"It's time I was going," I said.

"I don't know why you don't just move in, like Evelyn," Gerald grumbled. "Then we would get this painting done much faster."

Evelyn replaced the cup he was drinking from in its saucer with an audible clunk.

"I have not moved in," he objected. "I am simply a treasured friend enjoying your extended hospitality."

I laughed. Evelyn looked cross, his brow collapsing into a frown. Gerald raised an eyebrow, in a way that only he could.

"I suggest you enjoy my company while you can. Soon my annulment will be through and I will marry Laura, and set up a domestic situation of my own again. No doubt I will soon be knee deep in babies and novels and you won't see me from one end of the year to the next."

As usual, my mother had been right. I squeezed Evelyn's arm and tried not to mind that my favourite bachelor was getting hitched again.

"I'm so pleased for you, Evelyn. You've had a horrid time, and now it's all ending happily."

"You're such a romantic, Penelope. Does it ever end happily? We are mammals and that means we are drawn to living in pairs and mating, that's all."

"If I'm romantic then you're the opposite!"

"I'm merely being practical. I simply wish the Papal committee would stop dragging their feet. They are taking an absolute age."

"I suppose there are systems for these things. Hoops to jump through," I commiserated. I felt mildly cheered to know that Evelyn wasn't madly in love with this Laura. "I'm sure everything will be resolved soon."

"Yes, yes. Of course it will." Gerald was supremely uninterested in Evelyn's love life, with all his attention still on his latest painting. "Darling. When will I see you again? Soon, I beg you. I want to paint while the muse is in the ascendancy. Tomorrow?"

"I can come at eleven," I said. "But now I really must go home. It will be dark soon, and I really don't feel like getting lost in the Chilterns and spending a night *al fresco*."

"Stable Moti here and let my man drive you," Gerald urged. "John would never forgive me if anything happened to you."

As the cold, foggy winter's afternoon closed around me, it was tempting. Oh to be even so briefly reminded of the luxury of wealth. A driver, a warm car with a rug to snuggle under, a groom to stable the horse. It would be so easy to say yes, but something within me felt it proper to return home as I had arrived. Besides, luxury was a kind of addiction. I feared one taste would not be enough.

"Thank you but no," I said. "I need Moti and the phaeton to get about." Gerald smiled slightly, as if he had known what my answer would be before I gave it.

"Really, Penelope, you are the most self-sufficient woman I have ever met. It must be that Empire upbringing."

I snorted with laughter. "What Empire upbringing?"

"You know very well what I'm referring to, my dear. Playmates to the Royal children. Tea parties at Windsor. The Grand Tour. Inja!"

When he said it like that, it sounded grand. But it had been my daily life, and so had seemed ordinary. Just as this – mucking out Moti, learning to cook, spending Monday to Friday without my husband – was my daily life now. I shrugged.

"I suppose. But it's all history now. The Empire's crumbling and the middle classes will rise. You'll see."

"Penelope the Social Forecaster," Gerald pronounced in weighty tones.

I whistled to Moti, who gave a last kick before trotting over obediently.

"Oh, very funny, Gerald. You are a scream. I really must get going. Thank you for your concern and your kind offer of your driver, but I'll be fine. I've ridden through much of the Himalayas. I'm sure I can manage six miles as the crow flies across the Chilterns."

I kissed Evelyn goodbye, and walked Moti round to the stables with Gerald. I tacked him up, attached him to the phaeton and climbed onto the box. I felt unaccountably weary. I waved at Gerald: "Until tomorrow," I said, with a slight smile. "Trot on, Moti. Trot on."

Chapter Twenty

The next day I woke early. The room was in darkness, with no sign of dawn trying to find its way through the pale floral curtains that hung at the windows. The room was cold, but under two quilts and a blanket, and wearing a pair of John's flannel pyjamas with an old cardigan on top and his best woollen bed socks on my feet, I was warm enough. I felt tiredness persisting, despite hours of sleep and I wondered if I was coming down with a virus. I was very bad at being ill. I hated staying in bed for days, and besides, on my own here without John or any company, it would be very dull. I swung my legs out of bed and dashed to the bathroom, but somewhere on the way the light headed feeling turned unexpectedly to nausea and before I could even think I found myself bent over the loo being sick.

I pulled the chain, and lent over the sink. Turning on the tap I swilled water around in my mouth, trying to rinse away the indelible taste of bile. I splashed my face, and looked in the mirror that rested above. I didn't look particularly pale, and I felt rather better now I had vomited. The light headedness had receded as quickly as it had come. My thoughts halted for a moment like Moti refusing a fence, and then I started to count backwards as slowly I felt my way towards a possible explanation Could it be? Dare I hope?

I walked back along the wooden floored corridor to my bedroom and climbed gratefully back into bed. Leaning back against the pillows, I wished John was here. I wished he could share this moment with me, this moment of hope and optimism, but as too often, the space beside me where my husband should be was just a stretch of cold, empty sheet. I could be wrong, there might be no baby, I could simply be sickening for something and, co-incidentally, late with the curse. These things happened, as I well knew, having had false alarms before. But here and now, a number of things potentially added up to make me feel something I had never felt before; that I might, just might, be pregnant.

My stomach lurching with hope, I pulled the quilt up to my nose for warmth and thought some more. Gerald was right, I was outwardly very self-sufficient – I thought nothing of wringing the necks of the chickens we kept when it was time for them to go in the pot, or of riding Moti through the countryside, or sleeping night after night here in this cold farmhouse alone – but I missed Tewpie. Marriage was about companionship-my parents had rarely spent a night apart. My mother had always travelled with my father, wherever he had been posted. John and I needed to be together much more than we currently were, and if what I was thinking, hoping, was true, perhaps it would persuade Tewpie to come home more. The trains were good, and he finished work by mid-afternoon each day. He only stayed in London to *see* people; people who distracted him from his real work of poetry, with their glasses of champagne and social chatter.

I lay back on my pillows and watched the morning light begin to slide in through the gap in the curtains. If he came home after work each night, we could have some wonderful quiet evenings together as we waited for our first child to arrive. I closed my eyes to further pursue this daydream. It wasn't, I thought, snuggling further under the pile of quilts, as if he even loved London that much. At the moment, he seemed to be rather off it, although he still enjoyed the going out. Of course he particularly loved the girls. His strongly emotional, slightly feminine streak, I supposed. He saw quite a lot of Billa – she was still living in London, still unmarried. She was my best friend, so that was alright – although of course I never completely forget that she had become engaged to him for a few days at the same time as me. Then there was Nancy. He always enjoyed Nancy's company, but I didn't mind that either, as I knew Nancy was the person who had encouraged John to marry me when things between us had started to wobble. I tried not to mind at all, whoever he met, as jealousy seemed such a petty emotional state. I also tried to get to London to visit him, to spend a night a week with him, but too often Moti, or the chickens, or sitting for Gerald, or just not wanting to travel to London, got in the way.

But John *had* been complaining recently about London, and not just to me-to any radio listeners who cared to tune in. He gave a talk from BBC Bristol – his first, and he loved it, and did it very well, I thought- and in it he'd called London 'a poisonous octopus' or something similar, a kind of ravenous beast spreading out and greedily swallowing up charming, unworldly, unspoilt villages. So perhaps luring him away from London wasn't a completely hopeless idea. I crossed my hands over my flat belly and decided to have a little more sleep before getting up for the day.

Of course I couldn't drop off. My thoughts just went round and round about the baby. Was there a baby? Might there be a baby? If there was a baby, would it be a boy or a girl? (I didn't care and didn't think Tewpie would either, fortunately he was not a dynastic, must-have-a-son kind of man). If there was a baby, when would it arrive? What should I do now? Should I call the doctor? Or Star? I immediately dismissed this last thought. I didn't want to tell anyone who mattered until I really knew for sure.

I threw aside the quilts and blankets and got out of bed. I went back to the bathroom and quickly began to wash. I'd get up and go to London to see my doctor. He was the person who would be able to tell me the true state of things. I couldn't wait to know, and why wait if I didn't have to? I'd already waited long enough. As I pulled a damp flannel over my face, I remembered Gerald and our scheduled sitting. I'd have to telephone and put it off for another day.

I returned to the bedroom and started to look through my cupboard for a suitable London outfit. Dress. Stockings. Coat with my diamond brooch pinned on the lapel. Hat. I'd tell Gerald something had come up, and I had to go to London. I just wouldn't tell him why. That was it. A decision. He would simply have to understand. Now I was glad I'd ridden Moti home last night – Jackie would be able to take me to the station in the phaeton. Suddenly it felt as if everything made sense, as if events were meant to be unfolding this way. Everything had been building to this moment and I just had to let it happen around me.

I laced up my shoes and went downstairs. I went into the kitchen, always the warmest room in the house because of the Aga. I filled the kettle from the tap and put it on the hot plate. I took out a small china teapot and put in some tea leaves, then put it on the kitchen table to brew. Pulling a chair close to the Aga I and sat and waited for the whistling that would tell me the water had boiled. I wanted to talk to Tewpie but I didn't know where to find him. I wasn't sure where he would be staying. I thought I remembered him saying he was spending the week with our friend Alan Byrne-Pryce, but I wasn't completely sure, and it didn't seem appropriate to call Alan only to discover that my husband wasn't there. That could embarrass us both and set a thousand rumours flying. Besides, it was too early to call anyone. Star, a stickler for good manners, always maintained that the etiquette with the telephone was never to call before ten in the morning or after ten at night. While I liked to disagree with my mother wherever I possibly could, on this I felt she was, unfortunately, right.

The kitchen clock revealed it was still not quite eight o clock. There was so much to do, but nothing I could start on yet. Horse, chickens, Betty coming to make breakfast, the doctor to telephone, Jackie to saddle up Moti and drive me to the station. I longed to be up and off, but all I could do was wait: for the whistle of the kettle, for the hands on the clock to catch up with my mind.

At nine o'clock, Betty and Jackie arrived. I asked Jackie to prepare the horse and cart, and told Betty of my plans for London.

At ten o'clock, I finally allowed myself to go to the telephone in the hall, and opened the address book that sat on the small table beside it. I ran my finger down the letters to G, and found the doctor's number. I picked up the phone and gave the number to the girl at the Exchange. The line crackled with silence. I waited.

"Hello. Doctor Gray's rooms."

"Hello. This is Mrs Betjeman. I need to see Doctor Gray today, please."

"Of course Mrs Betjeman. Let me see what he has available."

There was the sound of rustling paper and of the doctor's assistant breathing into the receiver.

"He has two openings today, one at noon, another at three thirty."

I wondered whether Doctor Gray had a long lunch planned. The gap suggested it. If so, I was surely better to catch him before it rather than after.

"Noon suits me very well."

"Marvellous. That's all fixed. We'll see you then. Marvellous."

I hung up. My stomach heaved nervously. I picked up the receiver again and this time I gave the operator Gerald's number. After a few rings, the butler answered. I left a brief message with him, cancelling the sitting, and then considered whether to make a final call to John, who would very probably be at work by now. I glanced at my watch. It was now ten past ten. The London train took an hour and left at twenty to the hour. Getting to Harley Street by midday was going to be tight. I wasn't sure I had time to spare to try and reach John. Besides, what was I going to tell him? I had nothing definite to say. Why raise his hopes only to possibly dash them a few hours later? I made a quick decision. I would go and see John after my visit to Doctor Gray, and if the news was good I would share it with him then.

I started to collect up my things.

"Betty," I called. "I'm setting off. Most probably back tonight."

"Very good, Mrs Betjeman. Jackie has the horse and cart round the front."

"Marvellous." I echoed the Doctor's secretary. Although Betty, along with many other people, did persist in calling my expensive and rather chic phaeton a cart. "Marvellous." Everything was marvellous. I felt slightly removed from things, as if I was watching myself from high up on the ceiling in the corner of the room. It was a disconcerting feeling.

"Come on, Penelope, buck up," I told myself, as I pulled on my coat and buttoned it up. I checked myself in the hall mirror. I looked pale. I fished out my lipstick from my handbag, and dabbed some colour onto my lips. I pressed my lips together and looked again. Better. I smiled at myself, unable to stop myself feeling a surge of happiness. I knew I mustn't get ahead of myself – it would make the disappointment so much worse. But enjoying the few hours when I might be a pregnant woman was impossible to resist.

I turned from my reflection, returned the lipstick to my handbag, picked it up and went to the front door. Outside, Jackie was waiting. He handed me up onto the box, which was less easy than usual since I was wearing a dress. I inhaled deeply, breathing in the pungent scent of horse, the leather, the wood of the box, the smell of horse dung and mud that hung in the damp air, and felt more settled.

"Thank you, Jackie. I'll drive to the station."

Jackie climbed up next to me, and I flicked the reins, feeling more like myself already.

Within minutes we were there. "Over to you, Jackie," I said, handing the reins to my groom who looked a little pale. Maybe I had driven a little too fast-one corner had felt a little tight-but I had always been in control. I wondered if I'd have to stop riding if I was pregnant. I hoped not. I scrambled down and rushed into the station. I purchased a return ticket from an unfamiliar man in the ticket booth – must be new -, and hurried to the London platform where several other people were waiting. I could already see the steam of the approaching train in the distance.

"Good morning, Mrs Betjeman," called the station master, hurrying out onto the line with his red and green hand signals. It was a tiny station.

"Off to London?"

"Yes. Some errands to run and the husband to catch up with," I shouted back. The puffing train was getting louder, and then it was there, hissing and steaming hot, in its glorious gleaming black and red and gold colours. I climbed in an open door and settled in a compartment, in the seat by the window. There was just one other person in the carriage, an elderly lady with white hair and a rather dated dark day dress that fell demurely to her ankles. We smiled at each other politely and then both looked away. I felt relieved that her rather severe appearance suggested she wasn't the type to break into conversation. I wanted to be alone with my thoughts, and to watch the Chilterns unfold before me, to glimpse the ancient chalk white horse on the hillside who just might have played a hand in a baby starting, and to witness the beginnings of suburbia, the point at which buildings began to take over the land, to Tewpie's ever-increasing fury, before we reached London Proper and Marylebone, my favourite of all the London stations. Smaller than the vast terminus of King's Cross in North London, Marylebone's Victorian edifice always seemed welcoming, and besides, for today's purposes it was very convenient: it was just a few minutes from Harley Street.

At Marylebone I went directly to the taxi rank.

"Harley Street, please," I said, as the porter slammed the door behind me.

It was five to twelve when I climbed the stone steps to the doctor's front door, and three minutes to twelve by the time I sat leafing through an old copy of Country Life in the plush, over-heated waiting room. Seeing nothing, reading nothing, the text a blur, my thoughts jumbled and almost incoherent, even to myself. I hadn't dared admit to myself before quite how badly I had wanted a child, how badly I had felt my failure to produce one. I wasn't sure why – I had never been maternal, had never been the type to cluck over other people's children, frankly preferring horses – but now, for whatever myriad of reasons I couldn't unpick, I was absolutely longing to start a family with John.

The nurse materialised in the doorway.

"Mrs Betjeman, the doctor is ready for you," she said. I replaced the magazine on the side table where I'd found it, and stood up. I bit back the word 'marvellous'.

"Thank you," I said instead, and followed her into the corridor and into Doctor Gray's wood panelled consulting room.

Doctor Gray, a thick set man in his mid-fifties with a shock of grey hair and a beard to match, was standing up behind his desk. He wore a dark charcoal three-piece suit and a crisp white shirt with a neat short collar – a Duke of York, Tewpie called them – and a stethoscope hung from his neck, perhaps forgotten about after a previous consultation.

"Doctor Gray," I said, sticking out my hand.

"Mrs Betjeman. How very nice to see you. Do sit down."

"Thank you for seeing me at such short notice," I began in a rush. I felt flustered.

Doctor Gray smiled slightly. "No trouble at all, m'dear. How can I be of service?"

"You may remember, I came some months ago when my husband and I were not managing to make much headway in the family department – "

"I remember it well. I believe I advised you to redouble your efforts." The doctor smiled slightly as he said this. "Not usually a hardship for young married couples such as yourselves."

I decided to ignore this remark, unsure of its appropriateness, and blundered on instead with my pre-rehearsed statement, devised on the train that morning, somewhere between Rickmansworth and Beaconsfield,

"The thing is, this morning, I got up and felt sick. And then I was sick. And then it occurred to me that I've been feeling very tired generally. More tired than usual. And|" – why did talking about this kind of thing with a male doctor make one blush? "Now I think about it-I'm possibly a little-late."

The doctor sat back in his chair and beamed. "That all sounds very promising, my dear. Shall we take a little look? I will call the nurse."

He crossed the room, opened the door and shouted into the corridor:

"Nurse! Could you step in, please!"

Immediately the nurse appeared, as if she had been listening on the other side of the door, waiting for the summons. Her face assumed an efficient expression. "Right you are, doctor"

"I need to examine Mrs Betjeman. Could you help her prepare?"

"Right you are, doctor," she said again, drawing the curtain around the bed in the corner of the room, and ushering me inside. Soon I lay in my bra and pants under a blanket, my hands crossed protectively across my belly. The doctor pushed through the curtain. "Mrs Betjeman. I'm just going to feel your tummy, and have a little listen. Apologies if my hands are cold."

I held my breath, while the doctor prodded my abdomen gently for a few moments, his eyes gazing over my shoulder thoughtfully. Then he pressed his stethoscope firmly against my tummy and listened. Finally, he stood up and beamed.

"Mrs Betjeman, I think we can safely say you are about nine weeks pregnant. However, it is early in the pregnancy, and you must look after yourself and not get too exhausted. But all being well, I think you and Mr Betjeman can expect to be parents by the middle of November this year."

"Oh," I said, tears pricking my eyes and threatening to spill out onto my cheeks. "Oh. OH! That's wonderful news. Thank you so much," I added, as if he had personally been responsible for making it happen.

The doctor smiled, and left me alone behind the curtain to get dressed and compose myself. I dabbed at my watery eyes with a tissue and glanced in my compact. I added a little powder, and some lipstick, and ran a comb through my hair, until I looked more like myself (my pregnant self!) before emerging from behind the curtain.

"Please take a seat for a moment. I am referring you to an obstetrician. He is extremely experienced and will supervise your pregnancy. He works from a clinic in Marylebone, which is where you will have the baby delivered. Here is his address and telephone number. You must register with him, and call him if you have any problems. If for some reason you can't raise him, call me. Here is my home number as well."

"Problems?"

"Any bleeding, any pain. Those are both signs of miscarriage. Most probably neither of these things will occur, but occasionally they do. Sadly it's nature's way of dealing with a foetus that isn't quite viable. What you can expect from a normal pregnancy, and there is no reason to think you will not have a normal pregnancy, is nausea and fatigue for the first three months, with a return of energy after that time. As the baby grows big, towards the end, you will start to feel tired again, but until then, I suggest you live as normal a life as possible. Do everything just as you normally would. There's no need to alter your habits."

I nodded. "Alright. Many thanks, doctor." I stood up to go. We shook hands. He smiled at me, and I left. I walked down the stairs in a daze, and exited onto the street. The air was cold and my breath made small foggy clouds in front of my face. Spring must surely come soon, I thought, nestling deeper into my rabbit fur and starting to walk in the direction of John's office. I would surprise him. We were to be parents. It was happening. It was real. After three years of trying and hoping and waiting and trying again, finally, I was expecting.

I had gone into Doctor Gray's rooms as one person, and had come out, with luck and God willing, as two. I put one hand on my stomach. In there was our first child. Slumbering sweetly in the darkness of my body, perhaps sucking his thumb, I thought, turning into New Cavendish Street. About the size of an olive, Doctor Gray had said, but growing rapidly, a bundle of cells dividing and multiplying miraculously into a whole new person.

I crossed Oxford Street and started to hurry down Park Lane towards Knightsbridge and John's office. My handbag swung in the crook of my elbow and the bright cold day was not unpleasant. I could hardly wait to see John's face. I descended down in to the underpass, and up the other side, on the edge of Hyde Park. Cutting through the park would be the fastest way, and the nicest. I had always loved Hyde Park, and now, with the slender green heads of daffodils pushing through the soil, and the cherry blossom trees waving their branches in the breeze, it looked particularly beautiful. Walking down to the Serpentine, I passed nannies pushing their charges in large navy-blue perambulators around the water's edge, while older charges ran alongside them. I smiled at a small boy – no more than four, I guessed – chasing a dog, oblivious to his nanny's shouts: "Edward! Edward! Come back here this minute!"

But Edward, dark hair flopping forwards, was not interested in listening to nanny, and only ran faster. I watched him for a moment, his skinny pale legs flying as he tried to catch his dog, a small brown and white Jack Russell. Was I going to have a cheeky, naughty boy like that, I wondered? I'd teach him to ride Moti, and feed the chickens, and perhaps we should have a dog too? I pressed my belly again, and wondered some more.

The sun was gleaming off the water, which had been whipped up a little by the brisk wind. Fat seagulls and pigeons intermingled in wary amiableness on the water's edge. The seagulls were strutting aggressively about in large and slightly menacing numbers, calling loudly to each other with puffed out chests like vulgar, overweight business men in off-the-peg suits.

I was nearly in Knightsbridge now. I could see the rows of town houses that backed onto Brompton Road. I exited the park and arrived at John's office. I entered the Shell building and the receptionist ushered me into the waiting room. As I sat in the second waiting room I'd visited in as many hours, I ignored *Country Life* and the dog-eared *Vogues* in favour of last-minute panic. Would John be as thrilled as I was? My head was full to bursting with ideas of the small boy or girl growing within me, but would John feel the same?

Suddenly John was in front of me, in all his familiarity. His favourite three- piece green tweed suit (matching green bits on his teeth), his polished brown shoes, his tie a little askew, his hair its familiar bird's nest, and the panic receded as fast as it had come, as I was flooded with a simple sense of relief. Here he was, exactly the same, exactly as I needed him to be, lovely, friendly, charming, funny Tewpie. Except he looked alarmed.

"Plymmie. Darling. What is it? Is everything alright?"

John came and sat next to me, holding my hand, his dark eyes warm with concern. How could I ever have worried, about John, about us? I broke into a huge smile. It was so good to see him. My doubts and anxieties receded like the tide going out.

"Oh John. Yes, everything's fine. Oh, better than fine. Darling, we've something to celebrate."

I watched John's features alter, from anxiety to expectation. I felt my eyes start to brim again. I never cried, or so rarely as to make it a remarkable event and here I was, blubbing twice in one morning. John pressed my face against his chest and put his arms round me.

"You're in pig, aren't you?" he said quietly, kissing the top of my head.

I laughed and cried at the same time, my head warm against his chest. "Don't be disgusting." I said. "But yes. Yes! I'm pregnant. Are you happy?"

John didn't answer, he just rested his head on my hair, and I didn't look up to see if he looked pleased.

Mutisher.

In pig. I chuckle now, recalling this phrase from long ago, but again, no sound comes out. In pig-that was Nancy's expression for pregnancy, dating from her childhood. She later immortalised it in one of her hilarious, dazzling novels – 'Love in a Cold Climate', or perhaps it was the other one,' The Pursuit of Love', I forget which.

I feel warmth running right through me like a current, from my uncovered head to my wrinkly toes, as I remember how happy John and I were that summer, when I was pregnant with Paul. Surely no child could have been more wanted by a mother. Tewpie came home in the evenings as often as he could, and we were more together than at any other time in our marriage. Gerald said he would hurry up with his painting – where is that painting now?- knowing he had to finish it before the baby arrived. In those days, pregnancy wasn't some altered state, where you had to go to classes and buy special clothes and practice methods of breathing. We just went on as before, letting out our clothes. It was only at the end, when I was very big, that I began to feel very fed up. That was about the same time when John suddenly realised what was coming, imminently, into our lives and began, metaphorically, to bite his nails.

Chapter Twenty-One

October 1937. Uffington.

I lay on the sofa, my vast bump rising above me like a watermelon I had shoved up my dress as a joke.

"Tewpie. I feel I'm going to burst."

John raised his eyes from the newspaper and took in my vast, reclining form.

"It does look like you ate a rather large breakfast," he said.

"Don't joke," I moaned. "I barely had space for a piece of toast. The baby's taking up every inch of me."

"Poor you, darling. Is there anything I can do to help?"

This was a very un-John like question. He never offered to do anything to help, and so I was especially touched.

"Could you massage my feet? They ache so badly and my ankles are all swollen. The things no one tells you about pregnancy. Swollen ankles, varicose veins, insomnia, exhaustion. Don't worry," I went, on taking in John's uncertain expression, "I was only joking about the foot massage. It was just rather lovely that you asked me if there was anything you could do. I didn't want to sound ungrateful by turning you down flat."

John's facial expression shifted from uncertain to bewildered. I continued to rattle on:

"Oh, just chalk it up to my being pregnant. I'm growing a whole new person, so I think I'm allowed to talk a bit of nonsense now and again, don't you?"

"Whatever you say, dear," John replied slowly, in a pitch perfect parody of a downtrodden husband, before going back to the newspaper.

I shifted uncomfortably on the sofa. My back ached. "Can this baby really get any bigger?" I demanded. John looked up again and sighed loudly. "Distract yourself, Yellow. Here. Read some of the paper." He leaned over, holding out some pages. I took them and for want of anything else to do, started to look at them for a moment, then dropped the paper in my lap.

"I can't concentrate," I gasped. "The baby's going to be a footballer… kick, kick, kick. What do you think it is, Tewpie? A boy or a girl?"

"It's an 'it' at the moment," John replied, without looking up.

"Soon 'it' will be a he or a she," I pointed out. "Aren't you longing to find out what 'it' is? Wouldn't it be marvellous if there was a way to know without having to wait until the baby's born. I wonder if doctors will invent something that tells us."

"Oh Propeller do shut up," John said, exasperated. "I don't care whether the doctors invent something or not, because if they do, it will be too late for us. We will find out what our 'It' is in a few short weeks, in the way that people always have since the dawn of time."

"I hope you're looking forward to being a father, Tewpie. Because your manner doesn't really indicate that you are."

John slowly lowered his paper with an air of weary defeat.

"I can't really look forward to becoming a father, because I don't know what to expect. But I will do my best to be a good one. I will teach it to read, whatever it is, and pay for it to be educated. I consider that to be a fulfilment of my fatherly duties."

I laughed and the bump heaved. "Oh Tewpie."

But John didn't laugh.

A thought dawned, not for the first time.

"Darling. Are you a bit nervous about it? I'm sure you'll take to it. Lots of your friends have babies and seem to enjoy them. Look at Bryan, how he loves his two boys with Diana, and now another baby on the way with his new wife. Besides, you won't have to do much for a while. It will just be a small bundle in the nursery for ages. And Betty is all set to help. You'll hardly have to see it if you don't want."

"I'm not nervous. It's one of life's milestones, and it's approaching rather fast, that's all."

"You make parenthood sound like a meteorite," I said, hoping to lift the darkening mood. John's words didn't reassure me. At times I detected a distinct lack of enthusiasm from him about the forthcoming baby, and this was one such moment.

"What shall we call it?" I asked, turning the conversation to one of the jolly aspects of imminent parenthood.

"'It' will do perfectly well for now."

"Oh. I thought perhaps Paul if it's a boy. Or did you want Ernest after your father? It's not my favourite name."

"Definitely not Ernest." John gave a little shudder at the suggestion. "Paul's alright I suppose."

I took this as an encouraging sign. A positive, even if qualified with an 'I suppose'. "And Rose, or Frances, or perhaps Candida, if it's a girl?" I suggested.

"Rose is very pretty. And I like Candida. Let's hope it's a girl," John said, his voice lifting. I watched him closely. How odd, he seemed to be more excited by the idea of having a daughter than a son. Most men were the other way round.

"Whatever it is, we are very blessed," I said firmly. I couldn't bear the notions of preference and favouritism, even between as yet unborn children.

"Yes," John agreed. "Now, please, can I go back to my paper?"

I lay back and closed my eyes. "Go on then. You are a bore, you know. Most men would be thrilled by the imminent arrival of their first child."

I said this but actually had no idea whether it was true. Would they? Men didn't have much involvement with babies. Babies were strictly filed in the 'Women's Department' of life. I was going to be the one whose daily existence changed. I was having the baby delivered in London at the clinic as Doctor Gray had advised, and would spend the first month after its birth with my parents in Avenue Road, convalescing. But at some stage I'd have to bring it back to Garrard's Farm. I pulled myself up sharply. Now I was doing it. Calling the baby 'it'. As if in protest, the baby kicked me sharply several times in my side.

"Ouch. There's no longer room in this body for both of us," I told my bump. It's high time you made your way into the world."

"It isn't due for another month," John said, without lifting his eyes from his paper. "If it comes a week early, it will arrive into the world at much the same time as my new collection of poems."

"Oh how very inconvenient! Anyhow, I thought you didn't want to talk about it any more. I thought you were reading." Now it was my turn to feel cross. John was clearly more excited about his forthcoming collection of poems than this baby. John Murray might be publishing *Continual*

Dew, to the excitement of a growing legion of Betjeman fans, but I was about to give birth to his flesh and blood. If men had to be pregnant, I thought, hauling myself off the sofa and waddling through to the kitchen to make some tea simply to keep busy and take my mind off the awfulness of the final stages of pregnancy, they'd have a great deal more respect for the process. I could barely walk, was too heavy to sleep well, and worst of all, hadn't dared to ride Moti, or have sex with John, for what felt like months. None of my clothes fitted any more. My body was not my own, and I longed for it to become so again.

"Not long now," I muttered to myself, pouring water from the kettle into the pot. I simply had to grit my teeth and hold on a little longer. Mother Nature left me no choice.

I wondered sometimes about the birth. I'd seen horses in labour , so I knew something about the process, but occasionally I dwelled on the fact that this big bump had a relatively small door to exit through. Frustratingly, no one ever spoke of this important detail. Everyone talked about afterwards – engaging a maternity nurse, ensuring we had a suitable crib, where would we have the baby christened, and had we thought up any suitable names? – but no one – not even the doctor-actually addressed the issue of getting the baby out of me. The obstetrician had simply said, "Leave that part to me, my dear", as if I was absolutely nothing to do with it. The closest anyone had come to telling me anything about it at all had been Star, and even she had been uncharacteristically indirect in response to my enquiry.

"Is it – awful?" I had asked her on a recent afternoon visit. At the back of my mind was the unshakeable memory of the grisly rumours that had done the rounds at boarding school after lights out, circulated by girls with much younger siblings, about their mothers writhing for days in unbelievable agony. There had even been one girl, Audrey Simpson, whose mother had died in childbirth. On her arrival, the gory recountings of the agonies of childbirth had largely dried up, in deference to her understandable sensitivity.

But Star had simply looked away, and then after a moment's silence, said it wasn't much fun but all mothers forgot it immediately afterwards, that was nature's way, such was the joy of the child. Besides, she added, I was in the best hands. And she would make sure I had enough rest afterwards. Then she'd started telling me about a new florist she'd found on Marylebone High Street and I'd known the subject was closed.

I put the tea out on a tray and carried it back in to have with Tewpie. The unknown was always more worrying than hard facts. Everything would go smoothly, I told myself firmly. No point frightening myself with ghoulish half-truths picked up from girls who hadn't a clue themselves. I had what Tewpie called childbearing hips, sitting squarely on top of the 'Broadwoods'. Surely, if any one could give birth to a baby easily, it would be me. I would be fine.

The Himalayas. The mid-day heat.
My skin is prickling and sweat is running down my back, but still I do not seek out the shade.

I had not been fine.

But I hadn't died either, so I had been more fortunate than Audrey's mother. I had been alright in the end, in a stitched-back-together kind of way, but it had been a bumpy and agonising time that I had thought would never end. How women say they forget the pain of childbirth had seemed particularly difficult to understand, while I was gripped by agonising contraction after contraction that never seemed to advance the process and had failed to produce the desired result, while my mind swirled with the giddy-making effects of gas and air. Paul Sylvester George had caused me to labour in agony for three days, and relief only finally came for us both with the administration of a general anaesthetic and a Caesarean, from which it took me weeks to recover.

I wonder now, hardly for the first time but more like the thousandth, if this birth, and my prolonged absence from home at what these days is recognised as an important bonding time, was why John did not take to Paul. With hindsight it was clear that the signs of his indifference had been there before Paul's arrival but it was as if the difficulty of his birth, coupled with the weeks that my convalescence kept me back home in London with my parents and so quite far removed from John, allowed his resentment of his own unknown child to harden into dislike.

Dear God, please forgive me. How often have I prayed about Paul? It cannot be enough. No amount of Hail Marys or newly lit candles or coins dropped into collection boxes will undo the damage that Tewpie and I, between us, did to our only son. So longed for, so wanted by his mother, Paul now lives in America to avoid his family. He got married without telling us. When I finally meet God, I feel sure he will have something quite fearsome to say to me about our parenting of our first born. John has gone ahead of me, and is already facing this judgement. Even John's closest friends saw that John was a terrible father. I cannot deny it. But what about myself, as a mother? I was far from blameless. I had wanted to be a good mother. (Who wanted to be any other kind?) At the time, when Paul was born, and later his sister, it had seemed like family life would go on forever. The wellies in the hallway, the discarded clothes on the stairs, the sticky fingers on everything, the endless production of meals. Every mother knows the litany of work that parenting involves. But it didn't go on forever. Nothing does. It came to an end, like everything. How had I not realised that would happen? And then, when they were gone, I was faced with an empty house and a resounding critical silence.

I had longed for this baby, and I had loved Paul. It is a defence, of sorts.

The sun is burning on my shoulders and I am glad.

Chapter Twenty-Two

March 1939. Uffington.

The mornings were getting lighter again. I pulled back the curtains in my bedroom and looked out into our garden. Daffodils, the traditional pale-yellow sort, rather than the new fat hybrids with centres the colour of egg yolk, were scattered under trees and against walls in clusters, waving their trumpets in the stiff breeze. In the orchard, Moti raised his head and looked, stock still and silent, in my direction, as if he could see me. I knew he couldn't – his eyesight was poor, as was always the case with horses. The new maid was hanging washing on the line, and Betty, promoted long ago to the position of the Powlie's nanny, was helping her. The Powlie himself was bowling around in circles on his plump sturdy legs, which were protruding from his crisp white baby shorts. I watched him: blond, laughter bubbling up in him, spinning round and grabbing at the damp sheets with his fat hands. I opened the window a little.

Faintly I could hear Betty talking to Paul – "You'll make yourself sick going round and round like that,"-in her broad Berkshire accent. Paul looked at her as if to consider what she had said but then continued as if he hadn't heard her. At sixteen months of age, he seemed to have decided that there were some things in life about which he had to make up his own mind, and he clearly thought this to be one of them. Seconds later, he bumped down onto his bottom, clutching in a vain bid to save himself at a wet sheet hanging next to him, pulling it off the line and down on top of him.

I turned from the window, laughing myself now, Betty's scolding voice rising and falling in the distance as she addressed Paul. A few snatched phrases – "Now, see, what a lot of work you've made" and "You have to learn to listen" floated up to me on the quiet spring breeze.

This was my second spring as a mother. I headed downstairs, struck by a sudden need to hold my son for a moment. These surges of maternal love that came without warning, flooding my body, making a hug with Paul a physical need, still surprised me, but I felt so glad when they did come, for in the beginning, the rather terrible beginning, I had been frightened they might not come at all.

Paul – or the Powlie, or Paulie, as we variously called him – had grown so fast from the small, shrieking bundle that had finally been cut out of me after three days of horror. At first I had been in pain from the Caesarean, and had found feeding almost impossible. I wouldn't have managed without my mother. Although I hated to admit it, Star was wonderful. She really was the most capable person I knew. She gave the baby to the maternity nurse to take charge of, and she took charge of me.

"Don't bother with all that," she'd said of breastfeeding, passing me tissues as I'd wept on about how difficult motherhood was, and so different to what I had expected.

"Formula milk is jolly good for babies. The thing you need to concentrate on is getting better. Let the people you've employed simply do their jobs until you're up and running again. The baby's with you for life, you know. There's no rush."

I took her words to heart, and stayed with her and Pa until just before Christmas. Oh, the bliss of surrendering myself to a heated and well-run household, to someone else planning and cooking the meals. Star also successfully fielded the many visitors who came knocking bearing gifts. Cossetted and protected and looked after, it felt as if I had reverted to childhood, rather than become a mother myself. John came to visit me most days, but with the night nurse there was no room for him to stay with us, so he now began the mildly absurd business of being in Uffington, while I was in London. He got crosser as time passed about being alone, and I knew I had to get better before Christmas. John was not good alone, as the Berlin experience had shown. I willed myself to recover sufficiently to be able to go and join him.

Finally, almost a month after Paul was born, with my scar healing, it was time to go home. By ten in the morning of the appointed day, the hall was full of any number of cases and I was waiting with my coat on for John to arrive. He was going to drive us-Paul, myself and Betty-back to Uffington. I had no idea we'd accumulated so many things in the month I'd been with my parents, and I wasn't sure it would all fit in John's car. Predictably, Star had already thought of this, and her driver was going to follow us down to Berkshire with most of the luggage. And so it was that the caravan of baby, mother, father, maternity nurse and nanny, finally set off to Uffington.

Once home, we settled quickly. Betty proved confident and no-nonsense with the baby. John travelled much more for his work now, to try to get home to us most nights. I presided over our household, and whiled away many hours in the kitchen. I unearthed more recipe books in the Oxford bookshops, and slowly worked on broadening my repertoire.

I discovered I really enjoyed cooking, I liked the art of mixing different things, and making more complicated dishes. With a husband and a child, cooking fell increasingly to me. Most afternoons found me sweating over Veal Marengo, Jubilee Chicken or Lemon Syllabub, but generally to good result.

I reached the bottom of the stairs and head went out into the garden, feeling the weak, early sunshine on my face. I longed for the sun to hit me with a punch, for the hot searing heat of India. This country's feeble imitation barely touched me, but at least when it shone, like today, it lit up the day. Paul was tottering slowly and erratically down the garden now, holding onto Betty's outstretched hand. He loved the outdoors, rather like me.

Had I given him that, or was it something all of his own? As a parent, one never knew, really, the source of things. I had faithfully done the things with Paul that I had day dreamed about when I was pregnant. I put him on Moti at just a few months old, and often drove him around the village in the Phaeton. I regularly took him to see Gerald, who was surprisingly sweet with babies, and now Powlie was on his feet, he came with me in the mornings or evenings to help me feed the chickens each day. He was a little frightened of the goat we had recently purchased in a bid to keep the grass down. It did have a particularly piercing bleat. Whether it was the bleat, or the sight of his miniature horns that alarmed him, Paul always trod warily past the goat's portion of the garden. I watched now, as Betty carefully led him on, giving the goat's area a wide berth, Powlie holding out a hand at the goat, like a policeman stopping traffic. "No!" he commanded, already seemingly alive with the authority of being a male. "No". It was one of his favourite words.

I walked quickly down the garden, catching them up in a few steps.

"Powlie," I said lightly, swinging him up in my arms, feeling his dense, damp weight sink onto my shoulder. I understood now why people said babies were good enough to eat, a phrase I had once thought ridiculous. But Powlie wriggled, he wanted to get down, he had just found a worm to look at and wanted to get back to it urgently. So I put him down again, surrendering him once more to Betty and the appeal of the worm. I watched for a moment as together they poured over the worm, faces close to the ground, before turning slowly back towards the house. I felt a stab, of something I didn't understand, of something it seemed best to ignore. It was a Monday morning. I had many things to do, starting in the kitchen with an inventory of the larder. Orders needed to be dispatched to the village shop and to the butcher. And I wanted to get up to the church for a quiet ten minutes of prayer. I had something on my mind, and I couldn't linger over a worm all morning.

It stemmed from the day before. Sundays were always special to us. We often had friends to lunch – yesterday it had been the Pipers, in deference to John's on-going crush on Myfanwy -but we always went to church first.

Sunday morning was also when John tried to spend a little bit of time with Powlie, but predictably that usually ended in some kind of disaster, as John would forget he was meant to be looking after Paul, and would start reading the paper, or scribbling a note to himself about a poem, and then wander off to read or write in better light, leaving Paul to his own-usually naughty and generally reckless-devices. This was how it went yesterday, which meant I shouted at Tewpie – was asking for half an hour really so much? Which meant in turn, that by the time we got out and on our way to church, we had already had a bit of a row. Yesterday morning, on the way back from Church, John had taken my hand and kissed it in an uncharacteristically romantic and gallant gesture.

"You know, Propeller. However much we argue, when we kneel down, side by side in our pew, it simply doesn't seem to matter any more. At that moment, I know that everything is alright between us."

And he had smiled, but I had not, because I had known that John was right. That was how it was between us, and how it had always been. And it would be best for us, I knew, if it stayed that way. But where, then, did that leave my wish to become a Catholic?

I reached the back door and went down the corridor to the kitchen, my boots slapping on the red clay tiles. I had been married long enough to see that a few key pressures could come to bear on a marriage. Not enough work meant money worries, too much work meant no time together. John and I worried about money, of course, although we weren't particularly extravagant. There was the horse, and we did like to eat well and to entertain, so our butcher's bill was rather ghastly every month-but we were better if we were together. I needed to see him, to spend time with him. (Even if we did spend much of it rowing. Last week, we'd followed each other round the house shouting at each other, walking from room to room, and in and out of the bathroom, failing to notice that two of our house guests were actually in the bath at the time. Afterwards, when we had made up, we had laughed about that row and the bathroom scene and had speculated whether the guests in question, the Connollys, would ever come and stay again. Luckily, they both had a marvellous sense of humour and had bubbled up with laughter when we'd asked them, and said of course they would, how could they bear not to?)

I gathered up the ingredients for pastry – butter, flour – and reached for a mixing bowl. I had promised to bake a pie for an elderly neighbour whose wife had recently died. John had said he would be back tonight, so I might as well make two. I needed to buy chunked steak and a couple of kidneys from the butcher, but if I made the pastry now, it could sit for a couple of hours under a damp cloth before it was rolled, and would hold together better. I opened the flour jar and saw it was nearly empty. I picked it up and headed back out into the corridor to the pantry to refill it, my thoughts still on John.

We had a lot that held us together, but since Paul, things were definitely altered. Inevitably, John could not always come first, with a small baby to tend to, and he did not like that. When he particularly resented it, he took it out on the Powlie, mocking him and calling him 'It', in a way the bemused toddler simply didn't yet understand, although he picked up on the tone of it, and that usually made him cry. I didn't understand how John could do that to our son. Yet, if I berated him for it, he sulked and things between us got even worse. I loved Powlie, but I loved John too. It had never seriously occurred to me that they would not love each other. Sometimes I felt as if I was in a love triangle, and being forced by John to make a choice.

Childbirth had also changed me. I was solid, and fatter since the baby. I didn't have to look very carefully to find a fine thread or two of grey in my hair. My cheeks were red and chapped from too much time spent outdoors in the biting winter chill, this despite my nightly application of the cold cream which Bim swore by. I'd always known that in some ways I was far from John's ideal woman, and

I wondered whether I would always feel that my tenure was temporary and insecure. Ridiculous, I knew, since John and I had so much good that was between us, and with our strong faith, would not consider divorce. The very thought made me bring my eyebrows together in a frown. But still I sometimes couldn't shake the feeling that I was not the wife John would necessarily have wanted, or, even, been best suited to: I was not the elegant, spirited kind of girl, like the many women he admired – Myfanwy Piper, or the legions of other female friends – and I was not flirtily female and submissive in a tea dress, either. I didn't treat John as if he was the master of the household, with the deference and adoration he would so like, but instead strode around in my old tweed jacket yelling orders.

Don't be silly, I told myself, as I wrenched open the larder door – it kept sticking against the door frame, having swollen in the last cold and damp autumn and our landlord had yet to sort it out – John chose you, and that's all that matters. As I stood there considering why we needed a larder, when the rest of the house was so very cold anyway, a mean, spiteful voice in my head spoke up.

But he didn't choose you, did he Penelope? You chose him.

CHAPTER TWENTY-THREE

1939.

John got busier and busier. He had started doing regular talks for the radio, on various seaside resorts, for a series called 'Sea Views'. Of course this meant he had to travel and he gradually slipped back to his old ways. Weeks were spent away travelling or in London, while I almost invariably remained in Uffington, looking after Paul.

Every Friday evening Tewpie would return, by train, or via a lift with a friend, full of the latest London gossip, and a busy, sociable weekend would invariably ensue, with the house stuffed to the rafters with our friends, for lunches and dinners and overnight stays. Quite possibly there would be a trip to Faringdon House for drinks or a dinner thrown by Gerald. We'd dress up and John would drive us and any guests over, crammed into the Morris, to be greeted by chatter and music wafting down the driveway to greet us. There the brightly coloured doves perched in the trees above the guests – a revolving cast including Gertrude Stein, an assortment of Mitfords, Billa and her new husband Roy Harrod, and Evelyn, married again now to his new young wife, Laura, who sometimes came with him and seemed sweet. I didn't see Evelyn nearly as much these days.

On one such evening, John and Evelyn greeted each other heartily enough – they kept up the pretence of friendship for their entire lives, fooling no one-before John wandered off to flirt with Diana.

I remained next to Evelyn, who started to regale me with a long and complicated mildly filthy joke.

"Where did you get that from?" I asked when he reached the punchline, nearly crying with laughter.

"My new brother-in-law," Evelyn said. "He just reels them off in lieu of conversation. God, it's good to see you, Penelope. It's been months. You never come to London. I've missed you. Where've you been?"

"Knee deep in domesticity," I replied. "Animals, the baby."

"Moti, I presume?"

"Of course."

"Those were the days. Moti, you, Gerald and me, taking tea in this very room. I wonder what Gerald has done with your painting."

I looked up at Evelyn. His eyes were twinkling naughtily, as if he was up to something.

"I believe it's going into his next show. Don't you want to buy it?"

"It's a little beyond us, I'm afraid."

"Don't you find it odd, the notion that you and Moti will be hanging on some stranger's wall?"

I glanced at Evelyn again. He was smiling at me gently. "Yes, I suppose it is. But wasn't it fun at the time? Now, tell me, how is Laura? Is she here?"

"No, she's at home with the baby, and expecting another. So I'm on my own. Just like old times, eh?"

"Just like old times." Except everything was different.

"Don't think I've forgotten about the novel I promised you. It's coming. It's slow, but it's coming."

I smiled. "Helen of Troy," I said.

"That's it. The title is 'Helena'."

"I can't wait to read it."

"Read what?" John had materialised at my side, looking cross.

"Evelyn's dedicating a novel to me, darling."

"Oh. Is he indeed?" No one made John more possessive of me than Evelyn.

"Yes. I find your wife inspirational. Don't you? I'm surprised you haven't written more poems about her, John."

John hadn't written a single poem about me, and all three of us knew it.

"Oh look, we're going into supper," I said hastily, linking one arm with Evelyn and the other with John, and towing them towards the dining room like two small squabbling boys. Evelyn could be impossibly provocative at times.

Gerald's food was always delicious (he had an Italian chef) and the company always sparkling and upbeat (this was part of the deal-dull people did not get asked back). John and Evelyn were placed far apart by the perceptive Gerald, and the rest of the evening proceeded happily enough.

There were many evenings like that. But underlying all our gaiety, as the year inched on from winter to spring, as the crocuses gave way to daffodils and the daffodils to apple blossom, were thoughts of war. We all knew it, as we sipped our cocktails at Gerald's house, or entertained at home. I followed the news from Berlin closely, that city I had briefly loved, and it seemed to get worse and worse. The smashing up of Jewish property, the confiscation of anything left unbroken. Kristallnacht. People disappearing. A flood of Jewish refugees swarming into England. Every man and woman was preparing or so it seemed, as the unthinkable began to unfold. Unbelievable as it might be, we had to try and believe it. A war was coming, again.

The prospect of war began to be the subject on everyone's lips and minds. John came home at the weekends filled with the latest news on the preparations in London, and that the general feeling was that it was now clearly inevitable. I dug up our flower beds and planted rows of vegetables to keep myself busy. I didn't want to think what would happen to us all, if Hitler, so clearly mad, pursued what seemed to be his intent – to expand Germany into other countries in Europe.

We went to see Gerald one Saturday afternoon. Despite food shortages already becoming evident as the Government began to stockpile and ration goods, Gerald still managed to give us as lavish a tea as usual, with cream cakes and sandwiches-and Pamela Mitford was there. In between devouring most of the plate of sandwiches as if they were the last she would ever see, she couldn't stop talking about her sisters, and what would happen to them if war broke out. Jessica, she told me, through a bite of cucumber sandwich, was in America and in danger of getting stranded there for the duration of the war if she didn't come home soon.

Much worse, it seemed to me, was Unity's situation. She was still in Germany infatuated by Hitler. I remembered, now, her threat to kill herself if war was declared. I felt rather sorry for the Mitford parents. As if Jessica and Unity weren't enough to worry about, Diana had married Oswald Mosley, leader of the British Fascists, in 1936, with Adolf Hitler as a guest. She and Oswald were huge supporters of the Nazis. Surely the British Government would have something to say about that, if and when war broke out? John thought it possible that they might even be imprisoned as a threat to national security. John had tried to calm Pam down – he'd always had a soft spot for her, in fact I'm sure at one stage, before he'd met me, or possibly even after, knowing John, he'd tried to get engaged to her. But even he couldn't make unpalatable facts more palatable.

Gerald seemed the least able of everyone to face the thought of war. He left the room abruptly when anyone mentioned the possibility of it, munching a piece of cake as if he didn't have a care in the world, or humming a few bars of "The Merry Widow".

My parents came down from London for a weekend, staying again at the pub, but coming across to us for meals. On the Saturday night I prepared my father's favourite supper, finding my way round the food shortages as best I could. Potted shrimps, Vichysoisse, Veal Marengo, a pudding and French cheeses. I knew proper cheese had been the food he had missed the most during his time in India, so an extra large piece of Brie de Meaux was spreading quietly on a platter on the sideboard.

Pa looked tired. He, too, took the notion of another war extremely badly. His generation had been decimated by the Great War, and such a conflict occurring again, just twenty years later, on such a scale, was impossible to contemplate. Pa had fought bravely, had endured and, unlike so many, survived the dreadful life in the trenches before being posted to Egypt and fighting in the battle of Gaza. He never spoke of the horrors he had seen, but by now, enough had been written about it for us all to understand. Words weren't needed. I knew he was also worrying about Roger, who would have to fight if war came again. Was another generation of boys and young men about to be cut down in their prime, like so many sheaves of wheat being harvested?

I'd lit the candles, and drafted in two village girls to serve. We also had several other dinner guests, including Gerald and Robert, the Pipers and the Connollys. Cyril was a friend of John's from Oxford, and in John's estimation, the poet of his generation. I hoped there might be enough intellectual distractions with Cyril's presence to keep the conversation light, but we didn't get beyond the potted shrimps before my mother brought it up.

"It's unthinkable," she said. She was in a full-length burgundy shot silk evening dress. A diamond necklace encircled her still firm neck, and several rings gleamed on her fingers. My father paused in the drinking of his soup.

"Unthinkable, yet we must think it," he said, shaking his head in bewilderment. I knew he was remembering: bodies, bloodshed, inconsolable mothers, a generation of fatherless children, the far reaching pain of war.

"It will change everything," my mother said, sensing immediately, after nearly forty years of marriage, my father's pain and reaching out to cover his liver spotted veiny hand with hers.

"It's just a lot of talk. It won't happen. I've planned to go to Rome as I always do this summer," said Gerald robustly.

My father stiffened. There were times when Gerald's frivolous take on things seemed inappropriate and this was one of them.

"Well, that should stop the Germans in their tracks," I said, trying to lighten things a little.

My father continued as if neither Gerald nor I had spoken, responding to my mother's remark.

"You are quite right, my dear, it will change everything, and not just in Europe. It's the end of life as we know it, I think. India, too, will go."

There was a questioning murmur around the table.

"Really?" John said. Too often he mocked my father – they had never become close as I had once hoped-but I could see he felt interest mingled with compassion now. He knew what India meant to my father. He knew what India meant to me.

"Oh yes. If the Indian Army puts its back into the war, and we will need them to if we are to defeat Hitler, the price will be their independence."

"No bad thing," I said. "I never felt comfortable with all of us in the top jobs in what is their country.".

"I know you didn't. Many people felt that way. Your friend Sir John Marshall, was one such. Perhaps that why the two of you got on so famously. Certainly that's why he taught the Indians to look after their own monuments. He always stressed they were their monuments, not ours."

"Well, Sir John was right," I said briskly. "India has some of the most marvellous artefacts. I often dream I am back at the Red Fort."

"I'm sure you do," Tewpie murmured, sniggering into his glass of Puligny-Montrachet.

My father gave John a look, before continuing: "I saw Sir John the other day. Up at the Club. Lives a very quiet life these days, somewhere in Surrey, with his wife. I do recall she was a frightful bore. Always yapping on about her children. Never do that, m'dear. Never become a bore about your children. There's simply nothing worse."

"Thank you for the advice, Daddy, I'll try not to," I said lightly, wondering if my father knew precisely what had passed between Sir John and me. I could feel Tewpie looking at me from where he sat at the other end of the table, hugely enjoying this unexpected turn in the conversation. The Connollys, meanwhile, sensing an undercurrent they didn't understand but definitely wanted to know more about, looked from me to John, and then back to me again in hope of clarity, but received none. Gerald, who knew all about Sir John, simply beamed with pleasure at the tease, full of relief that the conversation was turning away from his most hated subject of all, a possible war.

Why had I ever told Tewpie about Sir John? I fumed silently. Ignoring him completely, I continued: "I look forward to going back to India one day, when this wretched war that's coming is over."

"I don't think I shall ever go back now," said Star quietly, a little sadly.

My father looked across the table to her. "Some things are better remembered the way you knew and loved them," he said. Their eyes met for a moment in understanding.

I knew what they meant. They meant they were getting old, and that their world was vanishing that had once seemed unassailable.

"Delicious soup," Gerald said brightly into the silence. "I do love soup at this time of year. So soothing."

The girls came in and with a nod from me, started to remove the bowls.

My mother picked up the change of subject.

"Penelope, you have become a very good cook," she said, admiration mingled with a thread of mild amazement in her voice. She had never cooked for anyone, had neither needed to, nor been expected to. She had been born at the height of the reign of Queen Victoria, and servants had been as indispensable to her life as a pair of legs. When I had been born, it had very probably never crossed her mind that I would need to, either. Now, the era of her birth must seem as irrelevant as my horse and cart in this age of the motor car. I smiled at her. She sat still and tall, soup spoon in hand, regal despite her years and mood.

"What news of Roger?" I asked my father quietly.

"They're all well enough," said my father a little heartily, referring to Roger and his family collectively. Roger had married a girl they considered to be highly suitable, a distant relative called Molly, a few years ago, and they had had a child, a boy they had named Philip after Pa. Philip was just a few months older than Paulie.

Roger had followed my father into the army and would be one of the first to be called on in the event of war. He was probably already busy with preparations, I thought, looking at the plate of veal that had just been placed in front of me. I wondered how he would cope. We had never been close, Roger and I, our temperaments too different and the four-year age gap to great to bridge, but I knew his sensitive, melancholy nature well enough to understand that he would not take well to active warfare. Roger had never been as mentally robust as my father.

The girls had laid out the veal just as I had shown them. Toast first, then veal placed half on top, half to the side, then not too much sauce drizzled over the whole. Dishes of leafy green vegetables – from our own garden – were placed on the table for the guests to circulate amongst themselves. I sat back slightly in my chair.

"Tuck in everyone," I said, as my father spooned greens onto his plate. "While it's hot."

Everyone attacked their plates, conversation still humming around the table. With change all about us, I thought for a moment of my parents' early days of marriage, and the inevitable contrast with my own. Of the glittering dinner parties I knew they had given when I had been small, with uniformed footmen and a butler and a clutch of housemaids, rather than a pair of village girls in smocks.

And yet, despite so many changes, their marriage, their love for each other, had prevailed and strengthened. I looked at John, flushed from wine and excitement, managing to regale his end of the table with an anecdote while peering down into the depths of Myfanwy's cleavage at the same time. Was my marriage made of the same tough fabric as that of my parents? An indestructible weave of love, commitment, shared goals, ethics and morals that was unbreakable, come what may?

John reached the punchline and the listeners roared. He sat back, satisfied, enjoying the moment of merriment he had brought. He looked up at me, and winked.

"Alright Plymmie?" he mouthed.

I smiled. "Alright" I mouthed back.

Chapter Twenty-Four

September 1939.

That long summer of hope against hope dragged on. Finally, despite all the efforts, and all the sacrifices made – Austria and Czechoslovakia fed to the lions and Chamberlain's plaintive attempts at appeasing the insatiable monster that was Hitler-the Germans marched into Poland on 1 September.

Two days later, Tewpie and I sat tensely on the grey velvet sofa in the living room, side by side, and like most of the nation, waited for Mr Chamberlain to come on the radio.

"I am speaking to you from the Cabinet Room at 10 Downing Street. This morning the British Ambassador in Berlin handed the German Government a final note stating that unless we heard from them by 11am, that they were prepared at once to withdraw their troops from Poland, a state of war would exist between us. I have to tell you that no such undertaking has been received, and that consequently this country is at war with Germany."

"That's it then," Tewpie said, turning the wireless off. "It's really happened."

I exhaled. I heard Paulie shouting something at Betty upstairs. He was getting quite determined. He would celebrate his second birthday, and who knew how many more, during wartime.

It wasn't a surprise. We had all expected it, all except Gerald, who had continued in his state of complete denial and had been about to set off for Rome against everyone's advice. He would now be distraught at the thought he might be cooped up in England without interruption for the foreseeable future and quite possibly for the entire duration of the war.

"It's what I do every summer, and I'm not changing my holiday plans for one jumped up German bully," was all he'd kept saying over the summer, when one by one his friends tried to persuade him of the lunacy of his plan. Thank god he hadn't set off yet.

I rode over to see him a few days later. He was very low.

"These countries are my life," he said. "They are like close friends to me. England and Italy, Germany and France. And now they're all fighting each other, and things won't come out the same the other side. You know they won't. Penelope. Admit it."

"Change is inevitable now," I said. "We don't know how yet, but this war will bring a lot of change. The last one did."

"It's the end of a chapter," Gerald went on. "And there's no place for me in the next one."

Apart from Gerald, no one else was surprised. The signs had been impossible to miss. The country had been preparing itself for some months. Children had been being evacuated from London since August. Volunteer organisations to help the war effort were springing up everywhere.

John, despite his age and general lack of fitness, wanted to fight for King and Country. "I have to do my bit," he kept saying fretfully.

"We all do," I replied impatiently. And we all would, it just might not be as glamorous, or on the front line, as Tewpie wanted it to be.

He had talked like this before, but I knew, because my father had told me, that he was considered too old to join up. Privately, I felt this made sense. The thought of John manning our defences made me want to laugh. We might just as well hand over the keys to the country to Hitler right now.

I put a hand on his arm, feeling the thick ribbed wool of his jumper, knitted for him by his devoted aged aunt.

"Everyone will find their niche," I said, "starting here in this village." We had attended a meeting at the village hall last week and had agreed with many other villagers that when war was declared, John and I would be part of the newly formed Air Raid Patrol. The ARP were to be responsible for making sure that everyone carried a gas mask at all times, and that blackout rules were strictly observed.

John was not my only worry. I'd also invited my parents to come and live with us for the duration of the war, but they were refusing to leave London. Roger, as I'd feared, had already been called up and sent to some training camp in Sussex. Molly and his children – there were two now – had gone to St Ives in Cornwall, to avoid the bombs everyone knew were coming. I could not imagine Roger at war, not the kind of war everyone said this would be, and I wondered how he would cope. He was a domestic man, and never happier than with his wife and children.

At the weekend, John could still talk of nothing else but 'doing his bit'. "I'm going to write to your father again," John said on Saturday after lunch, heading for his study. "I must be able to do more than just make sure everyone's got a gas mask."

I sighed, trailing after him, knowing this wouldn't end as John wanted. My father, also worrying about Roger, about the coming war, and about where he and Star should ride it out, had told me he found these letters self-indulgent and frustrating.

"What does he want me to do?" Pa had asked me last week when I dropped in to see him for tea.

"He says he wants a job in the military. He wants to make a difference. He's just desperate to do his bit," I'd said.

Father had looked at me. "We all are, Penelope. But this is a rare instance of John and I having something in common. We are both too old to be of use to the military."

I had taken my father's hand then. I knew how much those words hurt him. If John felt useless, and was desperate to play his part in this conflict, how much worse was it for my father, a man to whom the military had been meat and drink for his entire working life?

I watched John through the open study door. He was scribbling away rapidly now. My heart sank a little. I tried to imagine John flying a plane and failed-the RAF was clearly out of the question. The Army? It seemed unlikely. Besides, John hated Abroad, and divisions of the army were already gearing up to be posted far and wide, to all corners of the British Empire that needed defending. No, it was glaringly obvious to anyone who knew him that a military career was not likely to meet with any kind of success. He was a man who sometimes failed to put two matching shoes on in the morning.

"Tewpie," I began. "Shall we talk about this for a moment?"

John didn't look up.

"Not now Propeller. Can't you see I'm busy?"

His face, bent over his work, fleetingly as earnest as a schoolboy. I shrugged. When John was set on something, there was no point trying to persuade him otherwise. He had to find things out for himself. There was nothing to do except to let life take its course. I shrugged my shoulders and went to the kitchen, where hundreds of green tomatoes were waiting to be turned into chutney.

Mutisher. Close to Midday.

War. So much happened to us in those six years, including and beyond the war itself. Gerald had what would now be termed a nervous breakdown, and never really recovered. My brother Roger was overwhelmed by it all and died. I can hardly bear to think about it, even at this distance. I say died, as if it were a passive act in which no one had a hand, but of course it was not, and my father and my mother and I, we knew it, even as we tried to hide the true facts from the rest of the world. Roger had been too fragile, and had not been able to withstand the challenges, and so had taken the only way out that he felt was left to him. He left a widow and two tiny boys and a scandal we did our best to bury. My father aged ten years overnight. My mother did what she always did – dressed for dinner and carried on as if nothing had happened. The British Empire had been built on women like my mother.

And John? He finally accepted that although he wanted to fight, no one would have him. His feet were too flat and his eyesight too bad, so instead he took a desk job writing propaganda for a while, and then he was given a job in the Ministry of Information and we all got sent to Ireland.

The Indian heat is making my head swim and hot sandy grit beneath my feet is working its way into my open toed sandals. Kingfishers and crows dart and call around me, and my tourists chatter together in the shade of a large mimosa tree, yet I am not here. I am not seventy-six years old, short of breath with unexplained dizziness, seated on the steps of the most perfect Indian temple in direct sunlight.

…I am thirty and packing to go to Ireland, where John has been posted as war attaché…

...I am thirty-one and so jealous my body aches. John has a new crush, this time on a girl called Emily who works in the Irish office. Will he, won't he? I lie awake until after two in the morning, having left them downstairs together. John doesn't come to bed at all that night.

...I am thirty-two and our daughter Candida is born in Dublin's general hospital, after another Caesarean. I lie back on the crisp white pillows and John takes her from the starched nurse, the white lacy bundle, and looks at her creamy peaceful face, and I see the very second that he falls in love with his daughter. I am glad he can love Candida. He still calls Paulie, 'It'.

...I am thirty-three and still in Ireland and John is having another affair, this time with a girl he met a dinner party. I was at the dinner party too, but still he managed to strike up something, and she reciprocated. It takes my breath away. I am homesick and miss my parents as if I was a young girl, not a married woman and mother of two. I tell myself to grow up, as I know my mother would waste no time telling me if I shared my feelings with her, but still the sense of missing endures.

...I am thirty-five and the war has ended. We are back in Garrard's farm, but packing up again. We have to find another house. The farmer can no longer rent us this one. He wants it for his son.

...I am thirty-five and after two babies, I am undeniably stout. My stomach sags in three folds that cascade downwards like steps, and 'the Broadwoods' have visible veins running up and down them like the new emerging motorways that John detests, for cutting up his lovely England. My hair is cut short and blunt, and I dye it to cover the grey, but the skin under my eyes starts to wrinkle. "Laughter lines" I call them, but I know it is the creep of age, and it frightens me.

Not much frightens me, but age does. It frightens me when I am thirty-five, and thirty-seven, and forty, because I am afraid it will mean I will lose John.

But I am getting ahead of myself. I am thirty-five at the end of the war, and my wonderful father, so solid, so dependable, so loving, so loyal, whatever I may do, comes to the rescue and buys us a house in a nearby village, Farnborough. We move in and straight away John hates it. He stomps off to London whenever he can, on the flimsiest excuses. Once again there is no hot water and no electricity, and it still puzzles me that while I don't mind, John so clearly does. He minds very much.

The children love the new house. Paulie starts at the village school. Candida runs about feeding the chickens until she is old enough to join him there. I teach them both to ride. I buy them small ponies and we take to riding about the lanes together. We grow vegetables, and I bottle the fruit that thuds to the ground every autumn in the orchard. John comes back on weekends, which makes Paulie pale and sullen and silent and as far from his free and easy weektime self as it is possible to be

At weekends we are very sociable, with all our old friends coming again for house parties and dinner parties and drinks. The Pipers have four children of their own now, but Myfanwy is as beautiful as ever and John's eyes still follow her. He has written several poems in homage to her beauty. I suspect she does not have rolls of fat around her middle. Gerald has picked up the reins of life again at Faringdon House, and we all try really hard, once again, to put a war behind us, but it is not the same. It cannot be. So many friends and family have been lost, and others irrevocably changed by it. Six long years have also passed. The whirligig of life seems to slow and invoke nausea and the gin has a less happy making effect on the riders than it once did. The whole world looks a different place.

Too often, I find myself watching, not joining in, going through the motions, wondering, where is the meaning in all this? What is the point?

One Sunday lunch, as I go to the kitchen to fetch more wine – there is very little help these days – and back again to take a pudding out of the oven, I think, what is the point?

And I know the answer. I know the point very well. I have known it for a long time. God – yes, God – is the point.

At thirty eight, with a continually unfaithful, increasingly successful writer of a husband, a silent son and a sparkling daughter, with spare tyres around my middle and legs like tree trunks, with my passion for horses undimmed, with my dedication to Indian art unfulfilled, with my beloved father, suddenly elderly and frail and a little defeated, sitting in the next room, with a steamed pudding in my hands, closing the Aga door with my foot, that is all I really know.

Chapter Twenty-Five

Summer 1946

The new house was very beautiful, but freezing cold in winter. Built of red brick, it dated from Queen Anne's time, with the easy good looks that typified the period evident in all the elevations. Five large windows across the broad front on the top floor, four below, with the central one lost to make way for a large front door. It had such stylish bones one couldn't help but be charmed by the house, despite the inconveniences. Water had to come from the village pump, and we still relied on oil lamps, as we had at Uffington.

We had barely moved in when without warning, my mother died. With the war just behind us, I thought I had become accustomed to death, but Star vanishing overnight told me otherwise. Her death came like a fork of lightening from a clear sky. One moment she was telephoning regularly to enquire about the children, hosting her celebrated dinner parties, running my father's life like a well-oiled machine, still observing every possible social convention as if it were 1930, and then the next, there was simply empty space where she had stood. So much space. It felt as if someone had removed a critical cog from our daily lives, and of course that was precisely what had happened. It had annoyed me so much that she had called every morning at 10am but now the phone stood quiet and each day I minded.

My father came to stay. Utterly lost, he arrived by train at the start of the summer holidays to spend a few days with his grandchildren. I fetched him from the station in my phaeton and gave him the most comfortable guest bedroom. He deposited his suitcase and came back downstairs to look around.

"It's like the dark ages, darling," he said, rather gloomily, perhaps because he'd bought the house for me unseen, and now he'd actually visited it, considered it to be a terrible investment.

"Oh Pa, it's not so bad," I said. I still failed to understand why everyone found the lack of hot water and light such a bore. One bath of water, heated at night, two or three times a week, was perfectly adequate for myself and the children, while the gas lamps gave a rather cosy atmosphere to the house. It also meant we hadn't ruined the cornicing and walls by covering them with miles of wiring and switches and pipes. John often went on in a complaining vein, which I truly didn't understand, as it was the daily and me who fetched the water. The only job John had to do when he was home was trim the oil lights, and since he was usually only here on weekends, doing this for two days a week was hardly arduous.

The children and their local friends ran in and out of the house as if it was their playground. Numbers at lunch were unpredictable as a result of the impromptu nature of my children's social life. I never knew who might or might not arrive with Paul and Candida at lunchtime after a morning spent playing outside in the sun. Inevitably I asked any guests to stay for lunch and they leapt at the chance as if their last square meal had been weeks ago. I relished this informality and the evident happiness my children were exuding, even though it was a time of sadness for us adults. At least they seemed happy the majority of the time and in some small way that was infectious, lifting us all temporarily out of our gloom. They were young enough to love life unreservedly; gardens and the village were their extended playground and they were spending their holidays getting to know every inch.

I had ordered a large ham from the butcher's a few days previously, which was providing this variable number of diners with lunch on a daily basis, together with homemade bread, a cheese plate and salad. Each day I'd go out at one o'clock and shout into the garden for whoever was around to come to lunch.

"You need a gong," my father observed. We had had a gong in New Delhi which had been rung loudly by the butler to call guests to dine.

"Those days seem a lifetime ago," I said. "Gongs are a relic from a different era." I immediately berated myself for my tactlessness, as my father's face took on a reminiscing expression.

"Although I'd like one. And I'm sure Gerald has one at Faringdon Hall," I added hastily. "Anyone who's anyone has a gong."

"A lifetime, and yesterday," Pa said quietly, as if to himself. I stroked his shoulder gently, before ushering all the children into their seats, inspecting their hands on the way in to check they were still damp from being washed in the bowl of water in the kitchen.

"With soap, I hope, everybody?" I said mock-sternly, pulling my fierce face that worried small guests but made my own children laugh, as they settled into chairs around the table. I began to carve the ham. My father settled at my elbow, and I felt his eyes watching me critically.

"Cut it straight down, Penelope, not across. You are exposing too much surface to the air. That dries it out."

"Daddy, there are so many of us, there isn't going to be time for this ham to dry out," I replied. But it was no use. He stood up and took the fork and carving knife from my hands and slid the ham on its carving board towards him. I shrugged and sat down. It was good for him to feel useful, even in this small way. He was like a ship that had lost its anchor, adrift and directionless on a flat and uninteresting sea. His face had developed crags and wrinkles as if overnight and I felt a swirl of panic in my stomach as a thought rose to the top of my mind like milk boiling over: without Star, how long would he last? They had been together for so long, that they had fused and become two parts of the same being. Now my mother was gone and my father was left bereft, just half a person. Even with my faith, losing him didn't bear thinking about. I needed him. Life was lonely and complex enough, without the loss of him, too. Tewpie had, more than once, teased me that I loved my father more than any other man, including him.

"First comes your father, then your various horses, and then me," he'd joked early on in our marriage. As with all good jokes, there was an undercurrent of truth. One of my great joys in life had been my relationship with my father. From my earliest memories as a tiny girl, he was there. Strong and light hearted, reliable and always on my side.

A heavy plate banging onto the table startled me out of my morbid thoughts.

"Well done, Pa," I said encouragingly, forcing a smile, as he handed the platter of sliced ham to the children. They started to circulate it around themselves, using the fork to place a couple of slices each on their plates, feeling my eagle eye on them and resisting the urge to use their much quicker fingers.

I poured Daddy a glass of whisky and glasses of water for the rest of us. The village water was delicious – crisp and clear, high up in the downs as we were. My father sat back down with the slow, careful movements of an old man anxious not to trip or draw attention to himself, as if he already wished himself invisible and somewhere else. How could this happen? This man had commanded armies. My heart swelled to bursting with love.

The ham plate reached me. I took a slice and a piece of the bread I had baked that morning, even though I didn't feel particularly hungry.

The children all went quiet, enjoying their sandwiches. I passed my father the butter, the salad, the mayonnaise, the mustard, and he looked at me gratefully. I smiled and slid my hand over the nearest one of his. Dry, slightly brown from so many years in India, as if indelibly stained by the hot sun; liver spotted, with a network of pronounced veins.

"Alright, Pa," I said. Roger gone. Star gone. Blow after blow. The pain of loss, the downside of love. There was just the two of us now.

He looked at me, another cautious, grateful look. We were a long way from those happy, heady New Delhi days.

"Yes, Penelope."

And so it was between us. By saying nothing of consequence, we both knew precisely what we meant.

After lunch, Pa went for a rest and the children returned to their games. As I ferried trays of dirty plates to the kitchen, my thoughts stayed with my father. He had always been there, protecting me from Star's sharper tongue, making me laugh, making light of my many errors, forgiving me for them quicker than anyone else. But somehow, without me noticing, the tables had quietly turned. Now I had to protect him, from the too noisy children, from loneliness, from the pain of an altered world. I wouldn't allow myself to let him down, I told myself, placing a tray on the wooden kitchen counter and emptying it before heading back to the dining room for another load. Despite all the other things going on in my life that needed me – children, Tewpie, the weekly column of recipes I had just started to write for *The Express* newspaper in a bid to pick up some kind of working thread to my life- there would always be, as was right and proper, time and space for Pa. I felt my mother at my elbow, trailing me back to the dining room. For some reason I pictured her in one of her favourite evening gowns, a long navy silk, and wearing all her jewels including her tiara, as if about to swan out to a state banquet. "Well done, Penelope. Quite right. You look after him." Second tray loaded and table finally cleared, I set off once again towards the kitchen.

John was in London as usual, not due back until the weekend. I feared he had a new crush, as he kept talking about a girl in the office. That was probably what was keeping him there longer than was strictly necessary, as was the fact he liked to avoid the noise and bustle of family life. While he adored Candida, the rest of us – the cows, Buttercup and Daisy, the horses, the children's ponies, the chickens, the vegetable patch, the visiting village children charging in and out, the water to be drawn from the well, the meals needing to be bought and made and served and cleared up-all this wore him down, not that he actually had much responsibility for any of them when he was here. Under the pretext of work, London offered him a continuation of his easy bachelor days. I tried not to mind when he returned at the weekend full of stories of drinks parties and dinners with friends of ours, but sometimes, I wondered how I had got quite so left behind. What had happened to the girl who had been so committed to Indology that she had considered quite possibly not getting married at all? She'd vanished in a sea of domesticity, I thought, answering my own question. As I had always suspected I would, if I got married. That was the well trodden path for a wife. But it was not for ever. Just for now, just while the children were small, just while John was so busy. And my column for the Express was a start.

I wiped down the table, and taking the cloth back to the kitchen, I saw Candida, blonde curls bouncing, running across the lawn after a slowly disappearing cricket ball. Paul held the bat and a child whose name I didn't know was standing watching Candida, clearly impatient to bowl if she could only return him the ball. It was funny, I thought, turning away, that such a quintessentially English existence should be too much for England's most 'English' living poet.

With everyone happily occupied and no meals required for at least a few hours, I went to the sink to wash my hands. The water in the sink was cold and already dirty from dishes. I looked at my hands – they had become hardened and calloused from all the things I now did in the house and there was soil under my fingernails. I considered attacking them with a scrubbing brush, but then remembered that I was taking the children riding later and still had potatoes to dig up outside. The scrubbing could wait, until a hot bath that night. The rest of the dishes could wait, too. What I needed to do now was write my weekly *Express* article.

I'd been writing pieces for some months and had become popular with the paper's female readers. Each week, I spent a lot of time researching and testing slightly unusual recipes before including them in my pieces. Last week I'd put together a recipe for a mild chicken curry, something that was unheard of in England but that I'd come across in Delhi. I always felt a thrill at seeing my name in print. I might not yet have done any of the things professionally that I had set out to do as an optimistic twenty-three-year-old, but at least writing these articles was creative work of some kind. Done in a quiet space, exercising my own neglected mental muscles. Quite a number of readers had written in to say how successfully some of the recipes had worked out. Encouraged, the editor had asked me to continue.

"You're getting the right kind of following. Be as inventive as you can, while bearing in mind the scarcity of so many day to day ingredients," he told me. I didn't want to let him down, but this week had been so busy, with the children on holiday for so long, and my father staying that I was going to have to cheat slightly and write up a recipe given to me by a friend in the village. This set out, step by step, the process of making home-made wine. I had the scant details from my friend, who had got it from her cousin, who apparently drank the wine she produced every year at a Harvest Festival celebration. I planned to embellish these details appropriately. I sat at the large walnut desk in the drawing room, took a piece of paper from the stand, smoothed out the scrap of recipe from my friend, picked up my ink pen and began to write.

"Many people swear by the refreshing properties of Elderflower wine, though I am not much of a drinker myself," I began. If I could get this straight in the next couple of hours, I could make the afternoon post at the same time as visiting the village shop for supplies.

With the children shrieking distantly in the background, the audible thud of a ball on willow, the occasional optimistic cry of 'Howzat?' drifting in through the open window, I wrote on, listing ingredients and then starting to outline the method. Soon I was on my third sheet and nearly done.

"Now all that is required is a little patience. Make sure the corks are tightly secured, and allow the bottles to stand for 6 weeks in a dark place, ideally a larder or under stair cupboard where they will not be disturbed. Return in six weeks – don't be tempted to cheat on this period, as fermentation must take place for this wine to reach its full alcoholic potential. Then all you need to do is find a reason to celebrate, although the wine will last 'til Christmas."

I sat back and read through my roughed-out efforts, before rolling a sheet of paper into the typewriter and starting to type. The recipe read well enough – in fact the words 'fermentation' and 'alcohol' gave it quite an air of excitement in these days of post-war rationing. The only bother was I hadn't actually made the wine myself. I resolved that next week, I would set aside more time and would return to some well-tested creation of my own. I loved to cook and I was good at it. It was simply a case of finding the time to work up something original. I pulled out the typed sheet, folded it into an envelope and addressed it, opened the top right-hand drawer and found a stamp. Sticking it on, I got up and went to fetch a shopping basket for the trip to the village shop.

The days blurred into a week and then two. John came home for the weekend, but left on Monday morning complaining about how travelling to London from Farnborough was so much harder than it had been from Uffington.

"I miss Uffers," were his parting words, thrown in dismal tones over his shoulder as he rushed out to the car, his well-travelled leather suitcase swinging from one hand, forgetting to plant a goodbye kiss on my cheek, as was fast becoming customary.

My father left for London too. I worried about him, rattling around in our house in St John's Wood on his own, but he'd been independent for sixty-five years and wasn't about to stop being so now. I had to accept that but worried all the same. He assured me he was busy, with things to do, including a trip to see Roger's widow Molly and their two little boys, Philip, who was now heir to Pa's title, and Christopher.

Tewpie took a week off and we motored to Cornwall for a beach holiday. The weather was fine and several days in succession we went to Daymer Bay, which was dotted with families sitting on rugs eating sandwiches on the beach, shoulders turning red in the unaccustomed sun. Candida went even blonder and browner and Paul learned to swim in the sea and played beach cricket with John. But it was mostly Candida who held John's fatherly attention.

"Wibz, wibzie wibz," he called her. He made up rhymes for her and played with her and couldn't seem to get enough of her. She called him Dadz in return.

After lunch on the third day, John and Candida headed to the water's edge together. Paul found other children on the beach to play with. I sat on the rug watching him for a while. The gulls called to each other noisily and an ice cream van sounded its musical call in the distance. I stood up and brushed the sand from my legs. I put on my canvas shoes and set off across the dunes that lay behind the beach, to the little church of St Enodoc. Once almost completely buried by a sandstorm, it had been excavated in the 1800's and restored as a place to worship. With a small surrounding graveyard, the inside was cool and dark compared to the hot dry air of outside. The pews smelt of furniture polish and a handful of peonies sat in a little vase on the altar. I pulled down a hand embroidered cushion, knelt and prayed. Eyes closed, silence in the air, my breathing settled and calmed, I felt God wrap around me. When He did, it seemed as if things simply didn't matter in the same way. After what felt like a moment but my watch told me was almost half an hour, I stood up again. I had to go back, to the children, to John, but in another life, I could have stayed here in the still comfort of this church, all day long. I put a shilling in the collection box and returned to the outside world, blinking like a mole surfacing after a long dig.

I got back to the beach to find Tewpie and Candida sitting on the rug. Candida was drawing a picture of the sea.

"Where have you been?" John demanded crossly.

"I went to the church," I said mildly. John and I had both visited it, many times. John since his childhood, and I since he had first brought me here in my early twenties.

"You were gone for ages," he complained.

"I'm sorry," I said. "I didn't think you'd miss me. Where's Paul?"

"Don't know," John said shortly.

"Don't know, don't care," I muttered. Tewpie looked at me sharply and I looked back. His face was red, despite being screened from direct sun by his hat and his mouth set in an irritated line. I felt the calmness of God dissipating rapidly into the ether. I scanned the beach and found the small slight figure of my son in the distance, playing beach cricket with a scattering of other children.

"We're ready to go," John said. "Aren't we Candida?"

"Right," I said, resolving to find the right time to speak to John about Paul. This couldn't go on. He seemed to take less notice of him each day.

That night, Tewpie and I climbed into bed together. I put on my flannel nightdress-these Cornish summer nights could be unexpectedly cold – and stood a moment at the window. The moon was new and the sky was a dark indigo, the sea black except for where it broke on the shore in a frothy white line. I turned from the window, leaving the curtains open. I liked to be woken by the rising sun stealing into the bedroom.

John was already in bed, his chest hair sprouting from the top of his faded stripy pyjamas. I climbed in next to him, trying not to immediately fall into the middle of the sagging mattress. I turned off the bedside light – we had electricity here – and the room fell into quiet, shadowy night.

"Tewpie. Can we talk about Paulie? You must include him more," I said, in my nicest, most tactful voice. I reached out a hand to touch him on the shoulder. "He watches you with Candida. He wants to join in."

John gave me a hard look in the darkness. The whites of his eyes stood out. "Oh, Plymmie," he said, before rolling over onto his side, his back to me. "You're like a broken record."

I looked at his pyjama clad back, a slab of stone against me, across the middle of our bed. Within minutes, John was asleep. I lay awake for what felt like a long time, squinting at a small round spot of peeling paint on the ceiling and listening to the distant roar of the sea. What was the sea trying to say to me? My ears strained for the advice I needed, surely somewhere to be found in the crash and the pull of the waves. How was it remotely possible that the older I got, the less I knew?

"Dear God," I prayed in the darkening room, as I always did, before I fell asleep. "Please help me to find the answers I need."

John, seemingly untroubled, chomped in his sleep beside me and emitted a gentle snore.

We drove home to Farnborough late on a cold and rainy Sunday afternoon to the abrupt realisation that the seemingly endless summer holidays were drawing to a close. The lawn was spotted with the first of the autumn leaves. No sooner had John unpacked the car than he was making preparations to go to London the following day. The children rushed off to find their friends while I surveyed the contents of the larder and wondered about supper.

A slew of post sat on the hall table. I picked it up, and leafing through the pile I saw a letter bearing the address of *The Express*. Hoping it was a cheque, I opened it ahead of the more obvious and depressing bills. I scanned the letter quickly. The news was not good. Bottles of fermenting elderflower wine had been exploding in larders and dark kitchen cupboards across the nation, causing any amount of mess and damage and a record number of complaints. It seemed I no longer had the right kind of following. There would be no cheque. I had been summarily sacked.

Chapter Twenty-Six

1947. Farnborough.

Conversion was never going to be the easy road, but what had God ever had to say about the easy road?

I had known from early on in our relationship that John would not welcome my conversion to Catholicism. Perhaps that was why I'd alluded frequently to my conviction that I would one day convert, alluded so often, loudly and clearly, as if that would prepare him in some way for the inevitable. I'd told him before we were married and I'd told him after we were married. I'd written to him about it from Berlin, and I'd reminded him with my determined support for Evelyn and any other convert we even vaguely knew.

When Evelyn had converted, and John had been so vehemently and vocally appalled, I'd hoped that at least in part his reaction was so strong because he'd gone off Evelyn (that had been happening for quite some time) rather than because he had converted to a church John considered a threat. But even as I'd hoped, I knew it wasn't so. It wasn't simply that John didn't like Evelyn, or that he was suspicious of Evelyn's continuing affections to me, or that he was enraged with him for stealing parts of him, most noticeably Archibald his teddy bear, and reincarnating them as Sebastian Flyte in his dazzling novel, *Brideshead Revisited*, or that he was jealous of his professional success, although all of those things were present in the complex mix that was John's relationship with Evelyn.

Evelyn was a thorn in John's side, but there was only one valid reason why John was so adamantly against my conversion, and that was because he was a High Anglican, because that was what he firmly believed, and he wanted me to believe as he did. He wanted to carry on worshipping in the same pew as his wife. To John, Anglicanism was enough, and no more. It was not too little, and not too much. Like Goldilocks in the fairy story, he'd found the perfect bowl of porridge. It was just right. High Anglicanism was a part of him, as vital and fundamental to his well-being as the ability to write poetry. And he wanted it-needed it-to be like that for me, as well.

All this I knew. But I was thirty-eight and speeding into my middle years. I worried that if I delayed much longer, I risked never doing it at all. I needed to become a Roman Catholic, The thought of dying without having converted was unthinkable; it would be as if I had never properly known God. The desire was too strong to turn away from, and it seemed like there were reminders and signals around every corner. Was I seeing Angels or was I going mad? I chose to believe it was the former.

I knew John would try and talk me out of it, but I was also aware that he had a great deal going on in his life – his London life – and that he might come to accept conversion as my choice, as I was forced to accept the many choices of his that I didn't like. This, I reasoned to myself, was sometimes the way of marriage, or at least it seemed increasingly to be the way of ours. One person could not control the other.

But of course I was wrong. First came the pleading – "It's vital we worship in the same church, Plymmie, it's the tie that binds us" – to which I replied mildly, "No John, the tie that binds us is called marriage". Then came the threats, usually issued in the middle of the night after hours spent thrashing around in bed, turning the sheets and blankets into a tangled heap, and generally involving angry promises to divorce me. The prospect of divorce made my stomach turn over and my future go blank-I couldn't imagine my life without my husband; but somehow my resolve, after so many years of procrastination and delay, was finally set and even I couldn't seem to undo it.

I pushed ahead. I wrote to the Black Friars in Oxford asking for some initial instruction. They wrote back, happy to take me on. I could, they told me, study with them, and be received into the Catholic Church in due course under their auspices. As I was already a practising Christian, the process wouldn't take very long. All being well, they said, I could plan to be received into the Catholic church by Easter next year.

I began my regular tuition with Father Conrad Pepler. I took the bus to Oxford once a week while the children were at school, getting off in St Giles. I crossed the busy road to the home of the Black Friars, the beautiful flat fronted college building on the Woodstock Road. There, in Father Conrad's cramped dark rooms overlooking the small patch of grass that mocked the traditional Oxford college quadrangle, breaking only for lunch in the communal dining room, I felt as if I was falling into a pair of familiar open arms that had been waiting patiently for me for a long time.

Outwardly, it was as if nothing was changing. I still ran the WI and organised fetes and rode everywhere and ran the children's lives. John still came home at the weekends. We entertained the same old crew – the Lancasters, the Pipers, the Mosleys – and on Sundays, John and I went to church together. That was the worst part of every weekend, as it reminded him that our days of worshipping together were coming to an end. Quite often it would kick off another rant. But the more he ranted, the more implacable I became

One Friday night, after a supper of baked fish and mashed potatoes dug up from the garden, with homemade tartar sauce, John and I took a nightcap into the sitting room. John had brandy, I had apple juice. I'd recently found an apple press, and churning through apples picked from our orchard that autumn resulted in the most incredible flavour. (If I still had my *Express* column, I could easily have written a printworthy article about this that wouldn't have caused eruptions in anyone's larder.) I sat down in an armchair covered in a faded floral print. John remained standing, crossing to the window and looking out. A deep silence thick with unresolved problems, differences that we didn't know how to start tackling, hung weightily between us.

"Must you, Propeller?" he asked softly, once again.

I took a deep breath.

"John, I had a vision," I told him, for what was the umpteenth time.

"Yes. I know. Of the heavenly host," he muttered. John refused to believe me, and acted as if I just wanted to convert to annoy him.

"If it bores you so, don't make me say it again and again. I just know – I have to do this."

I looked into the depths of my cloudy apple juice. I wanted to add, 'I do nothing for me, nothing at all. Let me have this'. I wanted to scream, 'You do everything precisely as you want – girls, work, travel, when you come home, you choose how you treat our children. So let me have this'. Once, I would have shouted all this. Now, too tired with arguing to explain myself again to someone who refused to listen, I took a sip of my apple juice and waited.

Tewpie turned to look at me a moment, his face revealing every feeling he was struggling with – incomprehension, confusion, bewilderment, dismay-laid over a canvas of weariness about the whole damn thing. We had been struggling with it for so long.

"Evelyn keeps writing to me," he said at last, turning back to look out of the window. It was almost dark outside, but the dominant shape of the beech tree was still discernible in the distance. "In support of your conversion." John laughed, a sound utterly without mirth. "After berating me about my lack of understanding towards you, he told me I should consider it myself."

My heart sank. Evelyn's letters had been pummelling John for months now. John had shown me some of them. Even by his persistent standards, Evelyn was surpassing himself.

"I've already asked him to stop. I'll ask him again," I said. Evelyn had promised to stop writing to John, but clearly he hadn't. In a recent letter to me, he'd written that he thought there was a devil at work in John. I suspected that, for his own reasons, Evelyn enjoyed doing this, bullying John, running him down to me, but John's dislike of Evelyn was growing daily, and Evelyn's letters only made things much worse in our marriage. I wondered sometimes if that was Evelyn's intention, but it was an uncharitable thought about someone I cared for, and I tried to suppress it.

John still had his back to me. "Penelope. About – Waugh." He spat the word. "Should I be concerned?"

I looked at John's stiff back, jacketed in his favourite ancient misty grey tweed, slightly bent at the shoulders, standing by the window, turned away from me. Despite the breath-taking hypocrisy of the question – how many nights had I lain awake waiting for John to come to bed, listening for his footfall on the stairs? How many crushes had he indulged himself in since we married? There had been so many I had literally lost count- I got up and went to him. I took his slack hand in mine, and squeezed it gently, raising it to my lips to kiss. John turned to look at me.

"No, John," I said, his hand held close between mine. "You don't have to worry about that."

John nodded, relief joining the jumble of other emotions. He put his free arm about me and drew me in to him so I could feel the musty warmth of his body. He kissed the top of my head. I wished my hair was cleaner.

"I love you, Propeller. I always will. That will never change, whatever happens."

I nodded against his chest, holding his hand against my cheek. The pads of his fingers felt a little rough from typing. For some reason, my eyes were pricking. It felt like a goodbye, but it couldn't be, because we were married, with children, and John had just told me he would love me forever. Nevertheless, I felt like a ship in a dock, with the ropes being loosened one by one, and John was the crowd preparing to cast me off.

"I know," I said. "And I will always love you," I added.

My chin was tucked in below his shoulder, pressed against the scratchy tweed of his jacket. His smell-of wool and brandy and ink and dust-was in my nostrils and lodged in my throat like a fishbone. I squeezed my eyes shut against the pricking sensation that wouldn't go away, then opened them again to stare at a small part of the pattern of his jacket.

Slowly, John pulled back. He looked at me, his eyes watery. "This will be our last Christmas together," he said.

I must have looked shocked, because he added hastily, "I mean, our last Christmas worshipping in the same church."

Again, the strange verbal paralysis descended which meant I said nothing. It was as if there was nothing left to say. We had said it all, shouted it all, wept it all, and all that remained to us now was silence. The silence of a difficult marriage, the silence of two people who were running out of steam, and into that silence all I could hear was God calling me, offering me a refuge.

CHAPTER TWENTY-SEVEN

March, 1948. Oxford.

The church of St Aloysius had become familiar to me now. The smell of incense was ever present, mingled with wax furniture polish and an unidentifiable mustiness.

This time tomorrow, I thought, kneeling in my pew, the arches of the church reaching above me. It wasn't a huge church, quite modest in fact in its aspirations. It had been built in 1875, for the small but growing Catholic population of Oxford. This time tomorrow, I would have been received here, into my new faith. I had been a practicing Christian for a long time, but still I had a feeling of rebirth. I had been re-baptised a few days ago, and that had emphasised the feeling. Predictably, Tewpie had found this too much, and had gone to Cornwall, thundering to the last about my 'betrayal'. As my words failed me, he increasingly found his, and they included 'betrayal', 'distance' and 'desertion'.

I made the sign of the cross on my chest, stood up and quietly walked to the back of the church. A large fresco depicted the martyrdom of the several Oxfordshire priests who had died during the reign of Henry VIII rather than renounce their God. Somehow this put the fury of my husband firmly in perspective. John would adjust.

I took one last look around the church and walked out and back onto the Woodstock road. I was staying in a retreat run by nuns on the edge of the park for the few days before my conversion, meditating, reflecting, trying to really *feel* the Glory of God and be humble in the face of what I was about to do. For parts of each day I sat at my desk by the window of my room overlooking the park, trying to be embraced by these thoughts, but getting distracted by the blossom trees, symbols of spring and new life, in full flower. Somehow, I often found God more easily in the plants and the greenery and the energy of all His living things, on the back of a horse, or feeding the chickens, than I did between the pages of the Bible Father Papler had given me.

I walked on, past the turning left into Cherwell Edge and straight on to the park. The garden at home would be similarly transformed when I got back and I felt an irrational stab of homesickness. I walked towards the pond at the back of the park, by the river. Mallards were quacking: the glossy, flashily dressed males preening, the dowdy brown mothers looking about them beadily, protecting the cluster of fluffy ducklings swimming close to her. A small girl in a pale grey coat was throwing bread into the pond for the ducks to eat, her nanny holding her firmly by one hand. She looked just a year or two younger than Candida, and my homesickness increased. I pushed it down. It was just one more test. I knew what I was doing, and I would be home soon enough.

Although the air still held a chill, the sky was a brilliant blue, and the world looked bright and clean, as if it had just been laundered and hung out to dry. I continued along the path beside the riverbank, watching a pair of swans swimming close together. A man with a felt trilby and a woollen overcoat was playing ball with a small grizzled terrier. Green leaves were unfurling on branches on almost every tree. I turned right, to head back to the gates again, past a groundsman rolling the cricket pitch in front of the picturesque Edwardian pavilion, in readiness for summer. Suddenly, after what felt like months of waiting for spring, it was unfurling in a matter of minutes. The roller looked heavy, and the groundsman's face was red with effort.

I turned away and started to walk back to Cherwell Edge. The nuns would be waiting for me, ready to help me through this final hour. I started to hurry. I needed to be with them, for while the world out here seemed to imitate perfection, as it often did when I really chose to look, I was about to make my vows committing to a different life. The company of the nuns, not unlike the mother ducks on the pond, would keep me, the novice, in their view and help me safely reach the altar. If anyone held the secret of the joy that was being close to God, it felt likely to be them.

Chapter Twenty-Eight

Farnborough.

So it was done. I was home again a day after I had been received, and it was almost an anti-climax. In practical terms, everything felt exactly the same. After all the fighting and the build-up and the friction, and my worry and my doubts, it was done and now life had simply returned to normal. I was home, running the house and gardens and the children as before. John stomped back from Cornwall, and after a few disappointed words went directly off to Denmark on a poetry tour. By the time he finally rang to say he was coming home to stay, I'd been a Catholic for over two weeks. Two Sunday masses, and a Hail Mary every night. I'd added a Hail Mary to the end of the children's bedtime prayers. The children took it completely in their stride, blond heads bowed, hands together. "Hail Mary, full of grace," they recited, momentarily transformed from free-roaming country children to small fallen angels.

Eventually, John came home again. I heard his car in the drive – I had been listening for it for over an hour-and opened the front door onto the darkening evening to welcome him. I was determined to make things alright.

"John," I said, kissing him on a ruddy cheek, taking the coat from over his arm so he could manage his suitcase more easily. "Oi have missed you. More than you can imagine."

John smiled slowly and we hugged.

"Propeller. It's so good to see you. I've missed you too." He pulled back from me: "Why, you look exactly the same," he said, as if I should have grown another head.

"You are a fool," I said, elbowing him. "Of course I do. Why wouldn't I?"

Together we went inside, and John quickly found a bottle of Margaux and poured himself a glass. I had some ginger beer. He went upstairs to kiss the sleeping children while I took our supper out of the Aga and set the table. Lamb cutlets, mash and peas. Mint sauce. A jug of water. I hoped it wasn't too Spartan for Tewpie, who loved three rich courses and glamour and company.

We sat across the wooden table from each other in the silent house, the grandfather clock ticking distantly in the hall.

"So how are you, Plymmie?" John asked, struggling to cut his chop.

"Oi'm fine, Tewpie. And now you're home it feels like nothing has really changed. Not for you and I."

"Oh good," said John through a mouthful of lamb. "You know how I hate change."

I smiled. "And abroad," I added.

"Yes. No doubt you'll make me go to the Continent next."

"Darlin' Tewpie, I won't make you do anything. I just want to go on here, living here with you and Paulie and Wibz, in the middle of all our domesticity. A few days away were a good thing for me, because it reminded me how much Oi have to cherish."

John put down his mouth and fork, took a sip of Margaux and looked at me across the table with watery eyes.

"Penelope. I wish I had more of you. The Catholic church – it is just one more thing taking you away from me. I feel jealous, I suppose, of everyone else who takes so much of you." He began to reel off a list: "The horse, the ponies, the cows, the chickens, the house, even the children, and now-God."

I put down my knife and fork, too. The notion that John was jealous was one that had simply never occurred to me. I thought for a moment. If that was the issue undermining our marriage, it was easy to solve.

"God doesn't take me from you," I said. "But let's make more time," I said. "I will come to London to see you in the week. And you could try and come home one night in the week, too." I had a sense of having had this conversation before, a thousand times, but if we both wanted to spend more time together it could be done. I hated parties and socialising, but one night a week wouldn't kill me. I'd still have six nights in Farnborough.

"Yes, what a good idea," John said, resuming to eat. "These chops are good, Plymmie."

"George," I said with a tilt of my head.

John looked appalled. "Oh, don't tell me," he pleaded. "It will only ruin my enjoyment."

I laughed, and raised my glass into the air. "To new beginnings, Tewpie," I said.

"New beginnings," he echoed, and we clinked and drank.

It almost worked. We almost believed it.

I believed it that night, curled into John's body like a newlywed. We could heal this scar, see, it was knitting over already. We were a ship steering safely round an iceberg. This knowledge felt like a surprise of a warm day in early November, just when one had accepted the long inevitable advance of winter had started.

John kissed the back of my neck, my hair, my ear.

"I love you, Plymmie, as much as I ever have," he said sleepily.

I was to hear that phrase, or to see it written down in letters, a great deal in the years to come, for the rest of John's life, but over time, it came to mean something quite different to me than it did on that night of reconciliation. But on that night, with John's semen damp on my thigh, and his body curved hotly behind me, it meant he would always love me, like this, as his wife. That night I believed in the cure we had found for our ailing marriage, and fell asleep happy.

Chapter Twenty-Nine

1950

So life resumed its old rhythm. John was in London for the weekdays as usual, and I was alone in the country with Candida. I regularly visited Paul at the Dragon School in Oxford where he was a boarder, and went to St Aloysius to give thanks. Weekends were the usual mix of guests and cooking.

"You see how the same everything is?" I teased John, one Saturday morning as he frowned into the mirror in concentration, half his face covered in shaving foam.

"Hmm?" he asked.

"My conversion. You idiot. You had nothing to fear," I said.

And superficially it was the same. The only real obvious difference was Sunday, when I went to Wantage to the local Catholic church, leaving Tewpie and Wibz to attend the local church together.

It was almost as if my conversion had never happened.

My father and I had fallen into a routine of having lunch every Wednesday. Sometimes we went out – to his club, or to the Savoy grill, and took a turn around the National Portrait Gallery together afterwards, but increasingly, I simply caught the train to Marylebone and went to see him at home. In truth, that was my favourite. Restaurants and clubs and white linen table cloths were all very well, but I found it strangely comforting to be standing in the hallway of my childhood home, surrounded by the familiar noises – the tick of the grandfather clock, the faint clatter of the maid or housekeeper in the kitchen – and things that I had grown up with. The smell of polish on the floor, the portrait of Star from days before I was born hanging above the fireplace. It was as if nothing changed here, in this world, and for a moment I could lose myself in that. Except, of course, it had changed. Everything had.

Pa had been looking thin. I had noticed that his jackets were hanging loosely on his once broad shoulders, but I had put it down to age. He was 71, after all. So I wasn't prepared for the news he broke, one icy day in March. Perhaps one is never prepared for that kind of news. We were eating watercress soup.

"Darling. I have cancer," he told me, putting down his soup spoon. "Terminal."

My spoon clattered onto the plate.

"Don't be ridiculous," I said, eyes blinking rapidly. My father, ill? He'd barely had a cold in his life. He was unassailable. He was my rock. He couldn't die. I knew he'd found life lonely and hard without my mother, but he still couldn't die. I wouldn't let him. I wouldn't accept it. I'd put my foot down.

Pa stretched out a hand and placed it over mine. It felt cold, as if the tide of his life was already ebbing. I looked down at it and my face shone back up at me, reflected in the high polish of the mahogany dining table.

"Penelope," he said quietly. I slowly raised my eyes to meet his. And then of course, I knew it was true, and that there was nothing I could do to change things. I could protest as much as I liked, but keeping my father here was not in my gift.

"Oh Pa," I said helplessly. "No, no, no." My napkin slid silently off my knee to the floor.

"It's alright, Penelope. You know that, better than most, with your faith. Everyone has their time, and this is mine."

A girl came and took away the soup bowls, and brought in a plate of roast chicken and boiled potatoes. She placed it in front of my father, with the silver spoon handles turned towards him. A knob of butter was sliding gently down a mountain of peas as it melted. But it wasn't alright, there was nothing alright about it.

"When did you find out?" I asked.

"Last week. Both lungs. Six months to a year at best. There won't be any pain. Doctor Saunders will make sure of that."

"Come and stay with us," I urged, but my father was already shaking his head.

"I'm better off here. I've got my routine, and Doctor Saunders has recommended a nurse for when the time comes."

He had it all worked out. It was as if he was welcoming it, almost.

When I left that day, I hugged my father close and held him for a little longer, "Goodbye, Pa," I said, "I'll be up next week as usual."

That was what my father wanted, and so it was what I would give him. Life, as usual, until, one day, it would not be there, for him, anymore.

"Goodbye Penelope dear. I look forward to it." I left him in the drawing room, completing the crossword in the *Telegraph* to the gentle crack and spit of the fire in the grate and the smell of lavender *pot pourri*, my mother's favourite, scenting the room. Already, I thought, now that I knew, he looked smaller, as if he was shrinking away from life in preparation for his permanent vanishing.

I decided to walk to Marylebone, one foot in front of the other, my hat pulled low over my eyes, half hidden tears freezing on my face, my eyes unseeing. How could it be so? And yet I knew it was. I felt five and forty at the same time. I would do what I could, while time was left. I would be the best daughter I could be to him. A year was quite a time, after all. We still had time. Didn't we? Time to make it count? I hurried into the station, pulling my fox fur tighter against the biting March air. I wouldn't be surprised if there was snow on the ground back at home. London was always warmer than the countryside and it was feeling freezing here. A porter was holding open the door to the carriage, and slammed it shut behind me. I sat down in an empty compartment by the window and looked out at the grey of the platform. The station clock told me it was just past three.

'Oh Pa', I thought.' How will I manage?' I knew it was selfish of me, but I couldn't help it. Roger, Star, and now, my father. Losing your birth family happened to everyone in the end, but no one prepared you for how hard it was. The train stuttered and tugged once, twice, and then began to pull slowly away from the buffers.

Of course, I reminded myself. I was lucky. After all, I had John.

"If it's too bloody far, let's move!" I yelled.
"Fine by me. I've always hated this house anyway, I was much happier at Uffers," John yelled back. "I'm too far to get to London and back in a day, there's no bloody hot water, and I'm sick to death of the smell of oil lamps. And

as for that menagerie in the garden that takes up most of your time..."

"Oh, they'd have to come," I said immediately, defensively. "The menagerie, as you call them, are family, just as much as the children are family. And there's no question of getting rid of the children."

John rolled his eyes and roared at the ceiling in frustration. "Obviously the children have to come. But only you, Propeller, would value your horse and your cows and your chickens on the same level as your children. Only you." He threw up his hands like a long-suffering martyr appealing for divine intervention.

"Oh shut up, John," I said. "That's simply a red herring you like to wave around from time to time. The menagerie matter, but clearly not as much as the children or you. Let's look at the real problem here, and if that is that you hate this house because it's too far from London and a little bit uncomfortable, if you feel it will make all the difference to the quality of your life, then of course we should sell up and move. There's a rectory in Wantage that's for sale. Robert told me about it last week. It's a small estate, not as grand as you might like, perhaps, but grander than here. And being the nation's *treasured* poet with four best-selling collections, not to mention famous television broadcaster, perhaps more fitting to your status than this house with its many and often mentioned deprivations..."

Now it was John's turn to tell me to shut up. He pretended to hate it when I called him grand, but we both knew it was true.

"Are our trajectories going in opposite directions?" I asked John slowly. "It seems to me you need ever greater comfort and fame and glory, while I can manage with less and less."

"What a question, Plymmie. I don't consider it unreasonable, since I am working hard to earn a daily wage, and not doing too badly by anyone's standards, to ask for some basic levels of comfort at home. A decent supper after a long day's work, a hot bath, an electric light to read by, a wife offering slippers and the paper rather than smelling of horse and a row. Is that too much for a person to expect? And, for what it's worth," he blundered on, "I wouldn't call this house 'a little bit uncomfortable'. We are in the 1950s now, not the 1880s. Electricity has been available for nearly a century. I am simply asking that we avail ourselves of the modern inventions that are pretty much standard these days, that in fact an awful lot of people take for granted, in a bid to make everyone's lives easier."

I looked at John. His face was ruddy from shouting, his arms flailing about as if to underline his point. I noticed his moss green jumper had a small hole in it by the neck. Things were literally coming apart at the seams.

I sighed. If a move to Wantage meant he was more likely to make it home on a weekday, then it was surely a good thing-no, an essential thing-for our marriage. After all, marriages needed tending, they were work, as Star had often reminded me. Now, as I sometimes did, I felt her at my shoulder, my father hovering close by. The months since he had died had been particularly bleak. The last of his fighting spirit had gone out of him with the doctor's diagnosis, and it turned out it had been less than three months rather than the predicted year. By June I had been standing at the side of his grave, throwing a handful of damp English earth onto the lid of his coffin, listening in disbelief to the rattle it made on the walnut, watching with unseeing eyes as the grave diggers started to shovel more earth on top. I missed both my parents in an abstract way that bit deep into my flesh just when I thought I had managed to put aside the loss. It struck particularly cruelly in the difficult moments of life, like now – when John and I were fighting, or when Powlie fell silent when his father came home; when the bills mounted up, when loneliness threatened to overwhelm. My parents had been such a stabilising force and sometimes my world seemed to tremble around me without them.

When I thought of them, which I often did, memories of earlier days fell around me like summer rain. Unlike John's memories, they didn't drop from a pen in easy stanzas, but appeared unexpectedly, in snatches of image or scraps of thought, prompted by smells or a word or a sound or an absence, and then I would remember for a moment, our small happy family group. Holiday periods particularly stood out: An eight year old Roger back from boarding school, excited to be released from weeks of what sounded like bad food and bullying and a winter term spent freezing in shorts; of our Christmas tree which had seemed so enormous as a child, erected every year in the wood panelled hall, with exciting-shaped presents laid out all around it. I remembered how the servants would join us for a glass of wine on Christmas Eve, and how in the lull between Christmas and New Year, Daddy would crunch through the snow with us to Primrose Hill, towing a sledge. At night our nanny would sit reading by a low light while Roger and I went to sleep, my mother's perfume still in my nostrils from her recently bestowed goodnight kiss. Was everyone perpetually haunted, as I was, by their past?

"Plymmie?" John said.

I shook my head, frowning, and looked at John, who was standing quietly now, looking back at me questioningly. Those days were long gone, yet my mother's voice was clear in my head: "Tread carefully, Penelope", I heard her say.

"You love this man you married, so tread carefully". More images flashed through my head, dazzling me like the headlights of a passing car. The perfectly set dining table at Flagstaff House, her elegant long evening dresses, the perfectly coiffured hair, the diamonds hanging from her ears, the welcoming smile and witty remark so often on her lips, the fact that she was always to be found at Daddy's elbow when he faced an even remotely tricky moment. How was it that I hadn't realised how easy and secure my life had been, until twenty years later, when it was all gone? Perhaps everyone's lives became more complex and difficult as they grew older.

"Plymmie?" he said again. I fleetingly wondered whether to try to explain what I felt to John, but I knew he would struggle with it. He didn't miss his own father and mother, and had never quite warmed to my parents. The early *froideur* had never entirely vanished, as I had once hoped it would. He couldn't miss them as I did, but in truth I guessed he didn't miss them at all.

"John. Let's sell. Let's move somewhere where it's easier for you. It would be marvellous if we lived somewhere where you managed to come home more often. If moving is what we need to do, let's do it."

John nodded back at me. "Why don't I enquire about the house you mention in Wantage? Has it any land?"

Spoken like a true aristocrat.

"Not really. About nine acres. Good idea, why don't you?"

I went out into the orchard to pick some early apples. As I picked, I wondered if everything John and I tried to make our relationship work was a waste of time. What if we couldn't get back the sense of closeness and security we'd given each other in the early days? What if we were becoming one of those couples who simply didn't have anything nice to say to each other? As I wondered all this, I also knew that it was for precisely this kind of moment that I had faith. Now I must draw deep, deep inside me, for the resources God gave me, to get through each day. Marriages were demanding, by their very nature, and certainly mine had been from the start. Husbands needed tending, but they didn't vanish, as a rule. It was a life long journey, and John and I had simply been on a bumpy part of the road for a while now.

Soon the basket was full. I picked it up, straining with the weight of it and headed towards the back door. A tall, thin figure appeared around the corner of the house. It was Paul.

"Mummy? Do you need some help?" He hurried towards me. At 13 he was on the cusp of thickening into the frame of a strong young man. His blond hair was darkening, the first signs of adolescent spots appearing on his face. I could feel myself clutching a little frantically at his childhood as it inexplicably slipped through my fingers like sand. I smiled at him, feeling like I was seeing him afresh, as I often felt when I took the time to look.

"Thank you Powlie. That would be a great help."

Powlie took the basket from me and we walked slowly together back to the kitchen. He had just completed five years at the Dragon School in Oxford, John's old school, and was destined for Eton in early September, now just a matter of days away.

Until recently he had seemed to like to help me with jobs in the garden, but I had seen less of him during these long summer holidays. He had long been adept at avoiding John, but now I felt he stayed away from me too. I wondered if jibes from Tewpie about being a mummy's boy had finally hit home.

He put the basket down on the faded farmhouse table in the kitchen.

"D'you want to make some juice?" I asked him.

He shook his head. "Things to do," he mumbled, and left the kitchen. A year ago, he had loved using my apple press. I shrugged, trying not to mind, and began to unpack the apples into a bucket half full of cold water in order to wash them. I hated the feeling that I wasn't really keeping up with any of the tiny, invisible changes that seemed to be going on at home right now, changes that took life in its own direction and out of my hands. Perhaps I was more like Tewpie than I acknowledged, I thought, rubbing the apples gently before taking them out one by one and laying them out on a tea towel. Did I, too, hate change? Certainly, when it was the kind of change that took away those I loved. Paulie, despite our sometimes troubled relationship, was growing up and away from me. That was the nature of a mother-child relationship, and so entirely to be expected, but still, it left me with an absence in my heart. What would I fill that space with? Candida, at eight, was a cheerful and constant presence at home, but too often now it was just the two of us rattling around in this vast house, with John in London or away on a tour, or visiting someone he had a crush on.

My heart fell further as I thought of Tewpie and his crushes. In my darkest moments, I knew that we could blame our problems as much as we liked on the house, or the distance John had to travel, but the real issue was the other girls. That had always been the stumbling block, from the outset. I was not happy to share my husband with others, while John found it impossible not to stray. Perhaps there were some people who genuinely didn't mind, but I wasn't one of them. Each affair was like a stab in my heart, and after so many years of fending off such wounds, I was vulnerable to each new blow. Of course it threw up inevitable questions of my own inadequacy. Why was I not enough for John? What was I doing wrong, to leave him so clearly unfulfilled with just me? Why did there have to always be yet another girl? Would it ever stop, or would I be putting up with his unexplained absences, until the end? This was not what I had expected from my marriage. I had underestimated the emphasis John placed on sex; I had thought we were an intellectual match and that that would be enough. But it wasn't. However clever John was, he still reacted on a more simplistic level, to flattery and attraction and flirtation, and somehow he didn't find all that in me.

I started to rinse the apples in the sink, my head throbbing as my thoughts galloped to a conclusion. What if – what if, now divorce was so much easier, what if, one day, John actually left me for another girl? I turned off the tap and collapsed down into the tired wicker chair in the corner of the pantry. Nausea rose in my throat as I considered this: it was not impossible. I knew that. The signs were that John was restless and discontented. His religion would be against it, but his religion was against infidelity, and he'd managed to get round that. Panic flickered within me. What would my life be without John? For the first time I felt glad my parents were not alive to witness that. I could hear Star saying, "I told you so." Why, with the arrogance of youth, had I known best and married John, when everyone had advised against it? Why had it taken me so long to learn that rules existed for very good reasons, and should be observed wherever possible? All my life I'd known best – my affair with Sir John, eloping with Tewpie – and look where that had taken me. Married to someone who – God help me – said he loved me, but whose behaviour repeatedly told me otherwise.

Married to someone who, it was possible, didn't want to stay married to me any more.

I put my head down into my hands. I had to keep the problem small enough to manage. John hated this house, and found the travelling too much. That meant selling this house was the sensible course of action. We needed to buy somewhere more convenient to John, so he could come home every night. John and I would spend more time together, and the need for other girls would reduce. In due course the children would grow up, and John and I would have each other for company. We were well matched intellectually and needed to build up some common pursuits based on that. We had so many friends in common and years of history inextricably linking us to each other. All that couldn't be dismantled simply because the Government now said it could. Marriage – our marriage-was far more complicated than an Act of Parliament. Breathe, Penelope, breathe.

Paul came back into the room. "I've come to help after all. Oh-Mumma," he said, "Mumma, what's wrong? You're crying!"

"No I'm not," I said, dashing my hand across my eyes and surprised to find it came away wet. "I had something in my eye, that's all. Dust from the apples I expect. I'm so glad you've come back to help me. Come on, let's get pressing."

I stood up and Paul loaded the apples into the drum of the apple press until it was full. He closed it up and began to turn the handle. Slowly the lid began to press down on the apples, tighter and tighter until juice started to pour out of the little spout and into the jug on which it rested. Pale green and frothy at first, the liquid quickly separated into transparent liquid at the bottom and a thick layer of foam sitting on top.

I took two glasses and filled it with juice. "Delicious," I said. "Don't you think?" Paul nodded, smiling slightly, an apple-froth moustache sitting on his lip.

"I'll go and give one to your father." Paul's face went blank, as if someone had wiped it clean with a single swipe. I took a glass through to the study, guessing this was where I would find John, writing away at poems, letters, articles. I reached the doorway and stood still for a moment. Tewpie sat in the dark wooden desk chair, a half-drunk tumbler of whisky squatting by his right hand. He was writing and showed no signs of hearing the tread of my feet.

I looked down at the glass of apple juice in my hand, and back to John's whisky. Sometimes it seemed as if every possible thing divided us. I hated drink. John loved it. I could hear the nib of his ink pen scratching on the writing paper. I strained my ears and could hear John's breathing. He didn't look up, and after a moment I turned away and went back to the kitchen. Paulie had gone. I leaned against the counter and drank John's apple juice slowly, preoccupied, but still relishing its sweetness.

Chapter Thirty

March 1951. Farnborough.

Knowing this was our last January at Farnborough made the crisp winter scene more intense. From our high vantage point, Berkshire dropped away from us in layers of fields and clusters of houses. Often, I found myself pausing at windows on the landing to look at the landscape.

John had followed up the lead on the house in Wantage. He had visited it and decided it would suit us very well, and we had an agreement with the current owner to buy it as soon as our own house had been sold. It was appearing in *Country Life* in a week's time. The residence of the well-known poet and broadcaster John Betjeman, a Queen Anne jewel of a house, available for only the second time in fifty years.

Candida knew something was in the air, in that way children have of knowing, a combination of having listened in doorways and instinct, so when she asked, I had no choice but to explain. She was not happy. She remembered no other home than the one she was in, but I persuaded her it was a good thing on the basis she would see more of her beloved father.

"Will we still keep the horses? And Daisy and Buttercup?" she asked one night.

"Oh yes," I told her, tucking her up. "We couldn't leave them behind."

"What about my school?" She currently attended the village school, but had been starting to outgrow it, so would have had to move soon, anyway. "And my friends?"

I wanted to say, "We'll see", that convenient parental fudge, but looking into her slightly anxious eyes, taking in the frown on her forehead, it didn't seem fair.

"They have good schools in Wantage, and we're only moving a few miles away, so your friends can come and visit, and you can come back and visit them here. In a few years you'll be old enough to take a bus by yourself, and then you can come as often as you like. "

Candida's eyes roamed my face for further clues.

"If Wantage is just a few miles away, why will it be so much quicker for Daddy to get to work and back, all in one day?"

"It's on a direct railway line from London," I explained. "That makes the journey much quicker."

Candida looked unconvinced.

"I don't see why we need all this upheaval for the sake of just a few miles," she said, her face like a cross politician making a good point.

I decided not to argue with her.

"Let's tuck you in," I said, flattening her pillow down. "Time for lights out. Let's say our prayers."

I told Paulie about the move one Sunday when he had come home for lunch. He'd just looked thoughtful for a moment, before saying:

"Well, it hardly makes any difference to me, I'm never here," which I thought was quite unlike him. I knew he'd loved living at Farnborough and had a lot of local friends he would miss. Even though they could come and visit, and he could take the bus back to Farnborough to visit them, it wasn't the same as living right on top of each other, as they had done for several years. I looked closely at his face. It looked more shut off to me than before, as if a term and a half at Eton had rubbed away the last vestiges of childlike openness.

John seemed happier once the decision was taken, but his cheerfulness could also have been down to his growing professional success. His poetry was selling well, and he was doing another series of talks on the radio. He was also in increasing demand for articles, regularly writing for the *Daily Telegraph,* and was always being asked to contribute poems to mixed verse publications. For a man who had a terror of failure and of being overlooked, such work and publicity were gifts from heaven to him.

"I'm glad you're feeling so fulfilled by it all," I said to him one Saturday. We were sharing a rare, relatively idle moment before an onslaught of guests were due to arrive. Tewpie had been away giving talks at a number of provincial cities – Bristol being just the latest.

"I don't mind what menial work I do – book reviews, articles and the such like – so long as I can find the poems too."

"You are finding them, John. You are finding them, or they are finding you. They keep coming."

"Yes, they seem to, thank the Lord. Heaven knows what I would do if they ever dried up."

"Well, let's hope they don't. But perhaps more quiet contemplation and less socialising in London might lead to more poems, coming quicker," I said, ever hopeful.

John gave me a sharp look. "I need to go to London, Propeller. You know I do."

I did know. John had been born in London and remained, despite fifteen years in the countryside, an urban man. Sometimes I felt it wasn't only the other girls who were my rivals, but London too. Despite periods of disenchantment, the city seemed to exert a pull on him that I couldn't compete with. Of course at the moment we were both swearing to each other it would be different in Wantage. But Candida, at the age of eight, with her direct questions and unwavering gaze, had the clarity of vision to see this might not be so. How could two adults, educated, informed, intelligent, really delude themselves into thinking it was the house that was to blame for the disconnect between them?

This line of thought, which came too often these days, made me a little low. I tried to shake it off.

"It's a beautiful afternoon."

It was – sunny and bright, with little wind.

"Let's go for a walk."

John didn't look up from the paper.

"Take Candida."

Candida was playing with friends in the village, and Paul, my other regular walking companion, was at Eton. After a moment, during which time it became clear John didn't plan to change his mind, I decided to go alone. Without John, I might as well ride. I went to the back corridor, took my coat and riding hat and some tack of the pegs, and set off down the garden to find Moti.

Moti was old now but together we could still make our way slowly around the local bridle ways. As I neared his field he spied me, and trotted immediately to meet me at the fence, as he always did. I took off his nose band and put on the bridle, and as I did so I wondered if he remembered anything of his youth, of those hot early days of his life in India. Of the red dust and how it had stuck stubbornly in his mane, and how he had lived in the smartest stables together with close to twenty other horses. That he had been groomed and rubbed by professionals on a daily basis, and taken out and shown monuments thousands of years old. That he had tactfully looked away when he had happened to see two people kissing. How, one day, he had been put on a boat, and sent to a faraway cold country called England. Now, he lived in a field in almost all weathers, with only a rug to help him through the coldest months, and there was just me and a local boy to care for him. I threw on the saddle and buckled it up securely. Moti's life had been lived in extraordinary times, I thought, pulling the reins back over his ears. I checked the stirrup lengths, gathered up the reins and mounted. From the splendour and heat of India to life in a muddy English field.

I leant forward and rubbed Moti's neck.

"What a lot you've seen," I said. Moti's ears pricked up. Sometimes I felt sure he understood every word. As we trotted out of the gates, I reflected that horses were so much easier to get along with than humans, and much more reliable.

Chapter Thirty-One

Summer 1951. Wantage.

John was in an effusive ecstasy about the new house. With its Gothic gables, it fed his passion for Victorian architecture perfectly, and the sense of being in his own small world, his own estate, pleased him. I was happy with it too. There were stables behind the house and two cottages. The nine acres of land suited the menagerie better, and being near a market town actually did make all our lives easier. We employed a part time driver called Gardner to live in one of the Victorian lodges. Gardner would whisk John to the station or even to London and wait for him, meaning that true to his word, John was coming home more frequently during the week. Nevertheless his work often took him around England for days at a time, or kept him in London. But the move was accomplished, the children seemed to have adapted well enough, and John liked the house almost as much Uffington. We had mod cons, as he called them – electricity and hot water – which made my life easier and led John to almost dance with pleasure.

"Finally, we can live like everyone else," he said one day, soon after we had moved in, wallowing in a newly- run hot bath.

"For someone who despises the bourgeois, this is an unusual desire to be like everyone else," I replied, hanging a clean towel on the cast iron radiator to warm it up.

"Hot water and electricity aren't bourgeois," Tewpie said. "They're progress."

"Whatever you say, dear."

John gave me a sharp look.

"It's unlike you to act the submissive wife".

"Is it?" I parried.

"You know it is," he said with a disconcerted frown. "You aren't that kind of wife."

"What, the upper class nanny type you like so much?" I asked. John looked up, a startled expression on his face.

I left the bathroom and went downstairs. The type who would have been the right kind of wife for John? Was I was the wrong kind of wife for him? I was the solid kind rather than the glamorous kind, and the outspoken kind, rather than the artfully arranged, supportive kind, but did that mean I was the wrong kind of wife for a man like John?

What kind of wife would John have chosen if I hadn't cornered him that day back in 1933, in the offices of the Archie Rev? Would he had married hearty Pamela Mitford, and been catapulted to the centre of literary gossipy life by her sister Nancy? (Although John had found his own way there anyway). Or Billa? She had developed a great interest in conservationism, like John, so they would have been like-minded on that. But she was rather bossy, and while John liked the idea of bossy women – one only had to think of his ode to Joan Hunter Dunn – in reality, like most men, he needed to be the boss. He and Billa had remained great friends and endlessly wrote each other long letters, swapping notes on conservation practices and jokes they had picked up at parties. Billa worked for the Georgian Conservation

Society, a job which John had helped her to get, and John had decided to ask her to write the *Shell Guide to Norfolk*, which was where Billa's family came from and a county she knew as well as anyone else in the world. Despite all this, Billa still found time to look after her husband Roy – an Oxford don – and make sure he always had a decent dinner to come home to and a welcoming ear ready to listen to the trials and tribulations of his day. She also looked after their children and mothered Roy's students as they arrived each year, uncertain and bewildered in this sudden step up to adulthood. She charmed Roy's fellow Professors, and regularly produced supportive dinner parties. Yes, in spite of the bossiness, Billa might have been the right kind of wife – the right mix of intellectual equal and highly competent caretaker.

Had John ever wondered how it would have turned out if he'd married someone else other than me?

For my part, I knew I had chosen the right John. Johnnie Spencer Churchill was already divorced once, with a child being raised by grandparents, and had remarried, though rumour had it that this marriage too was rocky. Star, in her wisdom, had been absolutely correct, I could admit that now. I would not have found a safe and secure perch with Johnnie.

Sir John would be seventy-five years old now and was apparently living an idyllic, retired life with his wife, Florence, in Guildford. I had recently read a glowing review of his latest book on India. I hadn't seen either man for years. I had no regrets I would rather cherish their memories and I had simply loved John the most. How could I regret that, whatever difficulties it had brought?

I went out into the garden, shouting for our new Italian maid, Gina.

Gina had arrived the previous month at eight o'clock on a Monday morning. I'd opened the door in answer to her knock, just as John was leaving to go to London, and was milling about in the hall packing his papers in his usual chaotic fashion. Gina took one look at us, clearly expecting us to be more settled than we were. She seemed shocked to find packing crates stood about the room, and John muttering to himself, stuffing papers into his case, with, I noticed, one brown shoe and one black shoe on his feet. I had the feeling she would have been off again given the slightest chance, so I grabbed her suitcase and hauled her inside. I desperately needed some household help – the house was a tip even by my rather relaxed standards-and these days good help was proving extremely hard to come by.

"You must be Gina," I cried. "Welcome."

"… to the mad house," John muttered under his breath, rather unhelpfully I thought.

"This is Mr Betjeman," I told her, firmly steering her through the house and directly to her room. If she got unpacked, she was more likely to stay. "You are not to worry about him."

Gina looked at me blankly.

"Oh good God. No English," I said.

"Si! Si!" Gina said, breaking into a beaming smile.

I knew only a little Italian from my school days but I still had passable Latin, and this combination quickly became our way of communicating.

"Gina," I called now. "The cows need milking," (I said in Latin). Can you come and give me a hand?"

The sound of pots slamming in the kitchen was all the answer I needed. I set off down the fields. I collected a rather grubby apron from the stables and put it on, and picking up a couple of pails, walked on towards the cows. Relieved by the appearance of a sullen looking Gina about ten minutes later, I went on to the chicken houses to check for eggs, putting several in my apron pockets, before finally detouring back to the house via my new duck farm. I had decided to breed ducks as an extra source of income – John and I continued to exceed our income: he on first class travel to and from London, and expensive meals out, both of which I considered to be a ridiculous extravagance; me on ponies and carts, which, needless to say, John considered dispensible. Predictably, we both stubbornly defended our passions to the other, and the result was we were permanently felt hard up. My plan with the duck farm was to breed ducks and sell them, as well as any spare eggs. Time would tell if this was to yield any great financial success.

Back at the house, I found Candida cutting the bristles off Gina's hairbrush. She'd been very naughty since we'd moved, and my patience was stretched as thin as it was possible to be without snapping. Gina made a huge difference in the house, and I could not afford to lose her. She was a hard worker and took up much of the domestic load, albeit often with a mood to match the task. She had a mercurial Latin personality and I made a point of not going near her on wash day, when she invariably had a face like a mangle. On those days, I prepared all the meals, but on other, less busy days, she took over some of the cooking. She had proved a quick learner in the kitchen.

Home life in Wantage continued as a round of animals and children and friends far and wide dropping in for lunches, teas, dinners, or an overnight stay. John came and went, busier than ever. His writings increasingly carried a religious overtone, and he had started to be viewed as one of the most important lay Anglicans in the country. I was still running the WI, and going regularly to the local Catholic

Church in Hendred. I'd had a falling out with the priest in Wantage, and had decided to switch. John had howled with laughter about this when I'd told him the story. Even he, he told me, had yet to fall out with a vicar.

Somehow it seemed we both shouted less, I thought, cutting roses from the garden for the house in preparation for another weekend with John at home. But just as I began to relax back into my marriage, with Candida happily settled at her new school, Paul growing up, the new house a great success, and to consider that perhaps we were weathering the crisis provoked by John's restlessness and wandering eye; to feel that after my conversion, and the wear and tear of years of marriage, we were moving to calmer, warmer waters at last, the hammer blow fell.

Some busybody London hostess decided to throw a dinner party including John, Anthony Blunt – not yet revealed as a spy – a couple of our joint friends, and Lady Elizabeth Cavendish, sister of the Duke of Devonshire; tall, willowy, and aged just twenty-five.

"John's marriage is going wrong," said the busybody on the phone to Elizabeth. "Do come, darling. You'll like him so."

I didn't know at first. John never told me about it. I heard it from a friend, who felt it was better I was told, rather than the last to know. It seemed I wasn't the wrong kind of wife as I'd feared, but I was instead in a marriage 'going wrong'. The discovery of this left me breathless. After everything – the move, the efforts to spend more time together, the constant letter writing, forcing myself not to comment on the relentless bullying of Paul – was it was to end like this? A much younger, caring, submissive, aristocratic and well-connected female – an upper class nanny?-pulled inexorably into John's orbit and refusing, ever, to leave it.

Mutisher.

People say that time is a great healer. They tell you the pain of a love lost fades if you just give it time. And perhaps it does for some. But not for me. Sometimes, one can forget about it for a while. But at other times, it hurts as if it has just recently been inflicted. Those years in the early 1950s, when Elizabeth first met John, were the most painful of my life. I carried on, because that was what one did. We didn't talk about it. I didn't go into therapy. There were no kiss and tell magazine interviews, no opening your house and heart to a magazine or colour supplement. I didn't take a young lover. One simply carried on as normal, whatever life threw at one. So I dug the garden and I fed the ducks, and I rode the horses and I scrambled eggs for tea and I fed the guests and I shrieked at Gina in Latin, and like a canker in my mind all the time was John, falling in love with Elizabeth.

I prayed and I confessed, and I went to mass. I said Hail Marys every day. I put more coins than usual into the collection. I prayed and I brushed my hair and I prayed and I bought a face cream with a silhouette of a young girl on it, as if by the act of rubbing it into my face at night, things might significantly change.

Sometimes, John came home for the weekend and acted as if all was well. Friends still came and went, and John and I laughed and fought and entertained.

But all was not well. In London, it was John and Elizabeth; Elizabeth and John. Which left Penelope and John, who knew where? I wanted to rail at John, to shout at him, to throw things, but for the first time in our twenty years of knowing each other, I found I could express my fury better in letters than in person.

COME HOME NOW, I would write, often with half the page in capitals and whole paragraphs underscored. He, in his replies, sent from London, fudged it. Fudged it, dodged it. I will love you forever, he wrote. I have never loved you more than now. I poured over these letters. They made no sense. How could that be, since he spent more time in London than ever, and still Elizabeth stayed, the central presence in his life. She was replacing me.

Was I to share him, I asked him? I would not, I thundered in a letter.

"I WILL TAKE NO HALF MEASURES. I AM FED UP WITH YOUR DIVIDED LIFE AND COMPLETELY FALSE SET OF VALUES. Have the GUTS to tell your smart friends that you are tired of the rush and worry of London and that you are clearing out AND WISH TO BE LEFT ALONE. ... if you insist on going on with the London racket and Elizabeth... then I shall ask for a legal separation..."

This is what I got back:

"My darling Plymmie, I miss you and love you and all the time think about you," he wrote.

Each time, hope flared within me.

Each time, Elizabeth stayed.

My breath comes in short, shallow puffs as I remember. I remember the anger, white hot and surging at first, slowly giving way to a dawning sadness that quietly draped itself over every part of my life like a shroud, that this was really happening. The stabs of painful humiliation as slowly, everyone started to know that my marriage was "going wrong"

The blows fell as if they were thought up to deliberately inflict the maximum hurt. Soon after meeting her, John took Elizabeth Abroad – this being my husband, the same John who had always declared he hated abroad – and with a group of people most of whom I knew, including the Barnes, who were **our** friends. He took Elizabeth to meet the Pipers, who were **our** friends.

He went to stay with Elizabeth's mother, the Dowager Duchess of Devonshire. Of course he loved that. I could see him holding forth at Chatsworth, testing his latest funny little poem on the intimate audience of his mistress and her immediate family. Winning over Elizabeth's relatives as twenty years ago he had never managed to win over mine, with his charm and his wit and his cleverness. I wondered if he had deliberately waited until my father was just dead before embarking on his next Great Love. He loved it there so much he fell ill with a cold and stayed an extra week, being nursed by a devoted Elizabeth and her utterly enchanted mother.

All I could do was hope and pray that it would pass, that it would be like all the others – a short madness, a bout of nasty romantic flu, that would be slowly shrugged off and then normal life would resume.

I tried to arrange to meet Elizabeth. Befriending the other girls John had fallen for had always worked, as if they became too ashamed to betray me once they knew me. But Elizabeth, clever Elizabeth, refused to meet me.

Slowly, John allowed himself to be stolen. One of the most prominent Anglicans in the land, he began to live a complicated life of personal hypocrisy. He spent his weeks in London, working and meeting Elizabeth, and many of his weekends staying with friends, in a party of people that always included Elizabeth. He came home only if the children were coming back from school, or if he had asked friends to stay. Then he would act as if nothing had changed between us.

I felt like the housekeeper. I shouted, I raged, I said things could not go on, that we had to separate.

"No, Plymmie, we will not separate. We will not," he told me. And then Sunday night would come and he would leave me behind in that big house, ear strained for the departing crunch on the gravel, which meant then I could let my face slide without risk of anyone seeing.

I cover my face with my hands like a child shutting out something frightening. The inside of my hands feel hot and damp. I realise I am crying. Even now, after so long, the charade of it all chafes at my heart and my mind like a rough leather belt tightening round a weeping sore, and I want to shout out, 'it's so unfair'. And *here I am, an old woman who knows about the intrinsic unfairness of life, as any seventy-six year-old would.*

Could I have done anything differently? I don't think so. I acknowledge now that John was gone from me that first evening, at the supper party, when he first clapped eyes on Elizabeth. Our bond, so long stretched and strained by our differences, by our choices, worn thin by our rows, snapped that night. The love that had been between us, that had felt so giant and unassailable and unique for so long, altered irrevocably, like chemicals heated in a burner. As sulfide becomes copper, so it changed, and nothing could change it back.

Chapter Thirty-Two

1954. The Mead, Wantage.

I packed up the last of the hen eggs into a basket, and put it on the kitchen counter ready to take to the café. I needed to be there by ten as usual, as the part-time cook wasn't coming today. I had a lot to do, which was good. I was better if I was busy. Less time to think. But I had woken early that morning – I wasn't sleeping well-and had been fighting against my thoughts ever since. When I allowed myself to think, I had to acknowledge I was living a strange kind of life these days. John was more often in London than here, although he still occasionally referred to Wantage as 'home'.

I lived mostly alone in The Mead, running the café John had started in a moment of enthusiasm during a brief friendship with a local woman. He'd taken a twenty-one year lease and set up King Alfred's, then he'd gone to London and left me to manage it. I also had the house and the menagerie to care for, and the children during the holidays. But rarely these days, a husband.

I poured some hot water into a mug, a practice I had learned long ago in India, and sipped. Water was purifying and calming to the system, and hot water in the morning was even better.

At least the children were fine. Paul was about to do his 'A' levels and leave Eton. Candida was happy at her boarding school. The café was hard work, but with the children nearly gone, and John hardly ever here, I felt as if I had come full circle, and was waiting for something to happen. There was an echo of time, something that reminded me of the early days of my marriage, when I was struggling to fall pregnant and spent all my spare time riding over to see Gerald and praying at the foot of the White Horse.

I cut a piece of bread, and put it on the Aga ring to toast. I wondered what had happened to the painting of Moti and me. Gerald was dead. He had died in 1950, the same year as my father. He had never really recovered from the war. He'd tried to resurrect the gay parties of the pre-war Uffington set, but despite his clever catering in the face of rationing – he somehow had eggs, cream, butter and meat, when the rest of us had second rate, powdery imitations – it had proved impossible to make life the shape he wanted. Life, as it did, had marched inexorably on. Robert had inherited Faringdon House and we still saw him, but without Gerald, of course it wasn't the same. At least, I saw him-these days I didn't really know who John kept up with. We weren't really a 'we' any longer.

Eating my toast and sipping my hot water, I thought of my successful, absent husband. He had produced another collection of poems – *A Few Late Chrysanthemums* – and a book of prose essays, *First and Last Loves*'. He was always being asked to write articles now, for T*he Telegraph*, and other papers and magazines, and he always agreed happily. He loved the limelight, and I was glad for him that he had found it, but sometimes he chose his topic less wisely than perhaps he should have done. He'd recently written an essay on marriage. I had been surprised – that had seemed a piece to turn down.

John said, "I don't see why," with a baffled look on his face. I read the piece. From it, one would have assumed he was defying temptation and remaining true to his own wife. He wrote of how one must work at marriage, and of the value that comes to one in the end, if one does so. Reading it at the end of a long day in the café, I nearly spat out my cup of tea all over my homemade shortbread biscuit.

I put down my empty mug. This was the trouble with thinking. Where did it take me? There was absolutely no point dwelling. I scooped up the basket of eggs and other ingredients I was taking over to the café and gathered up my keys and purse. Dwelling was, too often, precisely what I did. My husband, despite his Anglican faith, now had an enduring mistress, one whom he showed no signs of giving up. No amount of articles would change that. Somehow he had managed to square his behaviour in his mind, and it was setting as if in concrete. I had been feeling the arrangement acquiring greater solidity day by day. Last night, I learnt that it had been settled even further. Cemented in bricks and mortar. John had taken a flat in London of his own.

"I can't keep staying with friends," he explained.

"Then come home," I retorted.

I packed away the goods in the carrier on the back of the bike, and climbed on. I started the engine and steered my Vespa out of the gate and along the road in the direction of Wantage. I came round a corner, narrowly avoiding a milk lorry approaching the bend too fast from the opposite direction. Wobbling slightly, furious, I sounded my horn several times, but the sound that came out was thin and ineffectual. How could he have taken a flat? He'd left me the burden of King Alfred's, a vast home to run, and rarely came back to enjoy it. We communicated on the children and other domestic matters almost entirely by letter. He wouldn't separate, but he wouldn't behave like a husband either. He told me he loved me, but this didn't feel like love, it felt like having your cake and eating it. What was it a friend had said the other day? "How does John manage to live the life of a bachelor while at the same time having a wife and a mistress?" Or something along those lines. How, indeed.

I drove through the market place and stopped the bike outside the café, relieved to have arrived in one piece. This bike was a recent development and not necessarily a good one. The 500 cc engine seemed a bit much to handle, particularly after years in a horse drawn cart. I wasn't sure why I had set on it. Along with everything else I missed that morning,-my husband, my marriage, the security of a married life, the certainty of being loved-I yearned for my simple horse and cart.

I removed my goggles and stood, blinking in the sunlight for a moment, the brightness of the light making my tired eyes water, before taking out the provisions. My head ached.

I went into the café to start preparing for the day ahead. I would do a lot of baking. Sometimes it was a relief not to think about it all, not to think about the mistress and the flat and the fact that my husband was never coming back, but just to get on with life and make a batch of scones. So I spooned out flour and butter and sugar and mixed and stirred until my arms ached, and as I did so, I felt the truth settle on my heart. The flat was the beginning of the end for John and me, or the end of the beginning for John and Elizabeth. John, Tewpie, *my husband*, had sailed into new waters, with someone else, to a place where I could not follow. A door had slammed shut, and John had walked on into a new life, a life with no place for me. I laid the scones out neatly on their baking trays and slotted them into the oven. Then I sat down at the wooden table, the surface of which was still covered with flour and smears of butter, put my head down on my forearms, and wept.

Mutisher

The sun is high in the sky now and there is no shade. I am breathing quickly, in and out, in and out. I feel something on my shoulder and my thoughts gather speed.

I burnt the scones that day, that day that marked the end of my marriage. The constant mistress, the flat, the going Abroad with her; Elizabeth, after so many had tried, was the girl who took John away from me, for the rest of his life.

Life carried on, as it always does, but John and I – we had reached the end of one kind of road, that day. John wouldn't admit it, but I knew it to be true.

Paul completed his national service, and went up to Trinity, Oxford, where he drove about in a vintage Rolls Royce he'd bought with a small inheritance from my father. Candida was abroad, learning French and hating it. John was mostly in London with Elizabeth. He won the Duff Cooper prize, and published another volume, 'Collected Poems'. I carried on running the café, but in between, taking time to travel, putting up a brave face for the world. The divorce laws may have reformed, but the emotions of marriage breakdown could not so easily filed away.

By 1960, with Candida out of school and in her first job, I made a decision. I picked up the reins of my personal ambitions. I planned a journey of my own. I rode across Andalucia on a horse, and wrote a book about it. John's publisher, John Murray, took it and published it. Tewpie told me he loved it. I hoped he was being honest with me, as his opinion still mattered; it always would.

And then I went back to India.

It was thirty years since my last visit, but I felt immediately twenty years old again when I placed a foot back onto Indian soil. I returned to Delhi and visited Flagstaff house. It was a museum to Nehru now. He had lived there from independence until his death. I stood in my old bedroom, and I tiptoed along the corridor to Sir John's, even remembering which floorboards creaked. It was flooded with light, posters on the wall about the Indian Independence, devoid of furniture, giving away none of its secrets.

I took the train up to Simla, and retraced a familiar route through the Himalayas, the same route I had taken long ago with my mother. Ghosts accompanied me all the way. On my way back, I crossed the Parvati valley, and documented my experiences in preparation for another book. 'Kulu: the end of the inhabitable world'. When I got home, I went to Oxford most days and wrote in the Bodleian library. It took me twice as long to write as I intended, but I loved my days spent in the quiet gloom of the library, the sunlight highlighting the specks of dust drifting in that rarefied air, the only sound the scratch of nibs on paper, of pages being gently turned, and of bicycle bells ringing in the distance. Then, I could forget everything for a while.

When it was published, John wrote to me that he loved it. We hardly ever saw each other by then. We only really came together for events that involved the children.

Candida had got married at Faringdon House, to Rupert, a handsome and aristocratic tailor. They bought a house in London and started a family. Candida was a writer, like her father, and, I suppose, like me.

Paul went to America, and never really came back. Between us, his father and I had somehow seen to that.

All around me at The Mead, property developers started erecting buildings on surrounding fields. Small executive houses that began as clusters of one or two and suddenly became cul-de-sacs of eight or ten. The house was far too big for me on my own and I *avoided being there as much as I could, for all it represented and reminded me of.*

Through it all, John's letters kept coming. He had left me, but it was as if he couldn't quite let go. Our frequent correspondence was all we had left. "I love you, Plymmie," or, even more painful to read, "Sometimes I wish we were back in our happy Uffington days."

I have never seen the point of regrets. I tried harder not to dwell. I got used to packing away my pain in just one corner of me, looking out at the world, and getting on with my life. I asked God to give me the strength to bear it without bitterness, without buckling. This mattered to me, for my own sake, but also for John's. I didn't want him to suffer as a result of his choices. Some friends didn't understand this, how I wasn't angrier, but I knew it was because I loved him.

We sold the Mead in 1970 and divided up the proceeds. I moved to a small stone cottage in Hay on Wye. Putting distance between me and my years of marriage, source of such joy and despair, seemed a good idea.

"Don't worry about me, I'm alright," I wrote to John.

Of course, he wrote a poem about it. 'On Leaving Wantage'. My lips move slightly now as I mouth the last few lines:

"From this wide vale, where all our married lives.
We two have lived, we now are whirled away,
Momently clinging to the things we knew –
Friends, footpaths, hedges, house and animals,
Till, borne along like twigs and bits of straw,
We sink below the sliding stream of time. "

Finally, after nearly twenty years with Elizabeth, John had written a poem about me.

We rarely met. I maintained my independence, my dignity, my own life, my own fiction that everything was fine, I didn't really mind. But as anyone who has ever really known love will understand, sometimes I could not help myself. Sometimes, despite the small, continual, dart-like humiliations – Candida declaring Elizabeth to be very nice; friends accepting John's defection and adding to it, fading out of my life and reappearing as Elizabeth's friend instead – I would get a stupid surge of irrational hope, that things could be fixed, and I would write to John and ask him to stay. That poem didn't help.

We had been young together, and grown old apart, and still I could not let the love go.

Hopefully, I put a bed in a downstairs room in my little house in Hay; I knew John's legs weren't that good at stairs any more. I waited for him to visit. He didn't like the countryside, of course. He told me that was the problem. I pretended to believe it, even though I knew he visited all his other friends who lived in the countryside. I wasn't stupid, even if people thought I was.

But he came a few times over the years. I think he was put off by the simple nature of my home, in contrast to the grandeur he was used to by now, from regular visits to Chatsworth, his own house in Chelsea, and from his grand invitations to stay with his grand friends. Also, perhaps, by the air of irrevocable sadness that descended between us when we were alone. In public, we kept up a spirited performance. A few jokes told against each other. Some happy reminiscing. A glance or two of understanding, for old time's sake. But when it was just us, it was hard to maintain, and all that had been lost sat between us like a sulky child.

"Goodbye John," I said, waving him off at the station after what turned out to be the last visit. I had driven him there in my trap. The motorbike had been a short-lived adventure.

"Goodbye Propeller. See you soon. Come to London! I love you!" he said.

I mostly lived alone, with my horses and my chickens. I read and I wrote and I cooked. I had visitors – loyal friends, whose kindnesses I will never forget, and Candida, who was always a daddy's girl, came to stay, sometimes with some of her five children, who called me Gramelope.

"It began when you converted to Catholicism," she once told me.
"What began?" I asked, but already knowing.
"Dadz. Being able to love other women."
"Oh," I said.

Billa said: "Affairs are one thing but marriage is for life".

A fine principle. If marriage is for life, then so is the unpicking of it. We didn't divorce. I didn't believe in divorce, although I did offer one to John to allow him to marry Elizabeth. For his own reasons, whatever they might have been, he didn't accept. I suspect his guilt wouldn't let him leave me completely. I always wondered if there was a part of him that rather enjoyed basking in his Anglican guilt.

Life wasn't dull. There were the trips to India. There was my riding. There were Candida and Rupert and the grandchildren. Occasionally, back from America for a visit, there was Paul. And letters, always, from John.

"Darling Plymmie," they all began.

"I love you more than ever," most of them ended.

The letters flew back and forth. That was all we had, now. Me, scribbling away in my spartan little hut in Hay, or from a trip abroad. He, now 'Sir John' and the nation's Poet Laureate, scratchy ink nib on expensive writing paper, from Chatsworth or his house in Chelsea next door to Elizabeth.

How far we had travelled, together and apart, and still he called it love.

I shy away from remembering his decline. John had always been so frightened of death. At first, the doctor thought his growing unsteadiness was due to weak muscles in his legs. Slowly it worsened, and then he was diagnosed with Parkinson's disease. John *got sadder and more frustrated by it. I wanted to see him, to help, but every time, I had to ring his secretary to make an appointment. Then Elizabeth would absent herself to avoid me. With John worsening, I tried once again to befriend her.*

"*Let us share his care,*" *I wrote. But she rebuffed me. So I hardly saw John, at the end. Instead, I carried on writing my letters.*

"*Do not worry about me,*" *I wrote to John.* "*I have had a very full and happy life.*"

On Saturday May 19th, 1984, I had just come into the kitchen from putting the pony away after an early morning ride, and the phone, only very recently installed and against my will, began to ring.

"*Mummy? It's Candida.*"

I knew, in that way you just do, that defies explanation in this day and age of logic and electricity and telephones and other mod cons so beloved by Tewpie.

As he had lived, so he was buried. It was a funeral with two camps. Elizabeth managed not to meet my eyes. I bore her no ill will. She had made John happy. She had been the kind of wife to him I had never able to be. Still, it seemed strange that **she** *would not meet* **me**. *After the coffin was lowered into the ground, she took some mourners back to Treen, the house John had bought in St Enodoc in 1960. It was to be her's now. I went to a friend's house with a few other loyal friends. The situation was quite clear. We were to remain divided to the end and beyond.*

Prayer helped. God sustained. A much-repeated plea. Dear God. Please help me in my hour of need. Hear my prayer. I did not have to die for my faith, like the martyrs depicted in the fresco on the wall of St Aloysius, but if Candida was right, I had had to give up my husband for it.

Had it really begun then, the beginning of the end, or would I have lost him whatever I did? Certainly John had acted as if my conversion was an act of betrayal, and somehow that had broken our sacred bond of marriage. But it feels a convenience.

I can't think any more. My head is full to bursting now. I have seen all three Johns again, but most of all, it has been about Tewpie.

My breath feels short, then shorter. I make a huge effort and take my hands off my face. I open my eyes, but still everything stays dark, the kind of reddish dark one finds behind one's eyelids in the early morning. John. The pain is paralysing me, making my chest feel it can't move at all, making my breathing, already so shallow as to be imperceptible, almost stop. Almost. Stop.

"Penelope," *a voice calls. It is my friend, Amy, who also happens to be a nurse.*

"Penelope. It's time to move on. Are you ready? We need to get going." *I hear the slap of her sandals on the dry mud. I almost feel her breath on me.*

"Penelope? PENELOPE?"

I hear more footsteps approaching. More than one set. Slap, slap, slap go the feet. They are in a hurry.

"She's not moving. I think she's – she might be…"

It's alright, Amy, I think. You can say it. I don't mind. And I find I really don't mind. The pain has gone now. I feel, for the first time in a long time, entirely pain free. It doesn't matter that my breathing has stopped. I don't seem to need breath any more.

The redness has cleared and instead the world is a brilliant splash of colours colliding to make a perfect picture. The blue sky arcing above, the red dust below, the pink and orange and lime green of the saris, the crimson and white and sapphire of the birds, the white of the flowers, the pureness of the light. The world has never seemed more alive. I know what is happening. I have waited some time for this. I have both waited and feared it, but I have been waiting more keenly these last two years, since I have been widowed.

"Dear Lord and Father, Yea though I travel through the valley of death, I fear no evil, for thou art with me".

And it is true. I feel no fear. I feel no pain. God is with me. I am light as a feather on the breeze now, high above my old self, drifting gently. I see Amy is holding my wrist, feeling for a pulse. She won't find one. Then she presses her index and middle fingers together, as if they were one fat finger, against my neck in two or three different places. Then she looks at me and shakes her head and murmurs quietly to herself, "oh no, oh no," and gently puts two fingers on my eyelids and pulls them down. She makes the sign of the cross on my forehead, then kneels in front of me, closes her eyes, and starts to pray. Two or three villagers, those who have known me for some years from my regular trips, start to cry softly. I want to tell them all, don't cry, it is alright. I am alright.

I have known it all day, since the moment I woke up early this morning. This is the day I am going to Heaven.

Epilogue

In the perspective of Eternity
The pain is nothing, now you go away
Above the steaming thatch how silver-grey
Our chiming church tower, calling 'come to me

My Sunday-sleeping villagers!' And she,
Still half my life, kneels now with those who say
'Take courage, daughter. Never cease to pray
God's grace will break him of his heresy.'

I, present with our Church of England few
At the dear words of consecration see
The chalice lifted, hear the sanctus chime
And glance across to that deserted pew.
In the perspective of Eternity
The pain is nothing -but, ah God, in Time.

Written by John Betjeman, 1948, on his wife's conversion to Catholicism, but not published until 1994, when both he and Penelope were dead.

Printed in Poland
by Amazon Fulfillment
Poland Sp. z o.o., Wrocław